by PETER DE VRIES

❖ ❖ ❖

THE TENTS OF WICKEDNESS

The TENTS of WICKEDNESS

by Peter De Vries

little, brown and company

boston / toronto

LIBRARY OF CONGRESS CATALOG CARD NO. 59–11106

FIRST EDITION

The poems appearing on pages 122, 141–142, 151, 266–267, 270, 271, 272, 275, and 276 originally appeared in *The New Yorker*.

The poem on pages 273 and 274 originally appeared in *Harper's Magazine*.

The quotation on page 88 (of which the last word is parodied) is from "The Hollow Men," in COLLECTED POEMS 1909–1935 by T. S. Eliot, copyright, 1936, by Harcourt, Brace and Company, Inc.

Lines from "Stopping By Woods on a Snowy Evening" in NEW HAMPSHIRE by Robert Frost. Copyright, 1923, by Henry Holt and Company, Inc. Copyright, 1951, by Robert Frost. By permission of the publishers.

*Published simultaneously in Canada
by Little, Brown & Company (Canada) Limited*

PRINTED IN THE UNITED STATES OF AMERICA

To James and Helen Thurber

You must not think me necessarily foolish because I am facetious, nor will I consider you necessarily wise because you are grave.

SYDNEY SMITH: Letter to Bishop Blomfield

❖ ❖ ❖

CONTENTS

the TREEHOUSE

We can be nothing without playing at being.

JEAN-PAUL SARTRE: *Being and Nothingness*

✧ ✧ ✧

1

CHARLES SWALLOW was taking a bath, and as was his custom on such occasions, he had undressed before climbing into the tub. Man is a creature of habit, but there was more to it than that. Since most of the clothes he'd been wearing were of the newfangled wash 'n wear, or drip-dry, variety, and equally in need of laundering, he might perfectly well have left them on and killed two birds with one stone. But Charles liked doing things the old way, even when they took more time and though the march of events had rendered them obsolete. It gave you a sense of tradition, and that, Charles increasingly felt as the years mellowed him into middle age, was something we all sorely needed.

He had lately been rereading the works of John P. Marquand, with enormous pleasure. In fact he had begun to fancy himself rather a Marquandian sort of hero. For one thing, he had this profound sense of the past. It more than greatly enriched his own life: to it he owed the fact that he was alive at all.

He could remember the time when as a boy of six he had swallowed a pin, a small pearl-seeded brooch which he had taken from his mother's dresser drawer on a rainy Sunday afternoon, and been rushed to the hospital for a bronchoscopy. They

3

had engaged the most brilliant surgeon in the East to perform it. No expense had been spared for the recovery of the brooch, which had been in the family for generations and was regarded as priceless both as an heirloom and on its own account. Charles smiled as he recalled the incident, still vivid in his memory though blurred in outline.

Suddenly the smile left his face as he heard his wife call something through the closed door. It sounded like "Have you finished *The Late George Apley?*"

Now why in the world would she ask that just then? It was an absurd query to put in the flutter of dressing for dinner, especially dinner with the Groteguts. Yet it had caught him precisely in the shifting, prismatic rigmaroles of self-inventory (underlined with rueful irony) that are the hallmark of the Marquandian genre. So it must be more than coincidence — it must be mental telepathy. In some way, it seemed to substantiate his claim to status as a Marquand hero, for whom things were always coming out of the blue to start the narrative ball rolling and make the protagonist wonder what the meaning of his life was. They were like nudges of a kaleidoscope which jiggle it into slight changes of pattern for the hero to squint a mental eye at. Charles squinted an autobiographical eye down the barrel of himself to see if he rated membership in this breed.

To begin with, Charles Swallow found scarcely anything in the world around him to approve of. The suit he had just pitched down the laundry chute was totally synthetic (were even the sheep any longer all-wool these days?) while his "hat" had been in reality derived from some legume grown in the Deep South (which perhaps made it edible in case he ever lost an election bet and were required to eat it). He had but to raise his eyes from the bath water to see the wallpaper, depicting people humorously caged in zoos of which the keepers were animals, that adorned the room. If standards were in visible decline on his own person and in his own house, they were in full rout in the world at large. The town rang with gimcrackery, human as well as material. There were the new owners of the old shore properties, people with allergies and two-toned cars, who had built swimming pools on the beaches. They sat around them eating frozen canapés and drinking gin-and-tonics with week-end guests who arrived on Thursday. The guests were those men from New York who ran things up the flagpole to see if anybody saluted, and their wives, metallic women with eyes like nickels who continually said "this." This I like, this I understand, this I don't get — surely one of the most irritating of locutions.

Well, all this Charles Swallow deplored with a genteel scorn (which a few intimates thought of rather as a mildly dyspeptic charm). As for missing the metropolitan life himself, to lay that ghost he had but to run down to New York for a day and drink it in in its present pure form. The Ritz was gone and the old Lafayette was gone, and as for the Algonquin — give it back to the Algonquins. Not that his home town of Decency, Connecticut, wasn't headed in the same direction. Gone from the local ice cream parlors were the nickelodeons that may not always have worked but which were better than the jukeboxes efficiently spewing their garbage into the streets till dawn. The trolleys that had once meandered leisurely around town were now buses that got you straight to your destination in five minutes or less.

Perhaps a subtler gauge of deterioration lay in the decline of reminiscence as such. He could remember a seagoing grandfather with a wooden leg, of the best teakwood, who had endowed the local marine museum. He died in a burst of nautical jargon, having beheld the dawn of the psychiatric. On hearing the term "autointoxication" for the first time, he had snapped, "I can hold with a lot of these newfangled notions, but drunk driving, no."

But this was really his father's memory; his own was merely

5

his father himself, a man picturesque only in the number of magazines that had rejected his articles, substantial only for the philosophers from whom he had cribbed to write them. Once his father had taken him to New York to the theater. After the entertainment they had gone to an uptown restaurant where his father had grown expansive about the play, an old-fashioned drawing room piece which he had liked. "That was a real comedy of manners, without any funny business," he had said, blowing cigar smoke in the boy's face. Charles had never forgotten it. There are few smells more delightful than the rich, full-bodied aroma of a fine Havana cigar provided someone else is smoking it. Puffing one personally only resulted in nausea for Charles, but he still liked the fragrance secondhand. The first thing he was going to do when his ship came in was not buy a boat, as so many of the fellows he knew did, but hire somebody to puff Havana cigars for him and blow the smoke in his direction.

As much more vivid as his father's recollections were than his own, his grandfather's had been than that. *He* could remember a father who ran a chandler's store on a waterfront still far from being improved by swimming pools, a pious figure with a gold toothpick in his pocket who quoted a brief portion of Scripture with every purchase of twenty cents or more. What, to complete the sorry cycle, would Charles's own two sons have to look back on? A man in a Brooks Brothers shirt mildly cursing chip shots on the living room floor.

No. Nostalgia, as his Uncle Joshua had said, ain't what it used to be.

Which made it pretty complete. Nothing was what it used to be — not even nostalgia.

Yet there were corners of his beloved Decency on which the blight of progress had blessedly not yet fallen. He loved to visit, each Saturday morning at ten, Matt Curtis; to ramble with Matt among the rooms of his old Colonial house, bumping his head on the original beams and smelling Matt's first editions; or over the grounds, to savor the sights and scents of long-established verdure, grounds kept at least semiformal by Tony the gardener and his idiot son Bonaventura, who grinned obliquely at you as he dug up weeds with his bare toes. There were still, too, the Irish and Italian quarters of town into which the marauding antiquarians had not yet swept, whose residents, still reasonably benighted, compounded from herbs with names like oregano and life everlasting nostrums of a charming uncertainty, and whose sons still ate yeast for their pimples. They always would. And there would always be Hallburton Hill, where folk of gentle birth still wet their finger before turning a page, a custom that has all but vanished from the human scene. He could no longer bear to look in on them: it was, as old Demosthenes had said, too high a price to pay for regret.

Professionally, he felt his life closing — not ending, closing — gently, like a bivalve, with the knowledge that he would live it to its end a newspaperman. There had been in youth a time when he had expected rather more from his typewriter, but he had settled for the realities — which was one way of propitiating the Furies. He ran a question and answer column. That was, simply, that. He did not yield to this destiny grudgingly but with a will; since we must all fall into a category it might as well be head first. All in all, it was a good life. His lines were laid in pleasant places and his heritage was fair. Life now had a felicitous monotony, bland as poundcake, of which the featureless days were the slices dropping with soothing regularity from the loaf of Time.

Yet there came to him sudden, inexplicable forebodings — hunches that Life might not yet have made its peace with *him*. That there might lurk somewhere yet a still unsettled account. He had it now in the bath, an intimation of — call it unfinished business, that seemed to chill the water in which he sat. He quickly nudged over the "hot" tap with his great toe. Which corrected the liquid temperature but not yet the freezing intimation with which he had been mysteriously struck. The premonition of events about to catapult him into another literary key, the fear that Something was going to Happen, was so overpowering that it routed out all his other thoughts. It invaded, like the thunder of an approaching tidal wave, the pleasant plash of reminiscence. What key?

As the water drummed into the tub he quickly and rather frantically reviewed the rules and unities of this Marquandian world into which he had so easily issued himself a life membership, as in one of the better clubs, to check once more his qualifications for it. What was it?

It could be defined as a Paradise without a serpent. But there was always, in the Marquandian apple, a worm. Be it a secret concealed in the rosy pulps of respectability or merely a gnawing discontent, or that social *bête noire* of larger scale, the Cost of Success (the price of money) — it was always there. What in God's name could it possibly be in his case? He had no money, so no one could be sending him a bill for that; and since he was only a peripheral success (as he was a peripheral New Englander) he need fear no moral duns on that account. A gnawing discontent everyone had — even the dull clods in the novels of Knut Hamsun. Then it must be some secret come to haunt him from his past.

But what?

Could it be something connected with what his wife had shouted, and was now shouting again through the closed door and the running water both, and that he had deliberately misheard the first time?

He heard it clearly enough now. Crystal opened the door and called into the clouds of steam: "Don't *dawdle*, for heaven's sake. You're late for Miss Appleyard already."

"Miss Appleyard?"

"The new sitter, the new *sitter*. You've got to pick her up.

8

What do you think I've been trying to tell you? You may have trouble finding her house because it's way across town, so allow for that. Shake a *leg*, Chick."

The name, penetrating his thoughts at last, scattered them like a truncheon dispersing a host of idlers. The wheels of memory spun; whirled to a stop. He sat erect in the tub.

"*Sweetie* Appleyard?" he said. "Surely not her. Surely not Sweetie."

"Miss Appleyard is all the name the agency gave me. And the address." Crystal opened the medicine chest and unscrewed the cap from a jar of cream. "Seven something Beacon Street. I've got it jotted down there. I think it's seven-eighteen."

"That's her. That's Sweetie."

He laughed — a chuckle of relief as well as of recall. Then that was all there was going to be to it. A flashback. He was going to be treated to a flashback. And what was more Marquandian than that?

Yet as he squeezed out the lathered sponge and felt the suds trickle down his back, he wasn't so sure he was sure . . .

Not all flashbacks are Marquandian, and this might be not the present flashing back at all but the past bolting forward, a missile held in long suspension and now shot from the abruptly let-go spring of time to meet you as you flew in antic retrograde to meet it, that name plucked out of all happenstance to exact not contemplation but its opposite, the reluctant recapitulation of all lost years, yourself a target with no less velocity than the arrow streaking toward it in bland outrage even though you knew it was already quivering in its mark, coming in monstrous javelinlike amplification both of speed and size through the clearing chiaroscuro of vapor billowing in violent dispersal through the open door, scattering now and possibly forever the ephemeral scented soaps and steams of old assumptions —

My *God*, what kind of stuff *was* this! He sat up in the tub now in genuine alarm. This wasn't Marquand at all! Then what was it? he asked himself shakily. What ominous vein was this in which his mind was running, in which it had galloped off of itself? He could place it vaguely but —

Could the Marquandian device of recapitulation misfire and, like a bungled rocket take-off or a bit of magic gone awry, land you in another world? Clear in that of, for instance . . .

No. He couldn't say it. It would be too awful. He wanted to stay in this world he knew, that enveloped him like this warm bath. The worm was serpent enough for him!

Yet he knew very well how plainly he was thinking it, the name he couldn't, or wouldn't, say, even to himself.

He knew all too well, now, what was happening to him.

2

So you say you knew this girl in school?" Crystal said, kneading her hands with the cream as she stood watching him bathe twice as fast as before, the water agitated as though by the same prose that was churning his head.

"Yes. Well, I'll be damned. Sweetie Appleyard turning up after all these years as a sitter for my children." He shook his head with that readiness for trite philosophy that the slightest sign of rhythm of pattern in our lives inspires. "It'll be like old times."

"How old?"

She flipped an electric switch with that effect of languor in which women cage their howling curiosities, letting in light as she had air, dispersing the gloom along with the steam in which he might for the moment have preferred to remain wreathed, the light imploding on his senses as the name had upon his memory. He averted his head long enough to gnash his teeth for this as for all human bother, softening it into a smile as he said, "Well now, I can't have seen her since . . . let me see . . . She used to visit a grandmother who lived on our street, and as children we played among the flowers and trees. At Sweetie's own house we'd climb the orchard boughs and all that jazz. Time passed. We found ourselves in the same grade for one year when they rearranged the school districts. Perhaps it was the eighth. Queer sort of girl, always running off into the woods and reading poetry. It must be ten years since I've seen her. Doesn't she ring any kind of bell, lambswool? Beth Appleyard! That was her name."

"Wait a minute. Isn't that the girl there was some scandal about in high school? Don't tell me." She put her hand to her brow like a medium in a trance, the light catching her bracelet, which had that look serene benedictive and forlorn that inherited jewelry has. The hand came down. "She cheated in an oratorical contest."

"You're right! I forgot about that. She got clear to the national finals with a speech lifted bodily from Daniel Webster. Horrible embarrassment in Washington, finals were to be in the Senate. But there she was in the papers, waving like a fool from the train platform with her arms full of flowers and her straw hat over her eyes. She hadn't known 'entries should be original and not assembled from available material.' How the principal must have slaved over that statement. That was our district champ. That was our Sweetie."

"Wouldn't it be a lot later than eighth grade? Yes, the contest was high school. And if you saw her ten years ago, it'd be even after that. When we were going together."

"Her grandmother hovers over my memory like a particular phantom," he said with that anger savage and defunctive of a cornered rat, thinking I don't mind being the rat driven through numberless doors behind one of which lies food, but I'll be damned if I'll be the food too. "The Appleyards and the grandmother were always exchanging visits, in those far-off childhood days, so we got to know the old woman too, God rest her. Well, she had a dog that chewed gum . . . Why do you look at me like that? Why should I lie to you?"

"I don't know, but every time you do you start this nervous gibbering." Crystal stood wringing her buttered hands with the most ludicrous air of portent, as though minding the theft, abduction, lust and murder with which the term "sitter" is latterly encrusted. The sitter is our latest American folklore, he told himself, who told himself also don't holler till you're hurt, but whose foreknowledge that he was going to be hurt was the same as being hurt already, the wound and the wretched wriggling to elude it one. "And you couldn't possibly have forgotten that oratorical scandal. Why did you pretend to? Changing the subject instead to those densely wooded areas you say she went to read poetry in — "

"I didn't say densely wooded areas — I said *in the woods*. Densely wooded areas is a tabloid cliché for where girls' bodies oh never mind."

"I know. But why did you omit that oratorical scandal? Some impulse to shield this Lovey as you call her?"

"Sweetie. It was her nickname. Her name was Elizabeth, I imagine. Her grandmother's name was Rodriguez or Bonheur or something like that, which was typical of the baroque strain that ran rather deeply in that family. So get ready. You know writers tell us that children's perceptions are the purest? Well, the first glimpse I got of the grandmother, it struck me that her fingers were like fried bananas. And I knew that if she had any legal documents they would be upstairs in ginger cans. That sort of thing."

"What about Sweetie?"

"Get the Faulknerian quality about this grandmother first, hon, and hence about that house from whose commingled bloods she, Sweetie, had been vatted out of all flesh and time; get what your correspondent saw in the grandmother in the very instant of her coming into the coalbin for us — the voluminous skirts imploding on our sight with the same violence as the imploding light when she pulled the string — that this was pure Faulkner: ornate, ramshackle, vertiginous and fine."

"What were you two doing in the coalbin?"

13

"Wait. Because I want you to know everything, so you'll know, no matter what anybody else may tell you or insinuate," he said, again with that savage defunctive anger. He knew as he rolled his eyes away that they had that shabby vestigiality of gnawed olives. "Get the idea of what I may have divined in that instant of shocked cognition; that all this — the documents yellowing in the ginger cans among the rotting ancestral lace and the suffocating potpourri, together with the imploding light and the horrible dark brown fried bananas — would one day burst into flower to win the Nobel Prize for Literature. That maybe she knew it too, without knowing she knew. Not just he but both of them there, locked in coeval fear and trust in the violated gloom. Doing in the coalbin?" he called through the open door through which he could see her bent over the dictionary in the corner, the pages riffled in sibilant outrage or anyhow exasperation or maybe both. "Why, reciting poetry more than likely. What else would anybody be doing in there? Because you see, Sweetie was one of those for whom beauty burns like incense in a million urns. To quote Teasdale. Remember how I used to recite Sara Teasdale to you before we were married?"

"Passing on to me what you had no doubt got from her. Whispering in my ear what she had in yours."

"Now you're doing it! The Faulkner. Now you're getting the hang of it. That repetition at once woozy and serene, sick with overimplication —"

"Oh, stop this idiotic rubbish!" she said, turning around. "And stop trying to throw me off the scent with all this hanky-panky, Charles Swallow, the way you always do." He loved her when she used both his names like that not only because it went with towns of from ten to twenty-five thousand, thereby draining off a lot of the nervous tension, but because it made her once again the girl next door. Not here. "At least in my house we recited poetry in the parlor. We didn't go down in the coal cellar."

"You forget one thing," he said. "You had oil heat."

He got to his knees and began lathering his midst with the same defunctive frenzy, thinking it's all right to unearth mummies and maybe even haul them up into the light of day but not to unwind the cerements in which they have lain and in which could they but speak they might themselves prefer to lie. Thinking too, who thought all this, *I have more to forgive than be forgiven for but I can never let her know it.* Because the wallpaper was her idea. The wallpaper with the zoo switch. Whimsy, of all sins the most difficult of definition and the least susceptible to reform, was to be forgiven daily and thereby daily unforgettable. He took in a scene over the corner window in which an ape on a bench, wearing overalls and the blue cap of officialdom, was eating his lunch in the noonday sun, a detail on which the ache of allegory lay keenest. A simian dressed in blue flannels and Homburg was thrusting a banana at a caged executive type. Swallow gorged himself on grievance till she was hopelessly in his emotional debt. Then he said:

"When I talk about when I 'saw' her last, I only mean visually. So let's stop this bone-grinding. She may have been putting flowers in somebody's mailbox, or shattering stars by walking through a rainpool. Because that was Sweetie Appleyard — loving Beauty every minute. If she had two loaves of bread she would sell one and buy a hyacinth. Her oranges were as sweet as the king's, and so on. She'd phone to call your attention to the sunset, then when you called her back after stepping outside to look at it she wouldn't come to the phone."

"Playing hard to get."

"Oh, my God." He rolled his eyes to the ceiling, where at least there was no wallpaper. "She *couldn't come* to the phone. It was more beauty than she could bear. Now do you understand it?" He squatted in the tub, reaching for the obscene sponge. "So the thing that'll be interesting to see is whether she still is."

"Still is what?"

"One of those for whom beauty burns like incense in a million urns."

"She apparently hasn't married, if it's 'Miss' Appleyard." Crystal stooped to retrieve a bobby pin. "Was there anything, I mean has she ever been disappointed in love, as they say?"

"Our good friend Nickie Sherman would say you had to be married to be that, now, wouldn't he?" he said, smiling affectionately upward.

"You're as slippery as that bar of soap, aren't you? But I think I may have you figured out by this time." She bent down and kissed him. "You tell me a story about a coalbin that's so ridiculous I couldn't possibly believe it, in hopes that I'll think there wasn't anything to it at all and not believe what there may be. Isn't that right?"

"You're pretty sharp yourself, and moreover your breasts are like two doves nesting in quiet places. Stay bending over me a minute — it looks like mighty pretty country down there. Why do we have to go out tonight? The question is rhetorical — a mating cry."

"Well, there won't be any place to go but bed when we get home, now, will there. That's rhetorical too."

"Is that a promise?"

"More or less. But the Groteguts said eight, and we're supposed to pick up Nickie and Lila on the way, so hurry." She rose and bustled into the bedroom.

"Right. But as for broken hearts for Sweetie, she had them every day, is what I'm trying to say. So don't pay no mind. A drifting leaf could shatter her into a thousand bits. They don't make them like that any more."

16

"Yes, well, you really must get a move on. It's after seven now, and if I have a new sitter to brief and all . . . Would you rather I went for this Miss Apple Strudel?"

"No," he said, springing quickly out of the tub. He drew the plug from the belching drain with his toe as he reached for a towel, recovering his balance with one foot on the mat. "I think maybe it'll be best if I do that," he added, and began to dry himself briskly.

3

AS he set forth with all speed to Beth's house, Charles bethought himself of the works of Jane Austen, in which he had by felicitous chance been but recently refreshing himself, as was his wont once in a twelvemonth. His purpose in so doing was more than to clear his mind and restore his sanity, urgent as these motives were. He wished to expand a certain recollection with which he had been visited, of Beth and himself dallying under the summer boughs with a volume of this author. The picture, if but sedulously dwelt on, must surely expunge from their bond all implication of guile! In a larger sense, Charles was striving to put Beth herself into focus as a Jane Austen heroine, or at least a girl who might since last seen conceivably have flowered into one. Imputing to her such wholesomeness must definitively exorcise all taint of blame, from which he likewise ardently longed to purge himself of any connection.

There were some small means in the Appleyard family, flowing largely from the grandmother, on her fair portion of which Beth might reasonably presume, and any young man of amorous intent reckon with in turn. Her reappearance as a sitter became therefore doubly an enigma. Of that alloy of human emotions, gold, however, our young friends were as yet blessedly unaware in the years when their companionship began. Those were childhood days, when they had scooped polliwogs from the millpond or picked berries on the hill, returning home with buckets heaped with sunkissed fruit or tadpoles congregated in obscene educational sacs, depending on the season. What sport they'd had in the orchard! Charles remembered arriving with a baseball bat one Saturday afternoon in autumn, and their going wild among the windfalls, smiting apples in all directions till the trunks were spattered with pulp. Beth had flung the bat into the laden boughs at last and run for the river that coiled away behind the house, screaming with pleasure.

Childhood ecstasies gave way to the more complex and literary ones of adolescence, embodied in images of Beth reading Shelley on the riverbank, or in the treehouse in the maple that spread its leaves over the gurgling stream, or pinking off unsteadily the nocturnes of Chopin at their parlor "grand." Once she threw herself into the open piano and embraced its strings. Though an "aesthete," in the mode of those days, and committed to beauty in all its forms, he had felt this to be a trifle overshot, the hum of the ravished wires unsettling. Urbanity had begun, in his case, to set in, and his tastes to shift rather toward those that would bear the scrutiny of the boulevards. There was also the other misgiving, which not even the most avowed *flâneur* could dismiss: whether a girl who habitually pitched herself into musical instruments would make a good wife and mother, let alone housekeeper. Her father once protested the presence of marigolds in his salad, though in all fairness to our heroine it was a question whether they represented a literal obedience on her part to the E. E. Cummings injunction to "eat flowers and not be afraid" or whether those poor blooms had merely depended onto his plate from one of the rather disheveled centerpieces with which his daughter was wont to garnish the familial board.

Friends and family by no means exhausted the range of those who had their lives enriched by Beth against their wills. In summer, she would climb into the elms that shaded the city streets and from there drop, one by one, upon dismayed pedestrians below, pages torn from the book of verses with which she had ensconced herself among the upper boughs. She did this not only with school anthologies but also with volumes drawn from the public library, on the ground that showering the citizenry with beauty outweighed the mutilation of public property entailed thereby. However, the librarians failed to appreciate this reasoning and eventually revoked her card and even barred her from the building. She was usually barefoot, and usually clutching an old beaded bag apt as not to contain a spray of laurel or pink, or a night moth, or a soft caressable gopher, rather than the keys and coins carried by the less imaginative for opening doors and paying fines.

It is a question whether her love for all living creatures extended to her mother, a gaunt pale woman who was generally to be seen bent over a sinkful of dishes or a steaming kettle in canning time. She was preserving the family fortune, she would have explained in that famously humorless tone of hers. When asked to lend a hand, Beth would answer with a vague shake of her head that pleaded impalement on some sensation too exquisite to deny and too far advanced to interrupt. "Humperdinck," she would say with a helpless gesture, if it were a record she was listening to, or "Millay" if a cloud of poetry in which her spirit was afloat, a cloud far more impenetrable than the kitchen steam that wreathed her mother's fading form, though not physically discernible. That was the idea. What effect all this had on Mrs. Appleyard is not known to man: she kept her counsel. But it got to be a nuisance to a young blade bent, as Charles was in the years of which we are now speaking, on the normal perquisites and pastimes of "dates." Love verses and erotic operatic duets were not, in however glutting quantities, enough.

20

It was their custom to go to Hickett's apothecary for sodas, and once when Christmas was approaching Beth asked what he should have liked in his stocking. "I want what's in yours," he told her with all the worldliness of sixteen. Mr. Hickett, a short nerve-ridden man who always looked as though he were trying to swallow his eyeballs, gave, on hearing this, a specially deploring, suffering version of this feat. Wiping fixtures behind the soda fountain at which they tarried, he rolled his eyes up till they seemed to vanish in his skull, fluttering his lids the while and twisting his mouth in a kind of outraged astonishment that such conversation could be held at all, let alone in his store. Nevertheless he hovered in their vicinity, powerless not to eavesdrop for more of what repelled him.

"Charles, you're so physical," Beth averred, poking her soda with her straws.

"For a girl who likes love poetry," he said, groping toward some fresh outrage for Mr. Hickett, for to *épater le bourgeois* was then the order of the day, "you certainly shy away from the subject. You fancy yourself some kind of Aphrodite sprite, so why all this skittishness when it comes down to brass tacks?"

"Aphrodite never married," was the terse reply.

"She had a lover, Vulcan."

It seemed Mr. Hickett's eyes were watching him intently, but it was hard to tell, for they were far from lined up. One was always applying to the other for counsel. Charles enjoyed tormenting him in the same way he had his father, whom his epigrams and paradoxes drove to distraction.

"I may be old-fashioned, but I still like the phrase 'pure as the driven snow,'" Beth went on. " I *like* being pure as the driven snow."

"Where would you like to be driven tonight?" our swain asked, and snickered.

"Oh, Charles, don't be so absurd! You're a sensitive person.

You have standards. Why do you always have to espalier the bourgeois, or whatever you call it? Why exaggerate the physical in this immature way?"

"It's not we who exaggerate the physical, it's you Puritans. For what is chastity," he said, pushing his soda aside and tapping a Melachrino cigarette on the lid of its box, for he now saw an epigram within his grasp, "what is chastity but an overemphasis on sex?"

Mr. Hickett's eyeballs disappeared. And the contortion was followed by his slamming the wadded washcloth down on the counter as hard as he could and walking to the back of the store, where he vanished in the depths of the prescription department, presumably to take something for his stomach or head.

Charles's "paradox" had been, of course, in the then burgeoning boulevardier tradition aforementioned, which had its headquarters on quite other premises than Mr. Hickett's. It was at the Greek's that the café-minded set foregathered. It was to the Greek's that Mr. Hickett's fit of temper had implied the youth should take his custom. He was right. And Charles saw something else as made incontrovertibly plain: that if he hesitated to take this girl to the Samothrace (the Greek's) for fear of ridicule by his more worldly friends, why, then she was not his "speed" nor he hers, and their relationship were best terminated. Before Christmas, to avoid the ritual of exchanged presents so indicative of a congealing bond. Besides, he was seeing another girl named Crystal Chickering.

Charles had a date with Beth the next evening, in the course of which she made a mysterious statement. "You ought to know why I'm skittish about sex," she said. He thought nothing of it at the time because she was forever talking in riddles; besides, she herself hastily dug out a record album and set *Tristan and Isolde* spinning on the gramophone. She hovered near it, refusing to come nigh the settle on which he lurked, both arms spread along its back whilst the smoke of successive Melachrinos issued from his nostrils. After an hour of this he simply rose, got his hat and walked out of that house. She did not even sense his departure. He left her standing beside the ever-grinding machine, reverently murmuring "Wagner . . ." That was the last he ever saw of her.

Until tonight, when he was doomed to confront her again in the unexpected role of sitter.

What on earth would he find?

The house at any rate was unchanged. It was the white cottage with the listing porch choked with wistaria that he had always remembered though never seen since, it being in a part of town into which neither business nor private purpose took him. One can live and die in a city of a hundred thousand and not see more than a handful of its streets.

A sound of eccentric but skillful piano music drifted through the open door as he mounted the three porch stairs, causing him to reflect that Sweetie had at least notably improved her playing in the interval. (Had a dream of the concert stage all the while been secretly inflaming her?) But when he reached the screen door and looked inside, he saw that the music was issuing from the same old phonograph, or a successor, before which she stood listening in the same attitude. He raised a hand to the brass knocker also remembered of old, thus reassembling a familiar tableau. He let the screen door swing to again after opening it to rap.

She gave no sign of having heard. She had her back to the door. He opened the screen door and rapped again, more loudly.

"Khatchaturian."

Whether this was progress remained to be seen. Certainly headway had been made in the matter of taste, of modernity, but she was rooted in the exact same spot in which he had left her more than a decade before, as though she had spent the interval neither eating nor drinking but only imbibing ethereal impressions. Even the dress she had on was the same, though that may have been an illusion cast by an old and apparently incorrigible addiction to white, and a way of always managing to look like a child playing grownup, with frocks of excessive length and chaotic fit that appeared to have been delved from attic trunks. She was barefoot.

"Sweetie?" He peered through the screen door, shading his eyes.

She turned. She turned by degrees, like those actresses who expose the secrets of their craft. Then she floated toward him in the half-light with an air at once intent and uncomprehending.

"It's me," he said. "Chick Swallow."

The process of recognition was, for Sweetie, one with the strain of incredulity, as well as of eviction from a trance. A smile dawned across her face as she pushed the screen door open with one hand and with the other drew him in.

"So you've come back."

A slight chill went up his spine as the screen door twanged shut behind him. "You're our sitter for tonight," he said.

"Oh, yes. Father said something about giving my name to an agency."

"It's kind of late. So if you want to pop into a coat . . ."

She raked him from head to foot in the darkening vestibule, taking in every detail of his appearance.

"So they've done it to you," she said. "They've put you in a blue serge suit and tie to match, and shiny shoes to go to work in. They've given you a swivel chair to sit in from nine to five, behind a desk piled with papers for you to do things with before they take them away again to other people."

Sweetie's "they" had always referred to the forces of convention, the materialist hordes who ran the world and to whose gross standards finer spirits must ever, in the end, capitulate. It

24

was paranoiac in nature but was applied on behalf of others as well as herself — all who combined to form a sort of beleaguered and perceptive Few. The powers in question had, in his case, it was clear, "won."

"Well, you haven't changed, Sweetie." He could not get over the dress, whose ill-fitting flamboyance recalled the shapeless folds in which Ophelia is depicted taking leave of her senses on the legitimate stage. It could all but have been a set of draperies plucked from a window in passing. Her face hadn't aged a whit, but resembled still a nerve-gnawed doll. It was to the great length of her lashes that Sweetie had attributed her flunking science in high school, claiming they prevented her seeing anything in the microscope. However, they had probably aided her passage through many another course. She fluttered them now as she reached to shut off the Khatchaturian. He was about to repeat that it was late and suggest a speedy departure and a resumption of the discussion on the way when something struck him with the force of a hammer on an anvil.

Behind such piping hot romanticism was all too often something stone-cold. What she had been lost in down the years was that lute-embodied, verse-bemused, high gutless swooning based on the illusion and maybe even belief that flesh could be reproduced without recourse to flesh; that you could multiply arms and legs and smiles and tears and hands and feet but without sex organs. Because now the Faulkner came roaring back with twice the fury, and who had been plucked out of New England and dumped clear in the middle of Yoknapatawpha County was now picked up out of nineteenth-century Surrey England and dumped in the middle of it. Not only because he had seen that she was not only not Austen but not even Brontë, but because he had simultaneously heard on the carpeted stair a tread that memory or instinct or maybe just fear identified even before his eyes turned to take it in, a step secretive and sibilant made by the polished shoes he probably remembered too, as he did the creased trousers, tweed coat and Ascot under the bland debonair face, a face that flashed from him to her a smile that moved so smoothly from courtesy to possession as to warn him of something in this house not just eccentric but worse. *So is it Mississippi or Massachusetts incest I'm up against?* The query roared along his bones, who reminded himself that there was Northern Decadence as well as Southern, the Puritan wintry hold-in as well as the semitropical let-go; *so I still don't know but what it's Marquand after all* — his mind swinging violently between the two extremes like the needle of a butcher's scale on which a joint of meat has been flung for weighing.

"Hello, Daddy. This is Charles Swallow. You remember him."

Appleyard was a man of light construction in his middle fifties. He combined what he himself obviously took to be a seasoned charm with a dryness of tone felt to be Anglo-Saxon. He lingered on the second stair to greet Swallow, perhaps for that interval to repair the disadvantage in height, extending one hand while the other remained in his coat pocket. The effect was a sinister geniality like that of those educated gangsters in bygone films, often depicted as emerging from book-lined hideaways to conduct, with as little loss of aplomb as possible, the necessary chores of violence. Sometimes the components of this blend in Appleyard were separately discernible; thus for minutes on end the learned charm would prevail in a smile turned up to full wattage, like Adlai Stevenson being acclaimed in distant lands; then that mask would drop and the smile turn taut, a secretive grin predicated on information about you which he happened to possess. In this constant shifting from one identity to the other he resembled those faces in drugstore windows which give the optical illusion of winking and scowling alternately at the passer-by, according to whether one has or has not taken the nostrum being advertised.

It was at any rate as Adlai Stevenson that Appleyard led him by the arm into the living room, after Sweetie had scuttled off in some direction, presumably to put on shoes.

"I remember you now, knocking about Granny's house as kids," he said, withdrawing the hand from the pocket to reveal in its grasp nothing more lethal than a pipe. "And then doing 'parlor duty' as I think you young bloods called it then."

"Not me."

"But somehow my most vivid memories are those when you were kids. Always racketing about, here or in Sweetie's grandmother's house. I was at Granny's one summer trying to get a book done in the attic. Vain dreams! I could hear you clear down cellar. By the way, wasn't there a bit of a ruckus down there one day?" he said, his grip tightening perceptibly on the other's tensed biceps. "What was that? Something out of Krafft-Ebing to hear Granny tell it."

"No o," he answered modestly, smiling at the floor. "Nothing like that."

Things were falling into place at the same time that they were going utterly to hell.

He remembered clearly now the fiasco on which Appleyard had been engaged in the attic, a life of Woodrow Wilson that had come to naught. Then he had run for mayor of Decency, waging a "literate" campaign. However, the application of Wilsonian idealism to the problems of garbage removal and road repair had struck few voters as possessing any great relevance, and he was defeated. Then for a while he owned a local movie house where he had gone bankrupt showing photoplays of distinction. A string of such misfires had no doubt done much to develop his acrid strain. He finally took some money settled on him by the grandmother and put it in, of all things, a bauxite mine in France, where the grandmother had come from. (What *was* her name? "Cinquefoil" kept coming to mind.) The investment had prospered, permitting Appleyard the life of cultivated leisure to which he felt by nature entitled. He spent a

27

great deal on his wardrobe, in which the pitiless recurrence of checks proclaimed him the man about town.

"What, exactly, happened down cellar?" Appleyard asked, straightening with his heel a rucked rug.

"Well, the thing was, Granny was a terrifying figure to us kids, but amusing nonetheless. There's a kind of grim humor in what I'm going to tell you."

Appleyard's face set itself into an exemplification of the former half of this quality, leaving the other to illustrate the latter. He chewed the cold pipe in his bright teeth, and sucking on it in that state drew from it an occasional death rattle.

"She'd go around the kitchen with a fly swatter swatting flies, and when we kids did something to annoy her, she'd reach over and swat us with the swy flotter too. I mean the fly swatter. I mean get the picture. She swinging that thing right and left at the flies, then with no warning giving one of us a flick on the hand, and going on swatting flies. She had a kind of authority. Call it an imperial something, that went out with her era. Everything she knew died with her. We shall not see her like again."

"Don't be too sure of that," Appleyard told him. "She's still alive."

"Alive! Where?"

He jerked a thumb at the ceiling. "Upstairs."

"But I thought . . . That funeral here some years ago . . ."

"Mrs. Appleyard," Appleyard said with lowered eyes. "Her mother is still very much with us."

"I'm sorry to hear that. I mean about Mrs. Appleyard. So her mother is still with us. My, my. How old is Granny now?"

"Ninety-three."

He whistled his appreciation, though the sense of eerie convergences, of accumulations and assumptions menacing to himself, continued to pluck his nerves. It was the sense of a plot,

28

ten years in the hatching, to hold him answerable, who at the same time thought: *What is it they think they're saying, that it's my skeleton in their closet or theirs in mine?* . . . .

Appleyard made a sudden nervous movement to the vestibule to make sure they weren't being eavesdropped on, there in the gloom, and returned, and straightening now a rug that needed no straightening, said, "I'm sure she'd love to see you again. She has all her wits about her, never fear." His smile was momentarily maniacal, and the presence in his get-up of the Ascot added to rather than subtracted from the effect of menace confronting Swallow; which was in part that of being up against someone "weak" who might by wildly misplacing responsibility get things out of hand. "As you can see, our Sweetie has never grown up past a certain point," he resumed with a smile of which the impression created was at once piratical and spineless. "Why? Did something happen to her, once, that frightened her permanently back into herself? A sexual scare thrown into her at an early age? Granny thinks now the incident in the coalbin may have had something to do with it."

"Rubbish," he said, feeling a firm line was called for here. "I don't even know what happened down there. I've forgotten the incident completely. What more proof do you want it was insignificant?"

"Insignificant for you, yes. But for a nervous, sensitive girl with a tendency to asthma — "

"Now look here. It was her grandmother that frightened *both* of us. Because I suddenly remember it all very clearly now. She who scared the holy bejesus out of us. So if you're looking for a villain, how about thinking of her? Has that been given any thought?"

"So you do remember the incident after all."

"That of being frightened, yes. Because we weren't allowed to go *into* the coalbin, so being caught there was in *itself* traumatic. We were forbidden to go in there because of all the coal."

"What was the matter with the coal?"

"It was dirty. So get the picture. Those two in trembling complicity locked, clutching one another in the still unblasted dark — You've read Faulkner, I presume?"

"Of course."

Because he suddenly thought now how he might get out of it. Not the thing's being Faulkner — he couldn't change that now, he was in too deep — but his taking the rap for it. Thinking: I've got it now. *It'll be what it is only turned around: I won't let them hang it on me, I'll hang it on them.*

"Because the thing has a kind of Gothic, Faulknerian quality. So all right then — here we go. The children locked in that conspiratorial dark while overhead and then outside the coal-bin door the footsteps come, and the hand that had wielded the fly swatter and might wield worse reaches for the latch, the feet and hands blended in that amalgam of familial power, that matriarchial Menace of which this is the one single feared avatar; and then the door swinging slowly open and for that suspended second the two still quivering in the still unblasted dark; and then the detonating light, revealing the shocked materialized old face beneath the upraised arm and the fingers like fried bananas still fumbling the light cord though the light cord has been pulled, the bulb itself dancing in frantic antic something-or-other overhead, disclosing, for her, the shocked one, the two innocents naked where they stand."

"Naked?"

"Not in the physical sense, but those clothes that covered them being themselves covered with dirt from playing in the hole so sternly disallowed them, naked the more to accusation and punishment." He drew a deep breath and continued. "So that they know, those two, that the same hand that pulled the light string will on the instant draw them by the ear and, the girl anyway, the tender floral She anyway, upstairs and into the bathtub. And more. Because this may be the point, so get this if you get nothing else: *By cackling insinuations about what that boy as ambassador of and from all dirty boys had intended should be done in that coalbin whether it had been done or no convincing the girl that dirt and the act adumbrated are forever one. Thus grinding into her mind what she was simultaneously scrubbing from her flesh — Filth. The old and primordial thought-muck. And locking her forever in that cloistral dream from which that sex who alone must waken her must by the same token be the one most powerless to deliver her."*

He sank into a chair, breathing heavily. Appleyard dropped into another, likewise greatly agitated. He packed his pipe with tobacco now, but then set it thoughtfully on the arm of his chair.

"It may not be all that simple."

"Aye-yi-yi!" said the other, slapping his brow. "How can I make it any plainer? What are you people trying to do to me? Get the picture again. That burgeoning and still unblackened trust — "

"No, no, please." Appleyard cut in with a wave of his hand. "Let's not go into all that again. Let's try to look at it from another point of view — Granny's. I'm afraid she won't know what you're talking about if you take this line. She doesn't know Faulkner. Granny," he said, a faint smile playing across his lips, "reads Dickens."

"God."

The youth rose and gazed out the window. A weight descended on his spirit, settling like an incubus there whose force could not yet be judged and whose tenure none could tell. Half an hour ago he was a free man. Now . . .

"I see. So now it's Miss Havisham in *Great Expectations*, a jilted virgin living out her days in a house where all the clocks stopped on the day the bridegroom never showed. Miss Havisham going slowly mad at the long table to which no guests will ever come; fingering the dusty goblets and the tarnished flat-ware; putting on her bridal robes never to be removed for any lover; watching the cobwebs gather on the tall tiered cake rotting in its frosting, in that shut-off room which is for her a tomb of memories. Is that what Granny sees? Is that the way it reads for Granny? Is that what Sweetie is — or may become — and I the culprit? Is that the way it is?"

Appleyard sighed unhappily into his interlaced fingers. There was a whisk of white on the edge of their vision, a pale streak running through the vestibule, a ghostlike fluttering of folds that was gone before they could turn their heads. All that remained was a cloud of smoke from a cigarette — which he suddenly remembered she'd smoked then, each one as though it were her first.

"She does seem to be, well, frozen in time, like the Miss Havisham to which you so quickly made comparison," Appleyard said. "Sweetie isn't very communicative — though she talks a lot — but she may very well have had Great Expectations of her own which — "

"But she was undersexed! She was against it, man!"

"Because of something that happened away back — "

"Oh, poppycock!" he said, pacing the room. "Why wasn't this put up to me before? I mean you sure waited a long time!"

"You know how those things are. What you see every day you don't see at all, till one day — And what could we . . . ? You were married and —"

"If it hadn't been for this sitter business we might never have met again for you to lay it in my lap."

"That's rather Dickensian itself. He creaked with coincidence."

"Just let me say this, apropos of Mrs. — of Sweetie's grandmother." He stood making a gesture which consisted in bringing the tip of a forefinger down into the other palm, like lost outdoorsmen letting which way spit goes decide what direction they will take. "You say she's ninety-three. Well, she's probably addled. Remember how old people distort their memories."

"I wouldn't tell her that to her face," Appleyard advised urbanely. "When you see her, as you certainly now shall — "

He broke off and craned forward in his chair to look into the dark vestibule. A sound on the stair arrested them both. Swallow listened to it stockstill, steeling himself for a Victorian beldame in black bombazine whose Dickensian world of black and white excluded any question of moral grays.

"Quick, does she have any other favorites? I'll never butter her up on Dickens. It'll never wash. Does she read any others? Quick!"

"She is passionately devoted to Proust."

"Sweet Christ in the morning."

There was a rustle of purple-black silk and a tiny woman clutching a massive cane appeared from the shadows. She seemed at first a mere solidification of the gloom from which she emerged, but as she acquired definition in the parlor light she was seen to possess a clear particularity, hatchetlike, with a face of the sort known as aquiline — though this derived from an incisive gaze more than from any cast of feature.

"I think you remember Mme. Piquepuss," Appleyard said. "Granny, this is that Charles Swallow."

She extended a thin claw which he took while trying to place her, for he did not think now that he remembered her at all. He would certainly not have recognized her on the street, or tumbled to her name. Perhaps he had never clearly heard that. She stood scrutinizing him also for memorable detail, and seeming to find none, said with a faint twitch of her lips: "So."

"You're still the same," he answered with the shred of a smile. "I remember you always had such sensitive hands. I was recalling to Mr. Appleyard how you'd smack us with the fly swatter," he continued with a glance at the stick on which she was nervously readjusting her grip. "Do you remember that?"

33

"You must come and see us again very soon," Mme. Pique-puss said with an abruptness suggesting that he had succeeded in definitively boring her in twelve seconds and was being sped on his way, until another rustle in the hallway made him divine her deeper purpose: that she wished all too firmly to see him on matters best discussed out of earshot of their subject, who now materialized with the wraithlike quality typical of this house. All the huggermugger was getting on his nerves.

"We really must go," he said to Sweetie, who had slipped, still barefoot, up to her father and handed him a rose. He put it in his trouser-pocket. "You've got to get a move on," Apple-yard said. "Have you had anything to eat?"

"I have a hunger food is gall to," said Sweetie, who always quoted from the best. Appleyard sighed.

"She can have a bite at my house," Swallow said. "The children will fix her something."

"We'll have to catch her," Appleyard said, for Sweetie had again glided from view.

That rang a bell.

For many years local artists had seen in her romantic possibilities as the Goose Girl or the Milkmaid, and thus it was that painters and illustrators, themselves representing versions of dishevelment, were often seen gesticulating down to the river shouting offers of employment, only to see her dive into the water and reappear, all Nereid, on the opposite bank to taunt them. Or clamber up the maple into the treehouse.

"Let's just forget it," Charles said. "We can call the agency and get another — "

"No," said Appleyard, whose idea it had been that she try a bit of sitting. But it was not he who brought matters to a resolution.

Mme. Piquepuss marched into the vestibule. Taking a position at the foot of the staircase up which Sweetie had whisked, she began flailing the newelpost with her stick in a manner that chilled Charles's blood. She looked at the post she beat, as though it were a head out of which she were bashing the brains. It was clearly a tested means of bringing the girl round, for here she came down the stairs like a summoned child, pouting and smelling yet another rose.

"She's an Emily Dickinson without talent," Appleyard declared. He grasped Swallow by the arm again and wheeled him back into the living room for a last word while the grandmother got Sweetie into some sort of sartorial shape.

"Now don't stay out too late," he told Swallow, with the first show of authority the latter had seen him make. "Get back by eleven, or twelve at the latest."

"Yes, sir. And don't worry, because the boys are reliable. They'll get her out of the house in case of fire or anything."

"Good. And one more thing. Don't let her make you pay her in things of the spirit, like books or flowers. *Make her take money*."

They stood watching the scene in the vestibule. Sweetie was seated on a Shaker chest while Mme. Piquepuss wedged high-heeled shoes on her feet. The elder stood with her back to Sweetie and Sweetie's foot between her legs, like a blacksmith shoeing a horse, tugging and grunting in a determined fashion.

"I'm most anxious to see how this sitting thing works out," Appleyard said. "We must all work together to get Sweetie out of her shell."

"She needs some responsibility, is what she needs."

Appleyard suddenly transferred his scrutiny from the hall to Charles.

"Say, this advice column you run in the *Picayune Blade* — what's the name of it again?"

"The Lamplighter. They won't hear of changing the name, though of course the old-fashioned banalities are a thing of the past. We use the psychological attack today, and I'm trying to get subtlety O.K.'d by the front office — "

"That's just what I was thinking — the psychological. By George, you may be just the man to get Sweetie straightened around. I never thought till just now — helping people with their problems is your *job*." He squeezed Charles's arm in an access of optimism. "We'll keep in touch."

Sweetie wobbled uncertainly on the high heels as, snatching up a beaded bag, she started for the door. Was it the same old beaded bag as always? Very possibly. A normal-looking flannel coat muffled the note of romanticism struck by the dress, though her unsteady legs — which necessitated Swallow taking her arm like a more experienced ice skater supporting a beginner with weak ankles — restored to their passage across the porch and down the stairs the element of the unusual. Sweetie looked more than ever like a girl playing grownup. A family watching from a porch across the street gave him the momentary feeling of "doing a fine thing," though where they imagined he was taking her God only knew. They crossed the lawn and climbed into the car to additional shouts of encouragement from the elders. As they shut the doors he heard, in the depths of the house, a telephone begin insistently to ring.

"Tell Mrs. Swallow we're on our way!" he called as, slipping the car into gear, he shot off down the street like a madman.

4

So we have the story of a man who wanted to settle down and be a comfortably-off Marquand character for the rest of his days but couldn't because of something Faulknerian in his past. So far so good. Or bad. The problem was how to get back. Back to the literary key from which he had been so violently transposed, the world from which he had been so shatteringly dispossessed, or, failing that, the compromise world in which he might settle in between. Mme. Piquepuss was a formidable figure and a Proustian phase might be indicated for brief intervals and for the lubrication of such diplomacies as dealing with her might entail, but to crystallize permanently in such a form was unthinkable. Likewise sustaining the Faulknerian pitch for the rest of his days: he would rather end them now — removed, cauterized out of the old and tragic flank of the world.

For the moment, why not put the problem out of mind? Its other principal was for the moment herself quiescent in the front seat beside me. I figured that I might as well improve the interlude — to drop the third-person guise assumed in order to objectify as much as possible the inauguration of events relating all too dismally to myself — I figured I might as well take advantage of the ten minutes' ride to my house by studying my burden.

Sweetie sat huddled against the door of the front seat as though on guard against unfriendly blows. Her great chocolate eyes, which watched me in silence as I drove, had the mute reproach of a street dog confident of its breeding in the face of widespread public disapproval, or hostility. Now and then she drew a gold locket back and forth across its chain with something of the apathy of the mad. I was glad to see her stop this and dig out of the beaded bag a comb and mirror with which she began to tidy her hair.

"Isn't that the rear-view mirror from an automobile you've got there?" I had noted a knob, as for a swivel joint, on its back surface.

She stowed the paraphernalia back without answering my question, and settled over again in her corner.

"I used to sing for you." She spoke with a rueful air, leaving unclear whether what was to be regretted was the time when all this had occurred or the fact that it had. "I have awful pitch."

"That's all right. I'm tone-deaf. So that was always all right, Beth."

"Shall I sing something now?"

"No, don't do that."

"Because we can't recall the past?"

I bore down on the accelerator, gnashing my teeth as we cut through traffic.

"Whom did you marry, finally?"

Finally. Dear God, must the assumption that there'd been a "triangle," that I might still not have her "out of my system" and all the silly rest of it, add its weight to the sum of nuisances flapping like vultures about my head?

"I don't know whether you ever knew a girl named Crystal

38

Chickering," I said. "Her father was an advice columnist on the *Pick*. I married her, and I now conduct the column."

"I don't place the girl but I remember the column now. Of course! You're the Muffin Man, or something like that."

She raised an arm to ward off my upraised hand, which I reached behind her to make sure the door against which she leaned was locked, as I often do with children riding in the front seat. "No, I'm the Lamplighter," I said. I mused rather sourly on my solicitude for one destined to do me harm — probably — a hunch that I now felt I had instantly had on hearing the name of the sitter in my bath. Sweetie took me in again with that air of evaluating not just myself but all life's unabating dismal developments.

"So they've put you in a tweed cap with little teensy checks and set you behind the wheel of a Buick and said, 'Be one of us. Conform.' They've given you a house to keep up the payments on and an office with a typewriter to sit behind — you, Charles Swallow, who used to read Shelley to me — and set you to work turning out platitudes for morons."

"Odd as it may seem, a good many people are helped by these platitudes," I answered. "They write me telling me so, and thanking me for my advice. I've even straightened a few lives out. How do you like that? I could show you letters."

"What are some of the letters? Not those you get thanking you, but the ones asking for help."

"Don't you ever read the column?"

"I never read newspapers. What are some of the problems people have?"

"Well, today, for instance, I got a letter beginning, 'Dear Lamplighter: I know I can make my marriage work if I can only find my husband.' Another went, 'My daughter has become engaged to three chaps. For years I've been after her to get a boy friend, like other girls, and get married. Now lo and behold she

39

gets three, making the situation hopeless. Where do we go from here? Is this what I deserve as a mother?' and so on. Cries of pain, pleas from the depths. Trying to help is a responsibility I take seriously."

"What will you write these people?"

"The first I'll probably refer to the Bureau of Missing Persons, and then when she's found her husband, most likely have them both in for a talk. The other woman is a different kettle of fish. I shall tell her quite frankly 'Madam, what prompts your daughter to acquire three fiancés is a fear of marriage. She *wants* the situation to be hopeless, because as long as it is she's free of the clutches of an institution you've discredited for her as something to be nagged and chivvied into, rather than a beautiful human relationship. Your daughter may be under-sexed — I would have to see her to find out. Please feel free to phone my office and make a date any time.' So sneer all you want. I at least do my bit to try to relieve suffering humanity. You don't know what goes on in the world, up there in your treehouse, Sweetie."

She tucked up the collar of her coat and shivered a little. "Maybe I know only too well," she said.

In the interval of silence in which we again drove, I felt I might have been a bit harsh with Sweetie; to repair the mood that had fallen between us I resumed chattily in the vein of old-school-friend reminiscence that her query about my marriage had in a sense generated.

"Do you remember a girl named Elsie something? Elsie Wayne I believe it was," I said. "She took ballet lessons every Saturday morning at Mrs. Meyer's. What ever happened to her?"

"They've put her in a frilly apron and locked her up in a chintz prison. A little jail with pretty chintz curtains on the kitchen windows, and there they keep her very well. They've put a broom in her hand and the last I heard she had four children.

40

That was several years ago. Didn't you have a sister named Lila? What's become of her?"

"Nothing's 'become' of her, Sweetie. Get over the idea that something 'becomes' of all of us. Lila married Nickie Sherman, my old sidekick."

"Are they happy?"

"Very."

This was not true. But all truth is relative, and I felt that what was called for here was a corrective to Sweetie's warped view of life, not an answer to her question. The problem was not whether the Shermans were happy but how to get Sweetie down out of the treehouse. I might as well begin on that now. It had been put on my docket. Urgency justified a false answer, one as false as I had given in reply to her estimate of the idiocy of my work, though that estimate was precisely one I had made that afternoon to my wife when she had taken, against me, the line I had just taken against Sweetie. Unable to bear Crystal's insinuations that I had a good job and ought to be grateful, I had flung my shirt and tie across the bedroom and declared that I could no longer go on pumping out bilge for morons. Just as, when next I encountered the amused smile with which Nickie Sherman habitually greeted mention of my employment, I would defend its value against the vacuity of wastrels like himself. Fidelity to large truths often requires betrayal of small ones.

"Do you know Nickie Sherman?" I asked, suddenly seeming to remember Nickie's having once described Sweetie as "the barefoot bluestocking." But it must have been someone else, because she shook her head and said, "No, I don't know him."

"Well, anyway, here we are at my house," I said, with no great stomach for that development.

Crystal was waiting for us under the porch light. Its rays cast a shimmer into her cropped hair and along the brown silk of her dress. She looked extraordinarily fresh and electric, up there, and I rejoiced in her appearance though it was one to which anger may have lent an additional sparkle. Overhead dangled a set of wind chimes we'd picked up on a "second honeymoon," motionless now in the numb June air but soon enough to be plucked loose and swept away by a hurricane. Crystal clattered down the wooden stairs to greet us, the racket she made excessive, I thought, punitive. I opened the car door for Sweetie and we repeated our impression of two ice skaters one of whom was teaching the other. Her ankles buckled violently as she clutched my arm.

"This is our sitter, dear, Miss Appleyard. My wife."

Slipping a pale hand into Crystal's hospitable grasp, Sweetie conferred upon her mistress that measuring gaze which was both shy and presumptuous. The scrutiny was prolonged to a full notation of the other's fine points, the felicities of face and form by dint of which "they" had been able to snatch me from freedom into bondage, to translate me from the intellectual anarchies of Shelley to that class of men who seriously purchase souvenirs like wind chimes for attachment to the front porch. Crystal sized Sweetie up in shorter order. Singularity is more easily pegged than normality, it being cloudless natures and clear façades that excite us to remarks like "I can't figure him out" or "She throws me," while devious and even dastardly behavior we take in stride as understandable in the face of life's complexity. Crystal had long ago ticketed the newcomer as a Nervous Girl while that girl was still imbibing the wonder of one able to look so spruce after a day in the Chintz Prison and to stand so affably poised on heels as high as her own.

"I'll introduce you to the children, and then we really must be off," said Crystal and trotted toward the house, again with a clatter aimed at meting out rebuke. I moved at moderate speed, not to be on anybody's "side." Sweetie wobbled up the stairs behind us, holding to the banister and developing a smile

42

of anticipation for the adventure. I held the door open for her while Crystal galloped ahead and set up a shouting for the boys. Mike and Fillmore appeared and were introduced, then Crystal took Sweetie into the kitchen for the usual sitter's briefing — phone numbers, where things were, and so on. Acting unhesitatingly on her title, Sweetie sat. She opened her coat and asked, "What about antidotes? I heard of a . . . ." I herded the boys into the nearby bedroom and gave *them* a few last-minute instructions.

"Fix her a bite of supper," I told Mike, who was just short of ten. "A sandwich will do and I think there's some potato salad in the icebox. By no means let her turn the stove on or anything of that sort. If you want to call us, we'll be at the Groteguts'. See that Fillmore is bathed and in bed by nine-thirty. Fill, see that Mike turns in by ten. Make sure Blitzstein has water. All this will give you ninety units for the week."

"This one doesn't seem very reliable," Mike said, peering worriedly down the corridor toward the kitchen. "She's funny."

"Read to her. Gain her confidence. We'll keep in touch — and we'll be back early."

I had a hurried drink in the living room, where, having finished with Sweetie, Crystal found me. Her mouth tight as a seam, she beckoned me off with a jerk of her head that drew a flash of fire from her earrings. I marched behind her toward the front door. From the depths of the hall closet I felt a hand clutch my coat sleeve as I passed, and Sweetie whispered, "She's *right* for you."

I drew her out and, shaking her roughly by the shoulders, said, "Stop talking nonsense! I must insist that you stop all this twaddle right away. Now there's an end of it!"

Crystal was kissing the boys good-by on the porch, taking care not to soil herself. She spread a hand across a large bow at the neck of her dress. She looked like someone bending over a water fountain to drink. Sweetie watched through the screen door with that smile which found the occult in everyday things. Behind the house Blitzstein could be heard baying at the end of his chain — dragging his house another inch or two across the yard with each leap into the air. Irked by the error of his acquisition, I turned on the boys and said: "Don't leave any telephones off the hook now, for heaven's sake. If you do, I don't know how many units I'll take away." We had extensions everywhere, including the laundry, which often resulted in people forgetting to cradle phones after passing a call on to someone elsewhere in the house, by means of a lot of co-operative yelling, or after taking their own calls to other rooms for privacy, etc. So that, though we had five telephones, we could rarely be reached.

I sped toward the Groteguts' with the same distraught haste as I'd driven home in, though I dreaded getting there. Nickie had described the Groteguts' dinners as food for thought; big and boring and symptomatic of the divorce between social life and friendship. Crystal had called the Shermans, canceling the plan for us to pick them up, as a result of my delay in fetching the sitter.

"What took you so long?" They were her first words in the car.

"We were talking about old times."

"How old?"

I reaffirmed my plan to check irrelevancies and all snowballing damned nonsense, from whatever quarter, and to give clear notice of this. On the seat between us was a novel Crystal had borrowed from a woman who would also be at the party. Briefly waggling which, I said:

"How did you like this?"

"Oh, all right. But why must novelists keep romanticizing prostitutes? I mean must we still have that? And the way they keep referring to it as a profession. Marriage is regarded as a trade."

44

"Wonderful," I said, taking honest pride in the quip. Was this the girl I married? No, thank God! She had come a long way from the provincial innocent I'd courted to the rather waspish woman of the world which a decade of marriage to me had made of her — no point in being modest about that. Of course her verbal humor was at its best when her mental humor was not, but that is the nature of wit, is it not? "What else? About the book. I know the man has a style as heavy as lead, but what else? Pour it on, ducks."

"Oh, this so-called realism." Crystal tilted the rear-view mirror to get a look at her hair, and having done so, swiveled it back. "Is it ever anything but exaggerating the seamy side? I mean God, I'm beginning to agree with that radio reviewer you intellectuals are always complaining about. I mean this book — they pop in and out of bed like seals in and out of water. They're *always* in the sack."

"They overdo it," I said, with a disagreeable feeling of "selling out," of capitulating to garden-club standards that made me avoid my reflection in the mirror when I gave it an extra twist of adjustment. "Why do modern novelists dish out so much sex? Why have they always got everybody in the sack?"

"Maybe they don't know the facts of life."

"Swell. Touché. Thou'st a nimble wit, I think it was made of Atalanta's heel."

My spirits rose, Sweetie all forgot. I even let up on the accelerator a little, not to get to the Groteguts' sooner than necessary; to enjoy the cool, delaying ride.

Crystal drew a stocking up and fastened a garter clasp.

"You said this girl and you were talking about old times. How old?"

I stepped on the gas.

"There was never anything between us."

I gritted my teeth. But what answer would not have been idiotic? It had been one of those questions to which no reply

45

is adequate since denial can't be made without automatically implying a situation about which it can be *said* that there is nothing to it.

"I love you," I said loosely. "You know that. There's never been . . ." I shifted up in the seat, gripping the steering wheel. I felt like the golfer in the comic strip who with every stroke digs himself the more deeply into the sandtrap from which he is trying to extricate himself. "Never been anyone else . . ."

I was glad to see the Grotegut house loom into view, a situation which I should not have thought possible.

My mood swiftly reversed itself on seeing the trap into which I had escaped.

The Groteguts were the sort of whom Nickie was fond of saying that they couldn't like people or they wouldn't have so damn many of them around. The house was a bedlam, though of motionless occupants. The guests exceeded by half a hundred the demonstrable maximum for a decent evening — say eight or ten — and stood vertically massed like passengers in a subway crush. Eager hostesses ought perhaps to have their living rooms posted with signs like those in commercial establishments which specify the number of persons occupancy by more than which is illegal. The chairs were all empty: they were inaccessible. A group near where I stood, hesitating before the plunge, was being well presided over by my boss's rather muscular, oblong wife, the veins in whose neck swelled in mid-emphasis of some point. Behind her was a large leather couch, on which I longed to pitch forward and go to sleep.

I spotted what I was looking for — Nickie at the other end of this room. I wanted a word with him, long enough to bring up Sweetie Appleyard's name and see if it rang a bell. Snatching a highball from a tray borne by a white-jacketed waiter from the caterer's, I began the long journey to his side.

To pass among a cocktail jam of this sort requires a special

46

kind of movement not unlike osmosis. One seeps and sidles through walls of flesh seemingly solid; nor is passage ever straight but circuitous, as counterpressures carry one off course. Delays are unavoidable as faces familiar to one swim into view and require pauses for greeting and graceful extrication. A man named Harry Larkin, a funny-story-dispenser, materialized in my path, ready with three new ones. He was moon-faced and a shade too expansive, and just now had a heavy summer cold which gave new meaning to the term "infectious laugh." I laughed dutifully at his three stories and oozed away to the left, and freedom. But not for long. Bearing down through heavy seas was the cultural freighter, Mrs. Adelaide Crewes, who in a twinkling could be saying to you, "But don't you think Tennyson . . . ?" By sagging at the knees I lowered my height six inches and hid behind a fat woman with noodles in her shrug, till the danger was passed.

One is, of course, contrarily, a chore to others. Two or three were visibly put out at having to take me into account. Knoedler, the German-born violinist who would play for us later, greeted my approach with an expression morose and even despairing. I hoped we would not get into politics, a subject on which he was aggressive without being informed. He had the thick shirts and high color of those who demand radical changes in government. What he did — with the obvious aim of scaling the encounter to my level — was to launch an account of a recent motor trip in which he had encountered several dead chickens on the turnpike. When I showed no interest in this theme he seized my arm and said, "But these chickens were plucked and dressed!" I thought of those film fantasies in which flocks of geese are plowed into by speeding airships to emerge, fully cooked, through the exhaust. Murmuring something about refrigerator vans, I twisted free of his grasp and made off. A woman I knew slightly named Mrs. Lumpey was next. She discoursed mainly on the absence of her husband from these festivities. "He has this peculiar pain in his stomach," she said. "I don't blame him," I said, and inched off. I squeezed apologetically between a woman with brown lipstick and a man to whom she was telling a story, so that a fragment, perhaps the climax, lodged in my ear: ". . . and held that ear of corn up for the dog and turned it for him while he ate it!" she said, grinning richly into my face.

A caterer hove near with a bowl of that fish paste into which one is bidden to thrust a potato chip, the body of which then breaks off in the paste, leaving a small residue for one to raise, dry, to one's lips. I declined the offering, which was by now replete with shards, and reached instead into my coat pocket for a salted peanut, which I slipped covertly into my mouth. Knowing what is served at these affairs, I often go to them armed with a supply of fresh nuts or even a few squares of Cheddar concealed on my person, on which to nibble privately. Such a practice is hard to justify, but it has become too habitual with me to give a second thought. I tucked a nut or two between my teeth and drank from my glass, which in the congestion I was obliged to hold at chest level, like a libation carried in an antique rite. To the conversational caldron, now deafening, was added the scent of mingled perfumes, growing steadily denser in the warm air. Before me loomed the powdered shoulders, flecked with rust, of Mrs. Tolliver. She was a pretty woman of middle years who smelled, herself, deliciously of soap, and I paused a moment to drink her in, olfactorily speaking. She stood with a young divine, new to Decency, named Harmon. They were gnawing triangular canapés which looked like pimples on toast, and both talking at once. Harmon spoke with an air of fluent worldliness that struck me as a bit spurious. I had heard him preach at a recent service, "Let us load the camera of our heart with the film of the Gospel, and set the light meter of our spirit at Infinity." So he seemed to me not quite the man to stand with a Martini saying, "Oh, really? And the Hewitts, are they off to Rome for the summer?" There was a note of imposture somewhere.

I mopped my brow, I hoped with my own handkerchief, and raised my glass for another gulp. It was getting decidedly hot in there. The voices mingling into one Voice were now a physical pressure applied to all the senses, a weight like water underseas, in which arms waved like dreamy fronds and teeth snapped at bright scraps dislodged from coral reefs by the pulse and thrust of the tide, or at twitching fish reconstructed back into their original forms out of the paste to which they had been reduced. To what end was all this? I knew the Indian dinner, complete with chutney, that lay in wait for us on the sideboard. "The Groteguts are perfectly matched for small-city social life," I formulated meticulously to myself. "She favors curry while he curries favor." "My parents are in the iron and steel business. Oh, they are? Yes — my mother irons while my father steals." That sort of thing. My eyes were growing heavy. They were ball bearings which the muscles assigned to their control could no longer support, and down they went, down the front of Mrs. Tolliver's dress. The promise of rest and airborne dreams after the long night of foolishness was over. The *what*, for God's sake? Harmon was looking at me with his own round eyes, the oustanding feature of his "sensitive" face. One was a plea for the humanities in a time threatened by overemphasis on technological skills while the other was a sustained flute note in turn resembling a single gull drifting over seas of measureless blue. I gave a nod intended to be meaningless, and holding my glass carefully, swiveled by degrees out of their vicinity. To find myself squarely in that of Oscar Shook.

Well, poor Oscar. Oscar was a nursery owner to whose rival I had let some recent landscaping work. Some hysterical compulsion made me bring the subject up. He writhed more wretchedly than I. "You see," he said, scratching his thin leg just above the knee, "I visualized a bank of evergreen trees as right for that side of your house, but passing by the other day I seen, um, I noticed someone had put in deciduous." What could I say? What was there to say? "Well," I answered, "I phoned your office at the time, but deciduous out," and laughed hideously. I was seeking a formula, not for conversation or even for sheer human amenities, mind you, but a means by which a terrible dismay with collective mankind could be reduced to an expiatory self-disgust. It would make disintegration honest, and thereby restore my membership in that race I had no call to fix in perpetual caricature.

It was now nine o'clock. I now saw my plight in terms of the postman in Dickens who plied his rounds in a quarter of London so tortuous that he could not get to houses he was in sight of. Nickie couldn't be more than fifteen feet away — half the original distance — yet he seemed as far distant as ever, due mainly to two enormously pregnant women who materialized in my path. I weighed the cogency of getting down on all fours and completing the trip in that position. It would be easier to thread one's way through human legs than among their owner's upper bulks, certainly. Nearby stood, again, my Boss's wife, who, glimpsed in sections, was trying to catch my eye, but I shifted mine well to the left and gesticulated at a nonexistent person, presumed to have a prior claim on my attentions, that I would be right over. This brought into my ken her husband — my Boss — which would have completed a nice dilemma were he not in a cozy tête-à-tête with a girl he was damn well not going to let anyone butt in on, judging from the way he flicked *his* eye away from *me*. . . . Hey, what's that just under your conscious mind, clamoring for attention? Which novel is it of Dickens, about the part of town so tortuous mailmen can't get around in it? Who can tell you? Mme. Piquepuss? Oh, no, let's not think about her now. Back to the Boss; that ogre will drive out any other.

He was thick-figured, thick-fingered, thick-necked, thick. He wore a hand-painted necktie depicting a scene of the kind more normally seen on bass drums. It was a woodland prospect featuring a waterfall, which spilled the length of the cravat, knotted so that it would. He had *taste*. He nodded at something the girl was saying, his head down and his chin, or rather chins, resting in a pleated assortment on the knot of the tie, just above the source of the cataract, affording one the fancy of its all running out of the side of his mouth. O my people, why are ye not home in groups of four and six, giving and taking in easy communion all that is pleasant and foolish and lovably human? Why stand ye here in this woman's house taking meat and drink in such wise that what cometh out of your mouth is no better than what goeth in? . . . That girl with the Boss was lovely. If hitching down her shoulder straps I sought her breasts as in the love of globed fruit, would I be accused of an unhealthy mysticism? But the dress had been designed to flatten away not only those hillocks but all of her. All of her. Most of the women there wore the shrouds decreed by fashion. The only ones with any shape to them were the two pregnant ones. Their bellies boomed out a praise of life. I wanted to stop by and say as much, perhaps laying a hand on their sweet burdens, but I would have been misunderstood. If a man acted on every instinct normal to the yearning to make a sacrament of life, he would soon be put away. But let's think about this stroking an expectant mother a moment. If it were made a custom, like kissing the bride or shaking hands, mightn't it have a salutary effect on our nervous systems? A palm laid ceremoniously on their middles — and most ceremonies are casual — would purge me of fear and boredom and lust for the rest of the evening.

A movement in the crowd suddenly cleared a gap between

me and Nickie. I darted through it to his side. He was talking to a guy from whom I knew he would appreciate being rescued, a feature writer on the *Pick* who had just had a volume of his humorous sketches of city life published under the title *How To Arrest a Policeman*. "They told me the advance on *Policeman* was seven thousand eight hundred and — " he was saying.

I reached out to tap Nickie on the shoulder. As I did so, I felt another hand come out of the mob and grasp my own wrist. Turning, I saw my sister Lila.

"I've got to talk to you," she said into my ear. "It's about Nickie. I know. But this time'll be the last. I promise. Because — come on, let's go into the library. There won't be anybody there."

She towed me through the edge of the crowd toward a pair of tall doors at the end of the room.

The library was the place for privacy, all right. No one ever went in there. Not even the Groteguts would dream of profaning the tomblike sanctity of those beautiful sets of books. It would be safe to say of George Grotegut that he had never even *heard* of some of the authors on his shelves. There was no vulgarity in this attitude, because no pretension: he simply recognized the contents of the room as the treasures of human genius for which he had provided a shrine best not desecrated by his frequent appearance. Grotegut manufactured commercial candies which were sold in tinned assortments bearing such labels as "Bridge Mix" and "TV Munch," with a "quality" line packaged in wicker containers later usable as sewing baskets. No, the books were safe in their noble ranks till Doomsday. First editions were in a special locked cabinet the key to which had been lost. I took down a volume of Lamartine's essays and opened it. It gave out a report like a pistol shot.

"Books like that aren't meant to be read," said Lila, returning with fresh drinks she had gone to fetch us.

"They're bound to sit upon the shelf."

She smiled at my little joke. She looked wan and tired, with circles under her normally bright blue eyes. Even so she was as pretty a girl as a man could want, with a figure shapely still after two children. I cursed Nickie for the trouble he caused. Not a month went by but some fresh facet of his impossibility came up for me to worry about. If only it were women! That would be something specific to be specifically dealt with. And if only he were not so likable. I steeled myself for another lament from Lila, to be followed by another pep talk from me — a simple airing of her feelings that would serve her till the next time. I was quite unprepared for what she told me now.

"What is it this time, Sis?" I asked, taking the glass. "What's he done now?"

"It's not what he's done, this time, Chick," she said. "It's what I'm going to do."

"What's that?"

"I'm going to divorce him."

She walked to the nearest chair, where she sat and drank from her highball as though it were a glass of water and she a child quite parched from thirst.

5

WHEN Lila told me she wanted to divorce Nickie, I instantly exclaimed, "But you hardly know the boy!"

She took this to be facetious. Actually, I was trying with gentle irony to remind her that I had opposed the match, just as firmly as I now would the divorce. I continued:

"It's all right for two people to rush into marriage, but divorce is a step that should be taken seriously. Splitting up a home! What will become of the children?"

"What is becoming of them now? If a judge decides, say, that they shall see their father week ends and three nights a month, that's just about the status quo. When he had a job, it could be said that he supported his family. Now that he's come into that ridiculous 'inheritance' he sits at the Greek's all day being a man of means. Maybe if a judge tells him to pony up five hundred smackers a month alimony it'll put some iron in his blood."

Lila had not overstated her case. The thumbnail sketch of her husband was accurate, though executed in bitterness and in a tone verging on hysteria. Life which mauls most of us into reliability (so that we can fruitfully for our allotted years ply the brooms and typewriters "they" put into our hands) had failed to deflect Nickie Sherman from his course, if you can call "drifting with every passion till your soul is a stringed lute on

54

which all winds can play" a course. So now, though married and the father of two children one of whom had malocclusion, he still carried a blackthorn stick and said things like, "I hate having my life disrupted by routine," and "I have only once heard Gluck made interesting, and that was by a conductor who misunderstood him."

This brought in no money. Nickie had once briefly worked on the local police force (an outlet I had urged as ideal for his inductive mind) but he had no more than settled down on the city payroll than an aunt had foolishly died and left him a small trust fund, the interest from which (roughly ninety-five dollars a week) he saw as bringing a cultivated insouciance once more within his reach, by conferring on him the status of Young Man With a Private Income. He had but to quit his job to become a free-lance sleuth. And quit it he had! So now we were presumably waiting for a hysterical woman *not* his wife to burst in on him with the news that her husband of a day had vanished, leaving no trace, and to press on him a retainer of ten thousand dollars. Meanwhile he was to be seen nightly at the Samothrace, the Greek's, quoting Cyril Connolly to the effect that he vegetated, while other people merely lived, when fresh out of aphorisms of his own. Of his indolence he said, "I'm developing character the hard way — with plenty to eat and drink and no worries."

"He's hopeless," said my sister as we sat in the Grotegut library that rotten night in June. "Not that you're much better yourself, at times. 'You hardly know him.' God."

"I'll stand by that remark," I said. "Two people should know one another inside out, till they can see in a clear and charitable light what *produces* the frailties that produce the tensions, and what if anything can be done about them. Nickie's tried, Lila — he has. He's sworn off being a Restoration wit several times for your and the children's sake, promised, like a drunkard taking the pledge, to come home and talk United States, only to go back to it each time, like a drunkard to drink. That should show you that, like drink, it springs from some inner conflict or problem that we evidently haven't gotten to yet."

"I knew him better when I first met him than I do now."

"You're a simple girl, without a bent for those paradoxes of his, the intellectual life and all, and I rather think that may be part of the rub. He seems affectionate enough, at parties and all, holding your hand and what not. The soul of domesticity."

"Shouldn't that begin at home?"

"It's because you're not up to the repartee that you say things like that, and are bitter. But try to understand what it means to *him*, what makes him tick, produces the particular *esprit* that is Nickie. Only when it's certain nothing can be done, that the ride will never be worth the tolls, should two people throw up the sponge and call a marriage quits."

"I've had enough tolls, not to mention bumps and detours. No, I want out."

We sank into glum silence. Lila dug a cigarette from a pack, twirling it characteristically in her lips to wet the tip. She snapped at a pocket lighter which at first resisted ignition, then yielded a tongue of flame that lapped the length of the cigarette and half her nose: the fruit of repairs recently made to it by the glittering lad under discussion.

I walked the width of the room, frowning in troubled thought. I gave my belt a hitch, and announced to her quietly: "Lila, Nickie has a touch of schizophrenia."

My sister laughed rather acidly through her burnt nose. "There's a lot of that going around, isn't there?"

"I'll tell you what I'm going to do with you, Lila. I'm going to give this thing my full attention."

She looked up in alarm. She set her glass down, now almost empty, and said:

"Chick. Chick, I'm going to tell you something straight from the shoulder. No holds barred, no punches pulled, no nothing."

56

She picked up her drink, but only to revolve its dregs in their ice a moment before setting it nervously down again.

"People are talking about you. You're the butt of a lot of — Now, wait. You run this column. Readers write you about their homey little problems — should they change jobs and how long ought a mother-in-law visit — and as long as it's just that it's fine. But when you bring them into your office and start messing around in their psyches — "

"I seem to remember having helped your husband once. Case of amnesia, wasn't it?"

"Into which you drove him with your therapy."

I really could not let this pass.

"I drove him into it?" I said, standing over her. "You did. By cracking that burglary case he couldn't, thereby making yourself so intolerable to his ego he had to forget who you were. A fugue, we call that. Your marriage very nearly went on the rocks then, baby. I pulled it through."

"And here we are again. Which brings me to the second of the ways you're playing with fire — marriage counselor. Now don't flap your arms around like a windmill. Here are the facts. You take this intellectual, this Ivy Leaguer, and convince him he should be a cop — a dick — "

"It was my considered opinion, based on a careful analysis of his aptitudes, that criminology was a good niche for him."

"That brings us to number three of the methods by which you spread confusion."

I stood at the window with my back to her, drawing patiently on a cigarette. I could hear, or perhaps just sense, her turning toward me in her chair.

"Chick, do you know what people call you?"

"What?"

"A triple-threat man. Because what you don't make worse with domestic relations or vocational guidance you use psychoanalysis on. Now don't stand there snorting smoke. I hate to do

57

this to you, but there's a slogan going around about you. Betty Franz told me, not to be catty, but because she felt she owed it to us. And I owe it to you to tell you. Would you like to hear what it is?"

"Not especially."

"What they're saying is, 'When you think things can't get any worse, see Chick Swallow.' "

I had become aware, by gazing through two windows into a room at right angles to this one, of something that had vaguely been seeming to insist on my attention out there. The other room was a sort of lounge, or den, fully illuminated perhaps in expectation of spillover from the party, and in one corner stood a statue of Venus with a radio in her stomach. I smiled at this. I liked it. At that juncture of a really rather painful scene it not only drained off emotional pressure through the loving valve of humor, but, by its reminder of the plane on which after all most human judgment is pitched, offered a bridge to forgiveness as well as a call to patience. It said to me: "Little children, love one another."

Turning back into the room, I twisted out my cigarette and said gently, "It's not just that he don't plant taters, he don't plant cotton. It's a whole view of life that we've got to knock out of him. Leave this to me. If I can only — "

She broke in with a shake of her head, looking into her lap.

"I don't want your advice, or anybody's, any more. That isn't what I called you in here for. All I want is your blessing, as my brother, before I go to Reno."

I stood watching her — watching what was an obvious struggle against tears. They would be damned up now, only to flow later, when she was alone.

"I withhold that blessing, Lila," I said, quietly. In the silence, the babel of voices could be heard like a surf beating monotonously against the closed door. "Instead I shall do everything in my power to get you two straightened out. I know that

58

mostly means getting Nickie straightened around, but I mean to take that on again whether you want me to or no. But I must have this one last chance with him. It's unlikely that I'll run into him here tonight, and a few words at the buffet table isn't the way to handle this anyway. I'll go beard him in his den first thing tomorrow. I want you to promise me you won't see any lawyers or go boarding any trains to Reno till I've had one more go at it. Will you promise?"

She shrugged, which sufficed as consent.

"What can I lose?" she said.

"Just you wait and see!" I said, and, taking her affectionately by the arm, led her out the door and back to the party.

6

THE Greek himself was at first all that I saw in the Samothrace. He was behind the cash register, "prostrate on a chair," as in his current self-pitying mood he called the sitting position when involving himself, turning the pages of an Athenian newspaper with a bored expression.

His present concern was to "favor his feet," which he had more than once described as on their last legs. He was forever going to chiropodists, meanwhile undermining what remained of them with health shoes, in which he cut gashes to relieve the pressure just as he would in any others, thus indicating to experts the futility of their measures. Nothing pleased the Greek more than the failure of any ministration or expedient, the mark of the true hypochondriac, and doubtless the chief satisfaction he derived from his visits to the podiatrists was that of regularly certifying their impotence. There was always some organ or area of his body in whose imperviousness to treatment he could take pride. A previous citadel which the specialists had been invited to storm had been his head, long the home of peculiar humming, or buzzing, noises; they had not, to my knowledge, ever been formally eradicated but they were no longer mentioned, having supposedly served their psychological purpose. His system was like a symphony orchestra of which each instrument was permitted a term of solo self-expression, according to the whim of the conductor. Now it was the feet. When I had once told the Greek that he struck me as a bit hypochondriac, he had replied, "Yeah, I wouldn't be surprised I got that too."

After greeting him and dropping a word of commiseration, I became aware that the restaurant was not empty after all.

Alone at a rear table, his back partly to the door, sat a figure in blue flannels reading a newspaper of his own, recognizable even from here as the London *Times Literary Supplement*. A cigarette burned in the fingers of one hand and a pony of something stood beside an empty coffee cup. At the sound of my voice Nickie dropped the *Lit Sup*, as he called it, and waved to me.

"Well, well. *Setzen Sie sich.*"

Drawing out a chair for myself here was no longer a natural act, though a familiar one. I had outlived the period it characterized. These were the same tables at which, suave and heathen, destinationless and suave, we had squandered the golden afternoons of youth, but I was no longer that youth. (To the resolute Proustian, steeped in that genius's time chemistry, I suppose they were not the same tables either.) Nothing is so alien as the once intimate, once we are parted from it. So that the Samothrace worked in my heart a reverse magic: it was not a café in which to partake of food so much as a museum of my lost self, reminding me — but without evoking it — of a past in whose fantastic spirit I had once broken bread. It had not the power to haunt me — I haunted it.

Seeing His Nibs still at home in the place did me no good either. His blackthorn was on another chair and under the table dozed his dog, a wire-haired Griffon known as Prud'homme. That Nickie saw the name as spelled that way, with the apostrophe, there was now no longer any doubt. A card from Majorca mentioning the animal had confirmed suspicions. The detail made my teeth ache, and injected an added hazard into a name I already had trouble saying, fond as I was of the creature that bore it. The Griffon is a medium-sized dog of great strength and vigor, with a harsh coat like the bristles of a wild boar, into which it is pleasant to rummage down to the relatively silky undercoat. Prud'homme was steel-gray, with splashes of chestnut, and had a very intelligent air.

"Well so! To what do I owe the pleasure of this visit?"

"Pause in the day's occupation," I answered drily, sitting down. "How did you like the party?"

"Bore."

"Why wasn't everyone else bored?"

"They may have lacked the discernment." Nickie twisted round in his chair and called the Greek. "How about a little drink for our friend?"

This was going to be worse than I'd thought. I had appraised his habits as a return to dilettantism, but nothing in the vein of the old days quite matched the sort of thing he was doing now. Boredom was a matter of discernment! I said I'd have a straight Bourbon, which the Greek affected not to have heard. He was always pretending not to hear orders, especially those from remote corners of the store, preferring to hug his own corner, and resisting to the last all attempts to dislodge and set him in motion. However, by dint of prolonged insistence on our part, bolstered by allusions to the Bill of Rights and threats of reprisal, we managed to establish our claim to service, and he shambled over with the whisky, with the customary show of pain and mumbling about his shoes.

"The Greek has a pedal obsession," Nickie twitted, jerking his head at him.

"Pedal my foot," the Greek said, and toiled away to his nook.

I tipped back half my whisky while Nickie sipped at his brandy.

"You were talking to Steve Coote at the party," I chatted.

"For my sins."

"Oh, now, I don't think Steve is fair game. It's all very well to poke fun at him, but those humorous sketches of his do bring pleasure to a good many people. He's going to leave the world a better place to live in."

"Yes, but *when?*"

"We could all take a lesson from him — hard-working, producing for his family. People like him are the backbone of this country, and they make up 99 per cent of it."

"I suppose it takes all kinds."

This was incredible. I was like a physician who having come to treat a simple relapse encounters at the bedside an altogether new strain of the virus in question, against which previous measures are no guarantee. By way of acquiring a more substantial "specimen" of the germ for study, as it were, I drew further samplings from quarters of the conversational bloodstream where it might be presumed most to be multiplying — the literary.

"What's new in the *Lit Sup?*" I asked, picking up that organ and opening it.

"Swell article on contemporary style," Nickie said. "The American novel is a fat slob, and as for the *mot juste*, that went out with Wolfe. Why bother with one word when three will do?"

"Here's a review of the Darrow biography," I said, my hackles rising. "Favorable, too. I'm surprised to find a character so American-grain so appreciated abroad."

"Well, by and large, Darrow is the kind of genius that crosses borders fairly easily. Like Lincoln. The appeal is universal."

"And have you noticed something else about figures with the tragic sense? They're the ones who buck the race up. Not the twitterers."

Here I sensed Nickie mulling an old gambit, that of agreeing with you by saying what you'd just said only better, which was more irritating than rebuttal.

"Yes," he said, moving his glass about on the tabletop, "it's interesting to note how much of our faith is derived from skeptics. Having squarely faced an empty universe, they are best bent on cultivating our poor corner of it. Having most nakedly glimpsed eternal snow and ice, they themselves most radiate warmth and light. No, you're right. It is not from optimists that we derive the courage to go on."

"Bunk," I said. "This all seems to me tenuous and far-fetched."

I closed the paper and set it aside.

Nickie sat appraising me over his glass as he sipped.

"Why do you always get sore when I agree with you? It's a curious habit."

I leaned forward and smacked the table with both hands.

"Where will you get the money to have Francie's teeth straightened?" I demanded.

"Where would I get it if I were working?" he answered, alertly. "If that's what you're leading up to. You needn't start another lecture. I'm perfectly aware of the needs of my children and perfectly capable of taking care of them myself. These orthodontists are all brigands! Dr. Quentin quoted a price of three thousand dollars for this job. I'd have to borrow it if I were still working, just as I would now."

"Why do you say 'would'? Aren't you going to get my niece's mouth fixed up?"

"Oh, my God," said Nickie, writhing into a fresh position. He spoke with an emphasis ill suited to the role of *bon vivant*, spreading his arms as he expounded some ideas, like a rug merchant extolling dubious goods. "Look, I don't hold with this current fad of running off to the orthodontist with every little thing, if that's what you mean. They've created malocclusion just as the psychoanalysts have created neuroses, by getting the term about. Every child in Decency has its mouth wired up like a bale of hay. Of course these men recommend braces. It's their living."

"Francie has an overbite."

"So does Ingrid Bergman. So does Loretta Young. I wonder where they'd be without them."

"It suits your purpose to wonder," I retorted, reaching across the table to tap his chest, a measure to which I had hoped I'd not be forced. "Bozo! You're just rationalizing your failure to discharge your obligations as a parent, such as correcting Francie's buck."

Nickie sighed and shook his head. "Oh, my dear boy."

He had spoken in a tone that was almost paternal. Now he screwed round in his chair in the manner of clubmen summoning waiters, and by flourishing our empty glasses in an authoritative manner very nearly succeeded in fetching the Greek. The latter grunted noncommitally, like a sleeper refusing to acknowledge he has awakened, and sat with folded arms and closed eyes. We returned to our ruckus.

"I could kill that aunt of yours," I said through my own teeth.

"That will hardly be necessary, will it?" Nickie answered with a laugh.

"All the trouble that legacy has caused. Ninety bucks a week! You had a hard enough time making ends meet when you were drawing a paycheck, but now — is there a merchant in town who doesn't have you on his Bills Outstanding?"

"All my bills are outstanding," said Nickie, leveling into his role again.

"The trouble with you, lad, is you want the privileges of marriage without the obligations, and that's not mature. Marriage *is*, after all, a give-and-take."

"I've never thought of it in quite that way. That's interesting. I must try to remember it."

"Don't you see you're living a romance far more moonstruck

than any shopgirl fiction?" I said, striking the table with my fist this time. "When you pounded a beat you at least had your feet on the ground, but now! What are you waiting for? Pete Cheshire to get out of jail? Your Moriarty free again to challenge your wits?"

"There were things in his early work that I admired very much," said my prince. "The question is whether he'll fulfill that early promise. There's so little creative talent coming along these days. He *is* due to get out soon, isn't he?"

I fell back like a collapsed puppet, unable to believe my ears. How could he have missed my satire? No intellectual is without his blind spots, where humor fails him, I reminded myself. Sophistication of the extreme sort always seems to carry a kind of built-in naïveté, as any café-society column shows.

I gave the screw of travesty another turn.

"Most criminals lack the imagination that excites a man's wit, you mean," I said, to see just how far I could go without his perceiving the mockery. "What one wants is an adversary worthy of his steel."

"Precisely. Pete has a certain low cunning. That we must give him. Whether he has the talent to go on to something really first-rate remains to be seen."

I thought of hands enclosing his throat in an act of strangulation, the thumbs joined over the larynx, the fingers well down under the collar — all quite undetected. We'd had a schoolmate named Joe Bond who by bobbing his Adam's apple up and down could agitate his necktie. He'd come to a bad end, driving while intoxicated on the Jersey Turnpike. In a restaurant across the street I could see a fat man at a window table eating Danish with a knife and fork. How could I be sure it was Danish, I wondered, at this distance? Because his movements had an element of surface absurdity, traceable only to some such source.

My inner mind flowed on in its separate way, like an underground river. It was thinking not of Joe Bond or Nickie or the man in the other restaurant at all, but of an article I'd read in one of the psychiatric journals to which I subscribed. It related a fascinating case — or I should say a fascinating treatment — involving shock. Not the customary electric or drug shock, but a deliberately aimed emotional blow which had shaken the patient up in much the same sense. The subject had been a shipping clerk in late youth who displayed marked anxiety about marrying a girl to whom he had been engaged for nine years. Agitation and night sweats had followed each mention of "naming the day." He was put under hypnosis, and on arousal confronted with data indicating latent criminal sexual tendencies. He promptly married, frightened out of his wits. The doctor had deliberately exaggerated, even fabricated, thus "shocking" him into the assumption of a normal bond for which, previously, there had been no alternative beside which it had seemed less appalling. He acted literally on the Pauline advice that it was better to marry than to burn — in the electric chair!

Why should Nickums not be given a similar roughing up? Was not some extreme possible which, by holding up his life to him for the mare's-nest it was, would administer a purging ridicule? A man needs his liver periodically cleaned out — why not his ego? The problem was to hit on some measure sufficiently drastic to drive home the parody I could not penetrate his vanity with by verbal chaffing. Some — some what? Wait a minute. I had it. Some *hoax.*

What kind of hoax? I puzzled over that as we continued to dispute.

"You know something?" I said. "You resent me. Oh, yes you do. And I'll tell you why. You resent me because of all I've done for you. It's human nature."

He nodded, tracing figures on the table with the base of his glass. He drew across it a design of continuous triangles of the sort that had become familiar in his pauses, and that are associated with Navajo blankets.

"You have a point there, I'm afraid," he said, again in the tone that warned you that your recent remark was about to be refined into an epigram. "It's easy enough for a man to love his enemies. The question is whether he can forgive his benefactors."

"Horse manure," I said. "I'm not going to sit here and listen to a lot of horse manure." I plucked my derby from a chair and put it on. I did not yet rise. I finished a last trickle of whisky with it on. "If you knew what a figure you cut, sitting there. What an ass you are, in the main. I wish I could drive it home to you. You've got no gumption, no get-up-and-go, no nothing."

"I suppose not," he sighed quite concurringly. "But then I have no ambition in the usual sense. Perhaps I was not meant to need it. I haven't your reputation, but then I can do without that."

Something in the way he was striking a match to light a cigarette set me seething. I lashed out blindly.

"Why does this dog have a cotter pin in his name?" I shouted, rising out of the chair. "Don't you see how ridiculous it all is? O God in Heaven, it's all too silly for words. Prud'homme!"

The dog, hearing his name barked in what he took to be angry summons, leaped from his sleep and wagged his tail at me in confusion. I reached down and soothed him with a few discreet words. Nickie had waved the match out, holding a mouthful of smoke uninhaled as he watched me. I felt myself perspiring, and my smile came tautly as I added, "Is he named after the French painter, Nickie? I've often wondered. Is that who he's named after?"

"No, no. The painter is Prud'hon. You're thinking of Pierre Prud'hon."

"Of course. How stupid of me."

I tried to summon the love necessary to go on with this, but it wouldn't come. Hearing his name further bandied — or thinking he had — Prud'homme looked from one to the other of us with bright expectation, panting. He had that expression of doting regard we like to call "human," though whether it is anything more than an echo of something canine in our own natures is a question.

"It isn't that I don't have faith in you," I said to Nickie. "I do. That's why I holler at you sometimes. I think you're worth saving." He nodded, breathing smoke as he consulted a wall clock. "Because you *can* amount to something. You have the stuff . . ."

I let the conversation coast to a stop, content to leave it so. Because the idea for the hoax had struck me all of a heap. It had sprung into my mind full-fledged, as the plot for *Uncle Tom's Cabin* is said to have sprung into Harriet Beecher Stowe's while she was sitting in church. This was my "plot," as indeed I might call it:

Saturday night would find us both at another party, the Flickendens'. Along toward the middle of the evening, there would be a phone call for Nickie. At the other end of the wire would be an overwrought woman's voice reporting that her husband had been murdered, and would Nickie Sherman please come as soon as possible. Nickie would high-tail it over to the address given, that of a former bit actress named Susan Markey whom I knew but Nickie didn't, and whose husband was an inveterate prankster. He, the husband, would be lying face down on the bedroom floor, clad only in pajamas, a lamp cord twisted round his neck and his tongue lolling out in a horrible fashion. Nickie would get to work gathering clues (in anticipation of the thick-fingered police), in the midst of which the corpse would rise and dust himself off. Everyone would get a good laugh, including the party guests, who would have piled into their cars and followed in the excitement. Nickie would put a good face on it, enjoying the fun at his own expense, but once home would take the lesson to heart. He would have been made to see himself as others saw him — at last! The jape would rock him to his roots at first, but then, his ego cauterized, stripped of his folly, he would come down to earth and maybe start a new life on terms with reality. Whether he would learn I was behind it was unimportant; if he did, he would live to thank me for it.

That was the plan.

"I must be off," I said, eager to get back to the office and look up the article again. "See you at the Flickendens' on Saturday?"

"For my sins."

I hurried from the reception room to my private office with my secretary at my heels, reading messages aloud as we flew.

"Mrs. Cherne called again to say that her husband now sleeps with a chest protector on. There's a letter from the Women's Club thanking you for your splendid talk on "The Problem of the Only Child." They want to know if you'll address them next month on "The Problem of the Only Parent." Like when the father and mother are divorced and the children live with one or the other," Miss McConkey reported as we trotted on through, the swinging door flapping in our wake. "Here, I'll take your hat, Dr. Swallow. A Mr. Appleyard phoned. He said you'd know what it was about and for you to please call him back without fail. Oh, and Dr. Swallow." Her habit of addressing me that way was a persistent one which I had decided simply to ignore since its correction would have entailed the removal of props vital to her ego. The reverse of Nickie, she needed building up, and nothing built her up so much as bustling importantly about calling me "Doctor." Now her voice dropped a tone to register the sense of portent which accompanied all her references to the Boss. "Mr. Bulwinkle has been trying to reach you all afternoon. He wonders where you *go*. He wonders what you *do*. Shall I get him now and let him know you're in?"

"Put him on," I ordered slavishly, "this very minute!"

"Right, Doctor."

She went out with her gelatinous walk, her flesh setting up within mine a useless contrapuntal greed, leaving in my mind a familiar mixture of tenderness and filth. If without preamble I raised her skirts and likened her limbs to marble seen by moonlight, would I be accused of Neoclassicism? It was painful to recall that the one time I had taken her to lunch, at a neighborhood restaurant, she had looked at the menu and exclaimed, "Ah, they have *soup du jour* today. I love that."

I sighed heavily and turned to the mountain of human documents awaiting reply on my desk. It seemed to me that the problems lost quality with each new paper added to the syndicate we fed, which now numbered eleven dailies in almost as many states. The first letter was from a woman who wrote:

> I've been married seventeen years and never had an organism. What are those? I read in articles and my friends tell me I am missing something, but don't know how to go about changing my ways. My husband refuses to discuss it with me. . . .

I threw the letter in the wastebasket (all that could be done with queries bearing no return address and not suitable for published reply) and picked up another. It was a complaint from a woman who had originally written in asking how to get rid of moles. Since we'd had no garden editor, I simply had Miss McConkey phone a drugstore for the name of a reliable mole poison and recommended it in turn to the reader. It was a pellet-form toxic called, I believe, Mole-Slay, which are put down into mole runs. The woman had purchased a package and swallowed one or two with a glass of water, necessitating her being rushed to the hospital to have her stomach pumped out. Which was the first inkling I'd had that she had meant not lawn

71

pests but face blemishes, and that her letter should have been referred to our Beauty Hints expert. Now she was sending notes threatening legal action, which it was a simple matter to keep from the higher-ups by putting them into the wastebasket also.

I rose and went to a refectory table on which were kept all my magazines, laid out by Miss McConkey in neat rows like those in clubs frequented by men of parts. I easily found the issue of the *Psychiatric Quarterly* I wanted, and sat down in an armchair to reread the article which so excited me.

It had originally been a paper read at a psychiatric convention in Lisbon, by a Dutch practitioner named Van Kuykens, and ran:

> There are times when the quickest way to bring a man down to earth is to blow him sky-high. Blasting is often preliminary to construction. Of course such a measure is precisely the matter of delicacy that it does not sound, and should be undertaken in only the most skilled hands, by someone with the fullest possible knowledge of what he is doing.

I raised my eyes to pause in reflection. I guessed I knew Nickie all right enough, inside and out, to gauge the degree of embarrassment that might prove stunning. I read on:

> For what we are talking about here is a kind of fission, if you will, a momentary furious splitting of the atom of Pride (of which let us remember that the notorious Ego is only the nucleus). Or to use a cruder metaphor, it is like one of these calculated kicks we deal a piece of broken machinery, which will make it work again if it does not destroy it utterly. . . .

My phone was being buzzed and I rose to answer it.

"Mr. Bulwinkle will see you now, Doctor," Miss McConkey said, "without delay."

I galloped derisively into Bulwinkle's office and came to a running stop on an island of coagulated stockings known as a hooked rug six feet from his desk. There I stood at a caricature of attention for some seconds.

"Yes, sir?" I said in a timorous squeal which took courage, lifting our relationship as it did into the realm of pure satire.

Bulwinkle shifted from ham to ham, like Sweeney in his bath. He sat in shirtsleeves because he was the Boss, while I had on a coat, being a shirtsleeve philosopher with some standing in the community. His tie hung on a rack as well as his coat; it depicted a girl manipulating a canoe in bright sunlight. He clenched in his teeth an expired cigar, which helped him strike the note of ferocity which he tended to confuse with high standards.

Bulwinkle had only recently taken over the *Picayune Blade*, which he edited as well as published. He modeled himself on the prevailing idea of the truculent, though inwardly sensitive, city-desk man, snapping, "Why can't I get decent reporters?" and "Call that a story?" in persecuted soliloquy. He fomented bedlam in both office and pressroom and tried to convey the impression, though there was always plenty of time to get the paper out, that we were operating under intolerable pressure. He cultivated chaos on his desk, among whose effects were the black coffee, aspirin and stale pie associated with the ruthless metropolitan dailies. On his assumption of ownership, he had summoned the entire staff to a lecture in which he told them bluntly that newspaper work was a brutal profession and that he could promise them nothing but long marches and hard bivouacs, which came as a surprise to numerous veteran employees accustomed to the leisurely, even apathetic, tempo under his predecessor, but who, however, obligingly broke into a trot when Bulwinkle came into view, pecked out copy with their hats on, had sandwiches and coffee sent in, and spoke of "getting the rag to bed."

"Look, Swallow," he said, relighting the cigar butt, "god-damn it, with Melton leaving we won't have anybody to handle Today's Chuckle. I was wondering if you'd care to take it on. It's open."

"I think not," I said. "Thanks though."

"You'd do a bang-up job."

I resented that. To be judged capable of turning out: "Waiter, do you serve crabs?" "Yes, what'll you have?" — to be regarded as just the man to beg, borrow, steal or fabricate a wheeze like that every day — filled me with rage. By way of pan-ning for a gleam of self-respect in all this muck I said, "It's not for me. Besides, my column takes all my time."

"It pays fifty bucks a week extra. We're going to run it boxed, on the lower front page, from now on. Just a two-line joke a day. You have a sense of humor."

It was what saw me through many such a scene as this, did he but know, and saw me through now. I smiled and said, "Thanks just the same."

"Okie doke." He shrugged and looked down at his desk. I sensed that he had something more on his mind — that the problem of succession to Today's Chuckle was the least of it.

"Swallow," he said, rising, "you have a hell of a lot of peo-ple come to your office. I see them in the waiting room when I go by. Just a minute. I know it's always been policy for the Lamplighter to be available to people in need as well as to answer their letters. But I've been told that you get some of them in there and psychoanalyze them. Is that true?"

"I wouldn't call it that," I said. "If you mean do I handle their problems in a psychological light, of course — that's the way they come in. It's the way people think these days."

"But do you represent yourself as a *psychiatrist?*"

"Certainly not."

He fiddled worriedly with a file of papers on his desk, behind which he remained standing. I noticed that he had only one sleeve rolled up, as though in the frenzies of journalism there had been no time to do the other.

"Your secretary calls you 'Doctor.'"

"It's a little notion she's picked up. I'll speak to her about it."

"See that you do. You're a newspaperman — not a head-shrinker."

I thought that ended the matter. Bulwinkle appeared to wish it might, too. But he hesitated again, then asked with visible reluctance:

"I understand there was some hullabaloo a few years ago, before my time, about you practising psychiatry on a girl. Lawsuit, wasn't it?"

I laughed, though my disrelish at the phrase "on a girl" was keen. "Oh, sir, it was nothing. The whole thing was a frame-up from the start, and I knew it. You see, I deliberately walked into the trap in order to get a case for my brother-in-law, a kind of amateur sleuth. I thought he needed building up then, but I know better now."

"The story is that this brother-in-law went into amnesia as a result of your treatment."

"That's a lie! It was a result of his wife's solving a case that had him stumped, involving a small-time grifter name Pete Cheshire, known as the Smoothie — "

"Another ward of yours, wasn't he?" said Bulwinkle, reading what appeared to be a full dossier.

"He was paroled to me, yes. My position in the community gives me lots of these extra responsibilities. We all went pretty much through hell on it, but I think we've won through. We're in the clear now."

"Is your brother-in-law all better?"

"Oh, absolutely. He doesn't even remember he had amnesia."

"Well, watch your step. We don't want the paper sued, you know."

Appleyard said: "Let's go sit in the garden. Though it's probably cooler here in the house. Stone foundation helps that much. The muggy days are here again."

I was glad to leave a house which I found oppressive not for reasons of humidity but because of what is called in journalism an unfavorable climate of opinion.

He led the way out the back and into a dooryard long remembered. The arbor sagged under wistaria denser than that which choked the front porch; the vines now supported in their clutch the crumbling latticework, rather than the other way around. I have always thought wistaria a disagreeable bloom. It lay in obscene bloated clusters at our feet as we made for a glider, scarcely less decayed than the arbor, at the edge of the orchard. Sweet trees of my childhood, standing suddenly in your flower like lathered shaving brushes; cool stream that rippled through the hot afternoons, beneath the sheltering maple in days long past. The treehouse, constructed of odd lumber and the sides of commercial packing cartons, was deep in the obscuring boughs, but I made out a patch of faded letters reading KELLOGG'S CORN FLA, and a face peering from that green lair: the Nereid was watching. In the astigmatic dusk, I had a sense of mythology encroaching on us, enveloping events. As if reality were still in control but only by a narrow margin, like the 51 per cent by which conservative businessmen struggle to retain possession of corporations threatened by unstable elements buying up securities on the sly. I had, indeed, the picture of sprites and goblins abroad, now that the sun had set and the moon risen, purchasing shares at a rate that might turn the tables against us if we did not watch out. How long would we be able to keep even our fragile hold on sanity?

"Now then, have you given any more thought to Sweetie?" Appleyard asked, unctuously enough, as he sat down on the glider. He was wearing freshly pressed denim slacks and a Basque shirt of red and white plaid, open at the throat; just what an astute stage director would have chosen for a weak character given to buck passing.

"May I answer that by asking another question?" I remained standing, holding to one of the metal uprights of the glider as I crossed one foot over the other and looked down at him. He was wiping his brow with a clean white handkerchief. "Would you say she's had a parental guidance that took account of her needs? Particularly, a strong father image in her formative years? Can you honestly say she's had that, Appleyard?"

"*Shh!*" Appleyard said. He pointed a thumb in the direction of the tree, from where we might be overheard. "Yes," he whispered, "I think I can say that, in all conscience. I was always good to her, and stern when the situation called for that."

"Who is the real authority in this house?" I asked, seeing another face at a house window, this one like a withered gourd.

"What do you mean by that?"

"What steps have you taken to mature that girl?"

"For one thing, we've had a telephone installed in the tree-house."

"An extension?"

"Certainly not! Her own private phone, where she can be reached. We thought it might encourage her to keep in touch." He sighed and looked toward the house. "Let's go inside for a breath of air. It's awful out here. And these damned gnats." He smote himself in the face.

"Just what did you expect me to do?"

Appleyard was uncertain; at least he hesitated. The light was draining away, and I could see the horn of the moon over the woodlot. After a moment he said:

"I was thinking if you were to begin all over again . . . I mean, take it from the scene in the coalbin where it all went wrong, somehow, and this time get it right . . . Do it finely, so to speak, and thus lead her out into normal daylight, like other girls . . . I think you know what I mean. You frightened her —

all right, *It* frightened her — into this Lady of Shalott character she's become. Who better than you to coax her out of her ivory tower, off that island, down to Camelot? Show her sex is beautiful rather than beastly."

There seemed now no mistaking his meaning.

"You mean make *love* to her?"

Appleyard had been a bit ruffled in stating his plan, but his composure returned now that the words were out and had not frozen us to stone.

"She's a 'good' girl for bad reasons, where the reverse might have some virtue to it. My daughter is ruined far worse than if she had been ruined! I make no bones about saying that only by proper — by someone *not* bungling, but rather — Where are you going?"

"Home. I'll have no part of this. I want out." I strode toward the porch.

"You're in it up to your neck whether you like it or no."

Appleyard's voice was so low as to be barely audible, yet it arrested me with one foot on the bottom step. I turned back to hear him out in this position. My coat was over my arm.

"You take a conventional point of view just where it serves no purpose. Do you call *that*" — he jerked a thumb over his shoulder toward the darkening tree again — "purity? Is that what you want to perpetuate? A virgin locked in amber? Do you think a moral quibble quite the manly thing? I don't. Not when you're probably the only man alive who can unscramble the mess we've got on our hands."

"You keep forgetting one thing. I'm not to blame for it. I thought I made that quite clear."

"All right, you're not. The accusations are withdrawn. Now will you see what you can do to help us? Or will you skedaddle like the frightened rabbit that I think you are? Or are you a coward clean through?"

I sighed irresolutely. "The situation is fraught with danger,"

I said. "You speak of the Lady of Shalott, and a neat comparison it is. But do you remember what happened to her, when she finally did go down to Camelot? It killed her. She had been too long in the world of Illusion."

"I'll take that risk. Things couldn't be any worse than they are now. That's why I'm calling on you."

Here was an unpleasant echo of what my sister had told me they were saying about old Chick Swallow, around town — and a moment's inkling of how they might have it all hurled back in their teeth. The most delicate piece of surgery one had yet been called upon to perform . . .

Appleyard crossed the grass to my side. He looked down, walking with that thoughtful tread with which people try out a new pair of shoes in a store.

"I've given this considerable, and very earnest, thought, and I believe it makes sense. Take up where you left off, and get it right. I'm a father asking you to seduce his daughter. Is that such an unreasonable request? It happens every day," he went on, backing me up the stairs and against the porch wall while in the wood the centaurs and the fauns were buying up stock like mad by the light of the moon. A faint wind stirred the leaves among which, over the chuckling river, Daphne hung between heaven and earth. Things were in a kind of unbearable balance, half real, half mythological, with myself planted with a foot in either kingdom. I stood woodenly, as if turned to a tree. "In baseball parlance, you once muffed a fly," Appleyard murmured gently. "Now I'm asking you to chase the ball."

"And if I refuse?"

He took my arm and steered me toward the kitchen door. "In that case," he answered with what I will call extreme unction, "I shall have to turn you over to Mme. Piquepuss."

Mme. Piquepuss sat in the cool gloom of the parlor drinking beer from a cup. I thought it was coffee she was sipping till I saw her go into the kitchen, later, and refill the cup from a large bottle of Budweiser. Her stick was propped against her chair, a high wingback embroidered with peacocks. She looked up when I entered, nudged forward encouragingly by Appleyard like a child pushed onstage, and said, "Can I give you something to drink?"

"No, thank you," I said, resisting all obligations here, even of ceremony. Appleyard gave a last glance over his shoulder into the room as he fled up the stairs, his footsteps swift and decisive as befit a man taking a firm line.

Dressed again in dark hues, Mme. Piquepuss was but meagerly perceptible in the half-light, except for her hands and the cup and saucer which caught a gleam of light from a street lamp, just turned on. I sat in a draw-up chair opposite her from where, without seeing her head, I could make out the white antimacassar it partially obliterated. The cup floated upward, lurked a moment out of sight, and returned to the saucer. I reached out and drew the tasseled cord of a floor lamp. "Do you mind?" I said as Mme. Piquepuss sprang, blinking, into view.

She set the cup and saucer on a table which also had one of those white tidies on it — they were everywhere. On the table I noticed something else. It was a sheaf of frayed foolscap, rolled up and secured with a fat rubber band. She touched the corners of her mouth with a square of cambric and said, "People don't like to sit in the dark any more. Is it because they're afraid of their own thoughts?"

"Twilight is more appreciated in rural communities than urban, and more in foreign lands than this, where we are a young and vigorous people eager to snap the switches and get on with the evening," I said. "And I'm not at all well. I had a restless night."

"Not sleeping any too well?"

Her voice was low and — "throaty" is not the word that comes to me so much as "furry." It reminded me of soft caterpillars and things proceeding cautiously in deep shade; it was something traveling up my spine as much as heard in my ear. The ghost of an accent came and went, subtly changeable, like the nap on her velvet dress, worn in defiance of the heat, or in observance of propriety to callers. She had emigrated from the Touraine in the 1880s. I noted again the twitching play of Mme. Piquepuss's lips, like the flickering origins of smiles that came to naught. As she spoke she tapped her right foot gently on the rug, as though somewhere she heard a melody being faintly fiddled; or as though — the notion thrust itself grotesquely in — she were one of those rare people who obtain radio broadcasts on their dental fillings — though this may have been the result of a jumble of musical impressions Mme. Piquepuss herself conveyed, and that may be analyzed in this wise: The color of her velvet dress was a deep purplish blue, like that with which the carrying cases of musical instruments are lined. Perhaps it was this association that made her thin arms, for the moment angularly at rest in her lap, remind me of a disjointed clarinet, and all of these thoughts together foster the illusion that she was humming under her breath.

"No, I couldn't sleep," I said, and added with a smile, "except when it was time for the alarm to go off. For just as Proust was awakened by the thought that it was time to go to sleep, so most of the rest of us are, I judge, rather lulled into slumber by the realization that it is time to get up. He was a special case."

"We are all necessarily troubled about Sweetie, and all most anxious to get on with this matter," Mme. Piquepuss returned. "I almost thrashed her to make her talk about the Experience, but she would not. The alternative is to make you do so." She reached out to steady the stick, which was slipping along the flank of her chair. "It is naturally very difficult for her to speak of what occurred Down There, but she did tell me one thing."

"Go on."

81

"Please do not interrupt. There was evidently some sort of commotion, or scuffle, she said, during which you reached over and tried to touch something."

There was a rain of blows on my legs. Pummeling my knees, I leaned out of my chair and said, "Now this has gone far enough! I will not have any more of this absolutely ridiculous kind of talk. I say that too many people are paying too much attention to the fantasies of a hysterical girl — yes! — suffering from repression, who *wishes* some of the things she accuses others of had happened. What we call in psychology projection. So there you have it!"

"It's what she said happened."

"What does she say I was trying to touch? May I ask that we be specific? Shall we lay it on the line, please?"

Mme. Piquepuss gave an uneasy shrug, and glanced speculatively toward the back door.

"Oh, don't call *her* in, for heaven's sake. She doesn't even know what she's *got* there, for a man to *go* after," I said. "But if you could give me a rough idea where it was located, and perhaps a word as to its function, I'd appreciate it." Mme. Piquepuss's head lay back on the tidy, on which it rolled from side to side, the eyes closed, while she raised a hand in a plea to desist. "What was your understanding about that? Is — well, let me put it this way. Are there one or two of them?"

"Please."

"I think I have a right to ask that. Are there one or two?"

"One or two of what?" she brought out weakly.

"Of what I was trying to touch. For on whether singular or plural depends the gravity of the charge. If we are asked to consider someone reaching down a dress, with the query 'Are they beginning to sprout yet, girlie? Let's see. Are they, eh?' uttered in all good humor, that's one thing. If reaching up from underneath — "

Mme. Piquepuss was leaning over the side of the chair, in an ominous suggestion of someone two days at sea. The strain was too great for her. She could not finish what she had begun. I relented, and went on more charitably:

"My own guess is that the first, or milder, alternative was meant. I say this for reasons that may at first appear occult, but are based on what can be demonstrated as a mysterious sensory connection in things. What has broken my slumbers, my dear Mme. Piquepuss, is a recurring nightmare that I cannot divest myself of the hunch is related to the Experience in some subterranean way, though my conscious memory yields no account of what you say. Related to it because the feature of this nightmare is a double image — the idea of *two*. In my sleep, I keep dreaming that I am on a motorcycle, speeding down a dark road toward a pair of approaching headlights, between which it is my intention to steer my flying course, supposing them to be two other motorcycles, one at either side of the road. However, at each meeting the pair of headlights prove to be not two motorcycles but one truck, hurtling me awake among the disheveled bedclothes. The dream is repeated, like that of the woman I believe M. Verdurin kept seeing in *Swann's Way*, the evil woman whose hand, holding a cloth, would reappear before his face each time he dozed off and wipe him awake."

"No, I think it was Bergotte who had that dream," said Mme. Piquepuss, quite herself again and sitting erect. "Yes, it was Bergotte, in *The Captive*."

"You read Proust?" I said. "Why, what a pleasant surprise! I've been dipping into him again of late. Well, well! So we have something in common. A strong bond, wouldn't you say?"

Mme. Piquepuss was looking toward the bay window in which I sat. There were several wasps in the room, some of which had settled on the curtain there. She rose, glancing up at the ceiling as for some opening in the wall through which they might have made their entry. Picking up an enormous pair of shears from a table, she stole over to the curtain without disturbing the insects. Deftly, she slipped one of the blades under a wasp and cut it in two. She did this with a couple of others before the remaining few took wing and dispersed.

"I can't stand to swat things any more," she said, returning to her chair. "I suppose we mellow as we get older."

I stared at the halved wasps.

"They have spray bombs for these things now," I said. "Slug-a-Bug is a good one. They've perfected them so they're non-toxic to people, and can be used anywhere."

"This is nontoxic," she said, clacking the shears a time or two before laying them by. She settled herself again among the flaming peacocks. "Now then, where were we?"

"Sweetie, and these fibs of hers. 'Mythomania' is the term we have for the compulsion to tell stories. We'll get her through this, never fear! But now, Mme. Piquepuss," I said, "here's a curious thing that must have struck you too. How can anyone, so shy of the outside world, in her one sortie into it pull a stunt so brazen? I mean of course that oratorical contest she went into with a speech stolen bodily from Daniel Webster."

"Yes? Go on." Mme. Piquepuss took her cup to the kitchen, where I saw her reach into the icebox and refill it from the half-gallon Budweiser. I hurled myself woozily into some more Proust.

"How can a shrinking violet do anything so unlike her — so *publicly*? That is what we say. Till we remember that the trait most likely to accompany an extreme is its opposite. For just as artists are found to be serving on town schoolboards while businessmen collect rare editions; just as we find the local clergyman conducting a liaison with a barmaid and the prostitute a devout observer of religious forms; just as the skinflint — following the principle of contrariety which decrees that to every action there be an equal and opposite reaction — dispenses lavish tips to waiters, and the son long remarked as 'Mama's Boy' is discovered, one morning, to have dismembered his mother with an ax — so it is precisely the nervous girl — shy, ethereal, cloistered — who must at least once in her life blaze a trail across the national skies."

"Why just once?"

Having leaned back with my own eyes closed, not in agony but the better to spin a sample of that erectile grammar which I had once observed to be the proxy pleasure of a man doomed to invirility — this in high-school days when I had used to read of Combray in bed long after my light was ordered out, so that mingled with the narrator's fears that his Mama would not come to his bedroom to say good night were mine that my Papa would show up in mine (a visit ill-mitigated by my humorously remarking, as I did one night, of the writer in which he found me immersed, that, once arrested by this author, we may expect long sentences) — but of which in this brief oral espousal I had suddenly another intimation vouchsafed me, a flash of insight so inebriating that I regretted not being able to share it with Mme. Piquepuss (under pain of prejudicing my status with her), namely that this labyrinthine syntax called for feats of respiration to which an asthmatic might in his desolation aspire rather than anything to which normal breathing is even remotely geared — having been thus disposed in my chair, I had not seen Mme. Piquepuss return to the parlor. She had walked so softly. When I opened one eye it was to find her standing over me, the roll of foolscap in her hand. She was tapping it suggestively in her palm, like a truncheon.

"What do you mean?" I asked, sitting bolt upright and un-crossing my legs. At the same time I instinctively put out both hands in a reflex of self-defense — in time to catch the roll as it dropped into my lap.

"Read these," she said.

I removed the rubber band, unfurled the manuscript and began to read — for the surprise of my life.

7

THE first of Sweetie's poems that I read was executed in telegraphic quatrains reminiscent of Emily Dickinson, in form if not altogether in spirit:

> *The cock that splits my slumber*
>   *Is a very raffish bird*
> *Who has had my number*
>   *Ever since he heard*
>
> *That I would rather be,*
>   *By a lengthy sight,*
> *Ravished into morning*
>   *Than jilted out of night.*
>
> *The lord of light is brazen;*
>   *I see his lance come nigh*
> *When at last I open*
>   *The aspic of my eye.*

The next page of manuscript suggested that I was probably not reading the poems in the order in which they'd been written, in the order, that is, of Sweetie's spiritual and aesthetic development over the years the material spanned. It was a series of couplets done in the offhand mixture of rhyme and near-rhyme of the early Auden:

> *No need to cry "Touché!"*
> *When scalped of your toupée.*
> *All that's false must go.*
> *Breast the future so:*
> *Comrades marching bald*
> *Of all illusion, galled*
> *By nothing but a fattish*
> *Sentimental fetish.*

> *Beware the well-groomed prexy*
> *Whose daughter wants your proxy;*
> *Don't pay for those coiffures*
> *Seen in rotogravures.*
> *Beware the smiling briber.*
> *Develop lots of fiber.*
> *Plan on growing thinner*
> *Of a reasonable dinner,*
> *And leave the past to puke*
> *Into its own peruke.*

It was odd to think of Sweetie embracing proletarian thought and sounding calls to revolution, till one remembered her old obsession with the vested "They" — now simply transposed into an economic key — and that she probably didn't realize what she was saying anyway. A more interesting question to me was how long it had taken her to play it down, to "throw it away" as they were saying in the theater at the same time that the antipoetic was proceeding on other fronts. Many influences must have been at work before the Oxford Group had their way with Sweetie, not least of which would be the conversational tone of more obvious origin as displayed in a poem entitled "Stopping at a Country Auction on a Summer Afternoon:"

87

> *Whose goods these are I think I know.*
> *His house is in the churchyard though;*
> *He will not see me stopping here*
> *To see how well his goods will go.*

"Brother!" I thought, very possibly aloud. This went beyond the question of influences. Sweetie was at it again — shoplifting. She had plagiarized from every poet who amounted to a damn since Whitman, sometimes riding about in her appropriations (taking stolen cars as the specific metaphor) without bothering to file the serial numbers off the motors. The result was almost a parody history of modern verse.

Knowing I was a fool, I kept an ear cocked for a note I had not heard before, that would announce our Sweetie had at last found her own style. I died hard, on the theory, I guess, that what obtains in legal burglaries must be true of the artistic, namely their requiring enough skill to suggest what the criminal might do if he went straight. While it was one thing to turn out yet another hieroglyphic of Cummings, complete with no capitals and looking as though it had been punctuated with a pepper shaker, and maybe not much better to note the swing to religion among intellectuals in a paraphrase of T. S. Eliot ending:

> *This is the way the world ends*
> *This is the way the world ends*
> *This is the way the world ends*
> *Not with a bang but a wimple . . .*

While these were, I say, one thing, it was something else again to forge a lyric entitled "All Isles Are Blessed While the Voyage Lasts" that would not entirely have disgraced its model, Elinor Wylie:

> *All isles are blessèd while*
> *The Voyage lasts,*

88

All harbors handsome
From the masts.

Living with you's lovely,
But I'd sooner
Go to seek you
In my schooner.

I took hope from my not being altogether sure whether it was Wylie or Millay bleeding through here; it had the strain of girlish irony running in both. And it required a bit of something or other to produce a mimicry of Wallace Stevens that I recognized as such even from the title — "The Courtesan Takes Cortisone" — some of whose further word-plays ran:

Perhaps
Her paps
Are not what was expected.

In short, Sweetie not only talked about poetry — she did something about it.

What was I going to do about *that?*

After reading about half of this goulash I asked Mme. Pique-puss (who had been going quietly about the room dividing hornets) whether I might take the manuscript home with me for more leisurely perusal. She saw no objections, except to my holding it longer than overnight, for she had stolen it from a drawer of Sweetie's desk without the latter's knowing it. So it was that midnight found me in my own easy chair, reading avidly. The foolscap was intermingled with sheets of ruled and punched notebook paper, many of them old and scuffed. The writing was in both pencil and typewriter.

For a long time it was more of the same. Jeffers, de la Mare, Yeats and even Rossetti passed in chronologically untidy review. I was grateful for all my past immersion in the originals, which stood me in good stead in spotting the thieveries.

As I approached the end of the manuscript, I came to a page that straightened me in my chair. Here was a beat that was new to me, and one that I found instantly exhilarating. Lush sensuous imagery and sheer reveling in words created an effect that broke over me like a wave:

While still erect as gravestones let us sing
How in the Sabbeth-gentled west the rose
Blooms from the groin of the sea where all
My long boatmen lie detained, whose salt blood ticks in my
*   wrist*
Here on the hill where bleeds the pubic spring,
And the bridegroom came.

I make this in a summer's dalliance, when all the lion-loined
And loaned and lying loves have left, and a clenching wind
Turns me to the ribbed shore beyond. In the field
Behind me waves tomorrow's bread. In ocean beds
The seamen in their beards are tweaked by every tide.
Then the red reptile in my vine of veins
Quickens to music from the fluting bones of birds.

So clutching that prophet pickled long in brine
I let his grandson pluck me from the Scriptures south
Straight to that shuttered room in Mozambique
Where a twist of the dial will shut the ectoplasm off,
Killing the suitor with the smoking gun, the débutante in
*   splints,*
The cross-eyed cop, and all the the's we got from Auden and
*   his boys.*

So all my mother tolled me is the clapper in the belle.
And all I know is what he rages in the dusk, the song
Whirled out of the wheat in Sunday's bread, the bread in
*   Monday's wheat:*
The last harvest is a shower of seed.

I rose, scarcely able to breathe. Could it be true? Had Beth Appleyard, the girl who had for so long gnawed her braids at an upper window, at last broken through her period of apprenticeship into a style authentically her own? Not only that, but one that would burst upon our generation with all the rioting imagery, wild-soaring music and plain juice-squirting joy in words needed to free poetry itself from its long calcification? And was I destined to be her discoverer?

Sweetie? No, it was too fantastic. And yet, why not? Stranger human organisms than she had produced the world's art. And how much infantilism was there not demonstrably at the heart of all talent? "You were silly like us" Auden had written of Yeats himself.

Trembling, I read the poem again, and two more in the same vein. There was no doubt about it. Here was an idiom I had not encountered before. It sent the chills up my spine. I hardly slept a wink that night. Still quivering with excitement, I hurried over to show my prize to the one man in Decency capable of appreciating it.

Nickie was sitting outside the Samothrace. He had his head tilted back to put nosedrops into it for some allergy he suffered this time of year, while in the other hand he held a copy of the *Kenyon Review* which he continued to read in the position required for this medication. It was a way of showing himself "dedicated," to all the lumpish and witless herd scurrying past his table. In our high school days, we had persuaded the Greek to let us drag a few tables out onto the sidewalk, there to sip our coffee in the evening air as true expatriates. The custom had persisted through every summer since, with only a little worried reluctance on the part of the Greek who thought we were talking about being "expatriots," and whose own wish to be a loyal American, albeit a dirty and sardonic one, was thus severely jarred. Latterly, he was hearing the term Existential bandied about, but he seemed to think it was the name of an insurance company. The only other sidewalk customer at the moment was a man named Pete Shotz who must have been as old as Mme. Piquepuss but in whom, by contrast, the vital saps no longer ran. He had lost all his illusions in 1919 when Shoeless Joe Jackson and his cohorts had thrown the World Series, thereby betraying both the Chicago White Sox and the sport of baseball as such. He rolled his own cigarettes from a sack of Bull Durham, spilling flakes into his beer, which no doubt gained in zest thereby.

"*Setzen Sie sich,*" Nickie said.

"Never mind that," I said, drawing out a chair so as not to disturb Prud'homme, who was snoozing under another. We lit up cigarettes, and then, in a pause, I drew from my bosom the three or four sheets of manuscript which comprised the samples of my discovery.

"What do you think of these?" I said, tossing them on the table. "Some poems a local writer gave me to look at."

Nickie smoothed them down and read, with no want of absorption I was glad to see. Once, turning a page, he raised his eyebrows in appreciation at some twist of phrase. When he had finished he handed them back to me, nodding.

"Not bad," he said.

"Not *bad*. Is that all you can say?"

"They're amazingly skillful pastiches, sure. Some of the echoes are uncanny. All that sea stuff, and the Sabbath-gentled west, catch him to a T. It's a favorite trick of Thomas's, making verbs out of adjectives and nouns. And that sort of sprung rhythm, which he got from Hopkins, of course."

Gritting my teeth, I turned in my chair to flag the Greek through the door. But the effort to get him out here was well-nigh hopeless, and I abandoned it. Nickie was nursing a beer which he had undoubtedly fetched himself.

"Thomas who?" I said. "You act as though he were a personal friend of yours." Apparently this new voice had *already* burst on the literary scene while I was tied up with other things than avant-garde publications.

"Dylan Thomas."

"That's better. Of *course* Dylan Thomas. Do you think I don't realize that? Of course every writer is derivative at first. I didn't come here to ask you *that*. What I'm trying to decide is whether behind the echoes there's enough individuality to warrant encouraging her, for Christ's sweet sake."

" 'Her,' eh? Who is she? Anybody I know?"

Now there was a funny thing. For days that had been the very thing I'd been meaning to ask him — whether he knew Sweetie. Another one of Nickie's high-school-day *mots* had popped into my mind, about a certain girl having "lovely lips but a cruel mouth," and I wondered if he had said it about her. I now told him her name. "She was called Sweetie."

He shook his head. "No, it doesn't ring any bell. Who is she? What does she want?"

"Oh, a half-daft girl with vine leaves in her hair, who hears the horns of elfland faintly blowing. She's going to kill us all yet. She's the one there was that oratorical contest scandal about."

"Oh, yes. I remember that, vaguely."

"Well, at least she reads. She keeps up."

Dylan Thomas, eh? I must look into him. Evidently the new thing since Auden and Co. all right. It might be pointed out in my defense that though Dylan Thomas had appeared here in print and had even cut that legendary swathe through Midtown Manhattan and down the Eastern girl's-school circuit that was to establish him as the most Byronic figure since Byron, he was still the pleasure of the few. This was the last poet whose pockets Sweetie Appleyard was to pick, and in whose arms she was destined to lie, but I couldn't know that then. All I knew then was that I couldn't sit here and discuss the Apocalyptic Movement with Nickie; I was too busy, with too many people to get organized, including himself. I would see him soon enough at the Flickendens' brawl. That was where *he* would get *his*.

"I suppose it'll be ghastly," I said. "Fancy dress, have you heard that? God. Why do we keep going to things over and over that drive us crazy, when all we need to get out of them is the guts to say the simple word 'No'?"

Nickie agreed with me. Nodding, he sipped his beer with narrowed eyes, perfecting my observation.

"Yes," he said at last, "it is to cowardice, rather than to courage, that we pay our tolls of stamina."

"Horse pizzle," I said. "I can't sit here exchanging horse-pizzly nuances about life. I have work to do. See you Saturday then. Do you know how you'll go?" I asked, rising. "I haven't decided on a costume yet."

"I may go as an ass," he said, "because that's certainly how I'll feel."

If you only knew the half of it, baby! I thought as I bade him good-by and hurried back to the office.

8

I WENT as a house painter myself.

I had spent the afternoon calcimining upstairs bedrooms and been struck with the inspiration of going as the early Schicklgruber, which combined with a ready-made costume the virtue of not having to dress for dinner. It went down poorly with Crystal, who had spent hours, if I shouldn't say weeks, assembling herself as the Mother of the Gracchi, on the assumption that I would go as Tiberius Sempronius, her husband. My last-minute resource, or rather the unpreparedness it was designed to meet, provoked a bitter quarrel. We had been in touchy spirits since four o'clock when Crystal had chided me for not having "done anything" about Nickie, which I analyzed as pique at her not having been let in on the secret of the threatened divorce. She had learned it that afternoon from Lila herself, in the form of *her* wondering when I was going to keep my promises about Nickie. She couldn't indefinitely hang on by her teeth.

"Wait till tonight," I had said mysteriously from the scaffolding, under which Crystal stood issuing her queries. "He may get his come-uppance. That's what he needs."

"What do you mean?"

"You'll see. He's what is known in psychiatry as too big for his britches."

When I declined to amplify, the exclusion from yet another plot added fuel to the fire, as I saw when I finished my decorating and went into our bedroom. I had knelt to pin the hem of her royal gown, and, impulsively thrusting my head between her thighs, murmured a small devotional. "Oh, Chick, for God's sake," she said. "Why does a man always think *that* will make a thing right? It's so easy, and so cheap."

Luckily the younger Gracchi wandered in just then. Children do indeed hold two people together, but as mortar does the bricks, by also keeping them a little apart. I rose and said, "Is Blitzstein still tied up all right, ye pampered sprats o' mine?" An incident involving the dog had contributed to the trials of the day.

A neighbor known to me chiefly as the owner of a low-slung foreign convertible had telephoned complaining that Blitzstein chased his and other cars in a way that constituted a menace on the road. The animal being a mixed Dane and German police of enormous size, he must run alongside any open sports car at about eye-level with the exposed driver, which I could well imagine was unnerving. However, when the fellow went on to protest that you couldn't drive a car "faster than twenty miles an hour around here for the dogs," I retorted that that was nearer the speed limit than his sort usually went when there weren't any dogs around to furnish restraining hazards, but only children.

As we all four discussed the problem, Blitzstein began to bark furiously in the yard. We knew what the trouble was before we reached the window. His leash chain was hooked to slide along a fifty-foot tie-out wire strung between two trees, which gave him that much mobility — except when, as now, he got the leash snarled around one of the terminals and couldn't move an inch.

"Oh," Fillmore groaned, "now we've got to untangle all that chain again. Come on, Mike, you hold him while I unwind it."

"No, no," I said, "that's not necessary. You let the *dog* do it. Watch."

We followed me outside. Utilizing the dog's instinct to caper in its master's wake, I walked around that tree in a manner reversing the entanglement, in ever-winding circles, till the dog was clear of its predicament and had the freedom of the run-wire restored to it. I became quite dizzy in the process, but the thing was done without any tedious disconnecting of chains, etc., and to the instruction of the boys for future purposes. I had just enough time to pick up the sitter — a woman we knew well, named Mrs. Healy — before hurrying on over to the fête.

We created quite a stir, arriving as Hitler and Cornelia, but quickly dissolved in the general grotesquerie. Our hosts had come — or rather were waiting for us — as Caesar and Cleopatra. A stuffed viper encircled Helen Flickenden's arm while Jack's brow was crowned with a victor's chaplet woven of rhododendron leaves. Its weight and bulk made it keep slipping down over his eyes, like a derby a size too large, in a manner that hampered his greetings by interfering with his recognition of the guests. A man in a moth-eaten leopardskin dragging a spiked bludgeon sauntered up and was introduced as a house guest. "I'm the bouncer," he announced facetiously. The Flickendens were in an income group statistically identified as boasting a servant and a half, but a swarm of white-jacketed waiters from the caterer's carried the field tonight. When we arrived they still outnumbered the guests.

The house was of the contemporary order undoubtedly dear to glaziers, and was set in a most uneven terrain. The property totaled seven acres, which had seemed ample protection when bought in a bygone July, but with the first shedding of autumn foliage were discovered to be mostly vertical; so that in anything but dense summer the Flickendens found themselves sitting in a nude hollow ringed by neighbors watching from nearby porches of a more traditional cast, like spectators in an amphitheater. Even now, barefoot children could be seen stealing down the wooded slopes to witness the revels.

"People in glass houses shouldn't throw parties," said a voice at my side.

Nickie had on a tight salt-and-pepper coat, jodhpurs and leather puttees, and a tweed cap worn with the peak behind. I took this in uncertainly. "I thought you were coming as an ass," I said. It wasn't until Lila twitched up to us in a short flapper dress and rope pearls that the idea began to take shape, and then only partially. We guessed she was a star of the silent screen, but Nickie's part in the gag wasn't clear until he explained, "I'm her favorite cameraman," executing a brief pantomime of cranking a handle. It was very cute, and one of the hits of the evening. Trust him to do something sweet and sec-ond-fiddlish just when you had your belly full of him.

It would be a mistake, however, to think that there could be any mood between us when he hadn't but to embrace an opinion for me to abandon it. To a knot of us forming there, I was expounding the position that women artists failed to equal the masterpieces of men because of an inability, or unwillingness, to plumb the dark side of life when I noted the nodding gleam which prefaced Nickie's adoption of your opinion for more brilliant summation, and prepared to scrap it in mid-statement. So that by the time he opened his trap I had certain rebuttals ready.

"Chick has a point there, definitely," he said, speaking for the special benefit of a lovely girl in a Japanese kimono who had just joined the group. "Most women novelists, for instance, don't really delineate good and evil, not by our standards any-way, but degrees of good. Take Jane Austen. A villain by her would pass comfortably for a stuffed shirt in the world of almost any contemporary writer."

"Oh, fiddlesticks," I said, through the girl's laughter. "You're oversimplifying it."

"But isn't that what you just . . . ?"

"Not at all. I was making a distinction between men and women, and you've twisted it into one between the past and present. Don't put words in my mouth."

There was a confused lull. At which Nickie flung out his own topic for conversation.

"Guess what," he said, darting a malicious glance at me. "Pete Cheshire is out. Heard it on the radio a while ago. Let out for good behavior. Did only a couple years of his sentence, if that."

"Oh," said the girl in the kimono, "isn't that the jewel thief who called himself the Smoothie? And didn't you put him away?"

In addition to giving Nickie the spotlight as Cheshire's adversary the news had for him the further value of irritating me. My ignorance of developments meant that Cheshire had been paroled to someone other than the Lamplighter, this time. Not that I wanted him in my hair again, God knew, but it injured one's pride not to have been consulted. Nickie launched a profound analysis of Cheshire's character that suddenly made me prick up my ears to the realization that it wasn't in the Conan Doyle vein that he fancied himself at all, but something a cut subtler. What literary wave length was this? Tantalized, I listened.

"All hopes of 'reforming' a bloke like that are futile because, while he has a morality, it's turned inside out. You see, the sin was in getting caught, so the redemption can only be the perfect crime — not going straight."

"What were you saying a minute ago about a tortured psyche?" I said. "Would you develop that?" It was coming to me, the literary beat here. A little more of this and I would have it.

99

"Morons, too, can be complex. I was trying to suggest that Pete's rather involved make-up requires him to live down, not his crime, but his arrest. It's almost a religious drive with him, this urge to meet all the clichés — you might even say the Ten Commandments — of his trade. He's got to Strike When Least Expected, and all the rest of it. It wouldn't surprise me if he pulled a job tonight — the day of his release. It's a kind of inverted Ethic with him, pulling a baffler — the final expiation for past shortcomings."

Graham Greene. Of course. Pinkie and *Brighton Rock* and all that tortured religiosity. I might have known Nickie didn't fancy himself anything so old hat as Sherlock Holmes. He wasn't just a connoisseur of crime — he was a student of sin.

"I see what you mean," I said as the others, out of their depth or distracted by newly arriving friends, wandered off one by one till Nickie and I were alone. "Vanity is often at odds with self-interest, and that's why we sometimes fail to recognize it. But it's there, operating in the other fellow when we least expect it."

I gritted my teeth, waiting for the transformation of this dross into gold.

"The Ego," Nickie said at last, nodding agreement, "is the conscience of the psyche."

"Cowplop," I said and, turning on my heel in time to see him in a wall mirror shaking his head after me, flounced out of the room. Area rather, for the house was of the one-vast-space variety in which rooms derive their identity solely from the arrangement of the furniture. Having flounced out of the living area into the dining, I got myself a drink at the bar there and sat down in a corner to get myself in a Graham Greene frame of mind. If that was the way he was playing it, that was the way I would have to play it — if I was to handle him intelligently and properly conclude what I had begun. I could look into the kitchen area and see the telephone — a stick of dynamite timed to go off at twelve. Two hours and a half to establish the evening firmly on Graham Greene lines.

Decency was for a Eastern city remarkable in the number of people who refused to be converted. They continued to burn coal. Old houses were the rule, Colonial cottages whose owners felt the purr of oil furnaces at odds with original floors buckled into precarious angles and beams on which heads were struck. These hazards had an obscure hilarity, as of New England consciences uneasily appeased, Puritan ancestors from whom the properties had been unworthily inherited permitted to rest in peace for another generation. Sleekly contemporary homes like the Flickendens' were still comfortably the exception; perhaps the suburban element they augured could yet be held at bay; the commuters stopped at the gates.

For this Decency was in a favored pocket of Connecticut. Beyond the commuting limits, it was outside suburbia, exurbia, and all the rest. But briefly during the summer there was a scattering of New Yorkers who week-ended at the waterside cottages. The Cape was too far for them, Westport not far enough. They were professional people mostly, and a handful of British UN personnel. There was a growing clique of the last whom American hostesses like Helen Flickenden yearned to mix with the local residents, in vain. The elements kept separating as inevitably as cream and milk in a bottle.

It was simple to tell the British from the Americans, even without the clues of speech and through the dense thickets of disguise. The English ate as they talked; the Americans merely talked while they ate. It was churlish to note the trick of style — there was a thousand years of history behind the one; no doubt a millennium would suffice for the raw young country straining in its materialist traces, sweating to produce more air conditioners, more snorkels and ballpoint pens than any other, while its parent would go on from prime to senility, dribbling her gruel and owing all the world. Meanwhile the hog bestrode the world, scattering its billions to all who wanted. It had not yet learned the civilized knack of the French to nick you for just what the traffic will bear.

Swallow felt an old pain beginning to throb. One couldn't help preferring the English as one's spiritual sort, yet the betrayal always exacted its price. Nothing so intimately bound Swallow to his own kind as the pathos with which he viewed their unworthiness. He sat with eyes hooded and finger tips grazing the green shag rug that lay like an indoor turf in half the American homes, while the cock crew and crew. The difference in the costumes crucified him. Contrasted with the quiet originality of the Englishmen's was the strident banality of the natives'. There were three or four pirates, a few skeletons, another troglodyte to keep the house guest company. A rangy man wandered by in a checked shirt and black string bowtie; leaving unclear whether he was a Bohemian artist or a cattleman of the olden time. A human fish swam into view, enigmatically flourishing a tuning fork. Its wife pointed to it and said "Don't you get it? Al's a tuna — *a piano tuna.*" The lash of pity came down. Swallow closed his eyes. He heard the fish say, making off, "Got to practice my scales." When he opened his eyes again it was to see Bulwinkle standing in front of him. Across his middle was a canvas vendor's apron, in the pockets of which he kneaded fistfuls of change. "Extra peebah!" he was saying. "Read all about it. Extra!" His fly was open, adding a fathom to Swallow's despair.

When Swallow dared to open his eyes again it was to see another chap from the *Pick* office, an advertising space salesman. Dressed as Satan, he shyly fingered a trident.

"You look like the devil in that, Art," Swallow joked.

Guilt demanded that he acknowledge his citizenship by calling out vacuities in the manner of Americans. That brought the knout down with twice its sting. The pain was an anodyne to guilt. He squirmed till a loose spring in his chair was wedged more uncomfortably against his haunch. The need to expiate never ended. He was glad to see a dead bug in his drink. When there was nothing else to wince under, he winced under the need to wince. He glanced at the telephone, braced for that anguish. A stick of dynamite timed to go off at twelve . . .

A couple entered of whom the man looked familiar. He wore a sort of dual costume. In faultless evening dress above the waist, he was in tramp's rags below. On his arm was a slender ash-blonde woman of forty, draped as Guinevere. "Charles has come as a schizophrenic," she laughed, and Swallow put his hands to his face.

He had recognized Appleyard in the tails and baggy pants. The latter's plot was laid bare in a flash, which also clarified to Swallow his own role as its butt. Appleyard wanted to marry again, and for that had to get his daughter off his hands. What woman, least of all this Arthurian beauty, would put up with the likes of Sweetie? Was this to be a fresh voice in the chorus demanding miracles of Swallow while they heaped him with slurs?

Appleyard had spotted him and was piloting his prize over. An introduction was impossible to avoid. Swallow experienced the wave of nausea we feel in the presence of superlative beauty. He rose, steeling himself to meet her. She was a seaboard type he certainly knew: the women with eyes like coins in whose metallic laughter lurked the ghost of girlish mirth, the years of Vassar or Wellesley, of autographed raincoats and furtive snacks after Lights Out; the love of boys so quickly hardened into competition for men, the husband who could give them what their mothers had scrupulously taught them to forage for: the fifty thousand a year and the house in Rye with the turf of rug like this, the servant and a half and the wine-colored Cadillac. And daughters to train to avoid what their mothers had them: the cottage in Tenafly with a man who left his spoon in his coffee when he drank, hooking his thumb around it, and children with allergies who played pieces; the winters of "activities" in the Godforsaken Methodist church and the stinking summers on the back porch with root beer and cookies and a neighbor baritone singing "Shipmates o' Mine." She would have buried or shed a husband or two already, and Appleyard would not be the last. But Swallow wanted her because her lipstick was ragged.

"Hello, hello." Appleyard smelled of some costly concentrate for men. Was this just the upper half of him, while he reeked of some abomination below? "I'd like to present Mrs. Bickerstaffe. Eve, this is Mr. Swallow, the chap I was telling you about."

A pair of pruned eyebrows rose in greeting. "Oh, yes. Of course. Delighted." The accent wasn't Eastern at all, but English. "We must have a little chat. Charles, do get us drinks."

She was unmistakably British. In her voice rustled the thin paper on which the air editions of the better English journals are printed, in America used for wiping eyeglasses and binding cigarettes. Perhaps the Americans saw too clearly to have vision? They lacked the touch of fog responsible for the mysticism that made English poetry great. Swallow saw her nose was irregular; he looked for more of the flaws that breed desire through pity. Her hair was darker at the roots . . . he felt the bowels of mercy stir. If her stocking seams were crooked, he would want her then and there.

He threw a stricken look at the terrace door, a thousand miles away. Through it swept a bell-shaped woman in dense veils who bore mercifully down on Mrs. Bickerstaffe and began a story about a waxwing in her yard that had built its nest of coleslaw strands. With the instinctive courtesy of the British, Mrs. Bickerstaffe turned her back on Swallow, no doubt sensing his embarrassment. Over his shoulder he saw the back of Appleyard's tailcoat. "I must tell Charles something," he murmured, and chased it toward the bar.

He tapped Appleyard on the shoulder.

"There's something I've been meaning to tell you, old man."

"What?"

"Ontogeny recapitulates phylogeny. It slipped both our minds. The individual relives the history of the race. Boys enact the hunting and fishing era, children naturally seek out caves, corners below stairs, any dark hole. That's ontogeny recapitulates phylogeny. Ask anybody."

Appleyard chewed a canapé plucked from a passing tray, wiping a finger across his brow like a squeegee across a pane of glass.

"Eve's crazy about you."

"But we've only just met!"

"I've told her all about you. She's delightful, with that charm that — understands. She wants to know you better."

"And how is Sweetie?"

"Granny told me she gave you her poems to read. Have you thought any more about it? I mean, really, what are your plans?"

"Why, to get her poems printed," Swallow heard himself say.

"You forget one thing. They're not publishable." Appleyard was picking a flaw in his logic politely, as one picks a bit of cork from a guest's wineglass. "I've read them. They're like parodies of everybody since 'The Man with the Hoe.' "

"That's how we'll publish them. As a volume of parodies."

Almost peacefully Swallow listened to himself go mad. Were he told it was on the strength of the nonsense he was jabbering that he would have to stand and deliver, he would have gone out and thrown himself into the Sound. Why not? The Atlantic deeps were more a home than this. He was thinking of those serious dramas that are so ludicrous out of town as to be hastily rewritten for the laughs they unintentionally provoked, and brought into New York as successful farces. But that only happened in plays themselves.

"They'll have to be completely reworked, of course. Beginning with a whole new viewpoint, a sophistication about *her-self* and what she's *been* doing, that we'll have to develop first. Old man."

Appleyard nodded, pursing his lips. "It might just be worth a try. Beerbohm . . ." he babbled.

Why must we bleed at every pore for one another, Swallow thought. He said: "I'll help all I can, of course."

"And I'll see that you're left alone together, you two."

Swallow stumbled across the turf to a divan where he sank between a knave of hearts and a man with his head in a scarf and gold bands hanging from his ears, from which hairs also verdantly sprang. The latter turned, smiling. "I'm a third of a gypsy esemble."

"Where are the other two?"

"They couldn't come."

There was no mistaking the stiff upper lip, the long Anglo-Saxon face. He was English all right, Seeing It Through. English to the marrow of his bones.

"My name is Gluckstern."

Mumbling that he had troubles of his own, Swallow apologetically rose and staggered back to where Eve Bickerstaffe was still standing, free of the birdlore woman and looking for Appleyard. Swallow had to know what she knew, quickly, before his nerves went.

When he gained her side, they stood grinning at one another. She tapped the front if his paint-spattered overalls and said, "*Heil.*"

"Have you known Charles long?"

"Oh, yes. Some months."

"Then you know the others. Quite a household. I take it you've met Mme. Piquepuss."

"Rather!"

"And Sweetie?"

"Ah." Appleyard's arm thrust a drink toward her. He didn't

106

join them, being occupied with someone else a few feet away. "Strange case." Eve Bickerstaffe drank, after a gesture to his health. She watched him as she sipped, as though waiting for him to speak.

"Yes, she is a strange case. No one quite knows what she's thinking. Of course I've been rather close to her — closer than anyone in some ways — and the family sort of expect me to — pull her out of it. Appleyard — Charles had told you some version of something, away back, I suppose?"

"It's too bad, of course. Yes, some brouhaha down cellar or something. I'm not quite sure I . . . What happened exactly?"

"I know now what it was."

Swallow drew a deep breath, taking care not to inhale the crumbs of a canapé, and looked over her head, analytically squinting one eye.

"You see, Sweetie always roused in you the protective instinct. That appealing helplessness . . ." he said. "You wanted to shield her, put an arm around her and . . . reach out, um . . ."

"I understand."

Eve Bickerstaffe drank again, watching him with a gentle gravity.

"Were you in prison?"

"No," he said, "I wasn't."

Among the people swirling like a bright lava through the terrace doors was Jack Flickenden, flushed with excitement. The crown of victory had slipped over one ear. The fish-man forged past, pointing to the bar. "Get stewed to the gills . . ."

The telephone rang at ten minutes to twelve. Swallow was standing alone in a corner, wincing under the need to wince, when he saw Helen Flickenden run to Nickie after answering it and whisper something in his ear. Nickie nodded, twisting out a cigarette, and rose.

Swallow put pity from him. A surgeon with tears in his eyes is worthless — a menace. God had no pity. He had compassion. Pity was the underside of the coin of contempt. It is the one emotion nobody gets anything out of . . . Such thoughts are scarcely beacons for an era verging toward its Night, Swallow mused. They relieved without dispelling the gloom, like fireflies garnishing a dusk over which hover the incurious and eternal stars. But they would have to do, both for the cruel brevity of life and its appalling length.

Everyone was piling into cars. Word had buzzed round about what Nickie Sherman had been summoned for, and a macabre gaiety was in the making. On the clipped lawn (resembling a rug so much more than the turf of shag inside) Swallow saw his wife glance speculatively over at him as she climbed into the Flickendens' growling MG. Swallow found himself in a congested limousine with Nickie on his lap. Lila sat beside them, a hand on Nickie's wrist; they had been like that all evening, affectionately linked again in the unity of their costumes. Swallow could hear her mind ticking: "This may be his Big Chance." Nickie's cap was switched to rights, the peak in front. Was it his elegibility for mercy? A word whispered in his ear that it was all a jape, and no one need drink up eisel. But wasn't the whole idea that someone drink up eisel? It was how the prescription read. . . .

The Markeys' house was a blaze of lights. Sue met them at the door in a quilted wrapper, her hair loose and gesturing hysterically. She had always overacted on the stage; it was why she was a housewife now.

Nickie bustled importantly inside, an arm around Sue, while most of the thrill seekers, chastened and a little ashamed, waited in the yard or on the road in their cars. Swallow followed Lila and Crystal into the vestibule, then on into the parlor.

The body was sprawled face-up on a couch, its head hanging over the edge and its tongue lolling between clenched teeth. The sight reminded Swallow of those faces scrawled on schoolyard walls with the caption, "Teacher." A length of cord, torn from some electric appliance, was twisted around the neck. Ted Markey was in pajamas.

Nickie Sherman went skillfully to work, combing the premises for clues. He avoided rather squeamishly the body itself, Swallow noted.

"When did you discover him, Mrs. Markey?" he asked, stooping to read the title of a book spread-eagled on the rug beside the couch. "I know this is difficult, but try to remember."

"Why, just now," Sue said, "when I called you. I had been washing some things out while Ted caught up on his reading. There's the book. I went in to ask him something and found — this. Oh, God. He was only thirty-four!" She buried her face on Swallow's shoulder. "We were so happy together. Why should anyone want to do a thing like this to Ted?"

Nickie opened and shut the drawers of a buhl cabinet, looked down out the open window. "Robbery was not the motive," he said. "Have you notified the police?"

"I wanted you to see it first. The police never *do* anything. Your sitter told me where you were and I called there. I hope you don't mind."

"Of course not, Mrs. Markey. The police do their best," Nickie said generously. "You might call them now. I'll have seen all I need before they get here and disturb the scene. This was a wanton crime, committed by a man of medium height or slightly under, wearing a dark blue sweater and sneakers with thick crepe soles."

"How can you tell?" Lila asked. "How did you know that, Nickie?"

"It's possible to deduce both from the position of the body and something about the window. Entry was made through the window, which was only a third of the way open, not high enough for a man of any size. There are footprints in the flower bed of a pattern made only by those thick gum soles. There's a snag of blue wool under this splinter on the sill. You see?"

Swallow was watching the figure on the sofa for signs of breathing, as playgoers do a corpse on the stage. No motion was discernible. Had Ted been in the theater too? Swallow couldn't remember. Could the wire round the neck have accidentally got *too . . . ?* He saw only the lewd judge droning sentence, the visitors bringing him tangerines on Sunday, the attempted suicide with rotten suspenders . . . Sue shifted a chair cushion and raked her hair. Evidently she was running out of dramatic resources. "He was going to get a promotion next month," she stated into a handkerchief.

Nickie at last stepped over and examined the prostrate form more closely. He bent an ear to the chest and listened a moment, then transferred his study to the tongue. He drew the bottom lid of one eye down with his thumb and examined the eyeball. Swallow closed his own eyes and prayed that Ted Markey had had experience on the Elizabethan stage, or even the Grand Guignol, to account for the total lack of rise and fall of the torso. Nickie turned away and glanced in his strollings at Sue.

"Perhaps one of the others can phone them for you," he said. "The police. You're probably in no condition to."

She buried her face in her hands, shaking her head distractedly. "I'd get the Fire Department."

The sofa creaked as the corpse got to its feet.

"Better let me do it, darling," Ted said. "You've had a trying night."

Those in the room took steps in varying directions. Then they all froze, and looked at one another like participants in a ritual of which the exact sequence had been forgotten. Ted and Sue grinned at one another, then at the rest, who somewhat woodenly followed suit. People seemed to be baring their teeth for the purpose of comparing dental work. One side of Nickie's face twitched up, like that of a man drawing a shred of food from his teeth. Swallow's wife whispered to him: "I *think* this is the *most* . . ." Lila heard it and glared at him. Swallow rocked faintly on the balls of his feet, like the Ghost in more sensitive productions of *Hamlet,* while a deep sunburn overspread Nickie's features.

Lila went to Nickie's side and took his arm.

"He knew it all the time, only he didn't want to spoil your fun," she said. "Come on, Nickums, tell us when you first knew it was a hoax. Play fair now, be honest. When did you first tumble, and what was it that gave the game away? How did you know?"

Swallow sat on the back porch of his house, on the worn glider, staring over the trees at the rising sun. A drained coffee cup stood at his elbow. He looked up "eisel" for the third time, in as many dictionaries. This one defined it simply as vinegar, just like the others, but noted its use in *Hamlet:* "Woul't drink up eisel?" As he set it aside he heard a footstep behind him. What is so personal as a tread? Like a signature on the stair. He knew Crystal was standing in the doorway in the faded flower wrapper.

"I didn't sleep a wink," she said.

"Do you think I liked doing it?"

"Oh, no more of that infinitely gentle, infinitely suffering business, please. You've been going around like a Graham Greene character all night. All that knowledge-of-weariness and weariness-of-knowledge, God-will-forgive-us-everything-but-our-optimism stuff."

"Can I pour you some coffee?"

"There's no more cream."

Seeing her shuffle onto the porch in a robe even drabber than he'd remembered, Swallow felt an old tightening of the shackle of love. Why do we celebrate beauty when it is a threadbare house garment, a new wrinkle, a sagging shoulder that bind us with bands of steel? He recalled that he had married her not in a tide of passion but because her mother had sunburned her face through a basket, making the whole family too ridiculous to desert. There was an aunt who sold Christmas cards so awful you bought three dozen. Love was the prisoner of pity; lust fed on the very shocks of intimacy, renewed itself on pain and rage. Every embrace is a collision. And so on. He leaned over on the glider and pressed his hands against the sides of his head, as though by squeezing thought from his brain he might still the throb of paradox.

"I got so tired of whistling down the wind with him, Chris." He willed himself not to vomit; what he let out instead was a gorge of verbalized misery. He spoke leaning over, and imagined what he said to constitute a widening pool on the rattan rug. "You see, the thing he had to be shown is that there's no *adversary* for him. Not that he isn't brilliant himself, but that life offers no Raffles to use it on. He's like half of a pair of scissors. Therefore, no *living* in it. And my sister with huge rents to pay, and my nieces going around with them in their clothes. Huge rents."

"Oh, Jesus." She leaned her brow on the window frame, her arms hanging at her sides as though her nervous system were losing touch with parts of her at an alarming rate. "He threatened to kill himself. Did you know that?" Her foot of itself recovered a mule it had lost.

"I simply had to get him down out of that balloon. More is not asked of a man than he can take. We think of the failure of theology when what we ought to get straight is the theology of failure. *That you have to deserve it.* Those not up to defeat are not picked for it. Ezra Pound said:

For God, our God is a gallant foe that playeth behind the veil.
Whom God deigns not to overthrow hath need of triple mail.

Kill himself? What's that you say?"

"Yes. Can you take that on your conscience?" Swallow

said nothing. He wiped his moist temples with the sleeve of his pajamas. "He's been walking the streets all night. Lila says he was home three times and went away again. He was last seen going in the direction of the waterfront."

It is because of our relationships that we suffer. What fools we are to fear solitude. Swallow remembered a week spent alone in Vermont in the dead of winter: the stark immaculate pines standing like Breughel trees, the snow falling like grains of Bromo-Seltzer. He thought: life is a tragedy perpetuated by the passion that relieves it.

"Have we any eisel in the house?"

He was not surprised to hear the telephone ring: stunned but not surprised. Crystal went to the kitchen to answer it. It would be Lila again, reporting.

When Crystal ran back from the kitchen the sound of her slippers was like a horde of rats hurrying in his direction. The sun was clear of the treetops. Where did it come from, what did it want? We groped in the dark, while the mysteries blazed down on us.

"That was Lila. She just heard a news report. A police bulletin from the waterfront precinct station."

Swallow had once read a fantasy concerning a country in which light traveled at the rate of ten miles an hour. Her fact reached him with that kind of dreamy leisure, while he stood apart from himself, as it were, witnessing its impact on himself.

"Whuh — ? Whah — ?" He opened and closed his mouth several times, as though by so doing he might trap the right words out of the air as a dog does flies. "You've known me long enough. Let me know in easy stages," he said. "One, did they find him wet?"

She came forward to the glider and smoothed a cushion on it. The female urge to narrate, to make a thing of tidings.

"What's he done, for God's sake, woman? Out with it, by degrees!"

"It's not what he's done. It's what somebody else has done. Chick, the Flickendens were robbed last night. Twenty thousand dollars' worth of jewels from their bedroom."

Swallow was on his feet. "Pete Cheshire — "

She nodded, her face radiant with the relief that was flooding him too.

"They called Nickie immediately to retain him. As well they might, the way they laughed at the poor boy. It's another chance for him, just in time to save his face. Or maybe even his soul."

"Where is he?"

"Safe in bed. Went to sleep like a baby when he heard about it. There's your other half of that pair of scissors. I'll take that coffee after all, with milk. Nickie called the shot too, that's another thing in his favor. Remember how he said at the party he wouldn't be surprised if the Smoothie struck tonight? Oh, it's like a kind of miracle. Just think, Chick. *Twenty thousand dollars' worth of jewels stolen.* It makes you think there's a God in heaven after all."

the DOGHOUSE

Convention has always more heroes than revolt.

BEN HECHT: *A Jew in Love*

✧ ✧ ✧

9

WHO kissed the Sleeping Beauty awake was none other than the Prince Charming of American letters. You know who I mean. That style was a glittering wand that had but to be flourished over the dreaming likes of Sweetie to make her sit up and rub her eyes. The long overtime childhood was finished. But it left in her a store of fissionable matter ready for the right sensibility to rearrange. By sensibility I do not mean that flabby impressionability thanks to which a man standing barefoot on a coin can tell whether it is heads or tails. I mean that almost ethereal attunement able to draw the data through shoe leather.

When I first mentioned Fitzgerald to Sweetie she thought I meant the translator of *The Rubaiyat,* and began one of those invitational and purely academic dashes through the gorse that were so much more wearing than the bacchanals would have been of which they were the empty blueprint. I thought to myself, "No, dearie, that ballet is over. Come meet your new chorcographer," and from under the wild cherry, bright in its dazzling pestilence of summer beetles, waggled *The Great Gatsby* and *Tender Is the Night* in my two hands. "I don't mean Edward Fitzgerald — I mean F. Scott. See how he parts his name on the side. Come here. He won't bite you. Have you read him?"

She came pouting back through the gorse.

"I don't read novels."

Then that was the whole trouble! She had been too long the prisoner of poets, who teach you only how to die, not live. This girl needed characters to ape, not verse forms — influences on her *conduct*. For if the principle of imitation is all it seems — and religions call believers to perfection by no other — then progress is a series of successful plagiarisms, and the good life a long, translucent parody on which God the Father will grade us at the last. All the world's a stage — in our development.

I tumbled those glimmering pages into her lap together with *This Side of Paradise* and the best of the short stories, and left her there. I left her for thirty days and thirty nights. If, as I thought, she was Poetry's little debutante, it followed as the night the day who must handle her coming out.

When I called again after dinner a month later I was met in the dooryard by another girl.

She emerged from the house carrying a glass of red wine from the dinner table. Her dress was a civilized summer print of a material known, I believe, as bleeding madras. The river of chocolate malted that had been her hair was gone — in its place a tuft of chopped gold. Even her feet were changed. She wore no shoes as yet, but there was something about them that it took me a second to place. She had been walking through money, that was it, lots of money, and you could hear it whispering like a green protective foliage in her path. (One hoped her father had enough to defray whatever little improvisation she had in store for us now!)

"Oh, Chick, we're all so beautiful!" she cried. "I had no idea. From now on I'm going to live! I'm going to live if it kills me!"

"How will you begin?" I sat on the porch steps fanning myself with a straw boater. There was a hushed, almost erotic expectancy to the night. The moon sailed like a wedge of Persian melon over the far trees. When Sweetie drank her wine I imagined it running directly into her veins.

"I want to work on my poems," she said. "I see what's wrong with them now. They're awful. Sweetie sorry. Sweetie ashamed." Instead of behaving childishly as heretofore, she deliberately talked baby talk, thus keeping at a fashionable remove from herself, which was something else altogether, and quite fabulous in its way. This gained degree of detachment put her poetry in its first perspective. "But maybe I can turn their very awfulness to account. Make conscious parodies out of the unconscious that you once mentioned. Maybe I could get a book of them published." She laughed into her wine and then laid a hand over the glass, as though she were trying to bottle the night's mirth, or had just jailed a bright bug. "Sweetie dying to go New York. Want toofums filled by someone better than old Decency dentist anyway. Sweetie want to see the Ritz."

"It's been torn down."

"Then Sweetie go Plaza. Sit in lobby and see if the music makes the palm trees quiver. Oh Chick, the sands are running — every morning I've been rubbing another night's worth out of my eyes and never knowing it. I want to *do* something. I've begun work on some of the poems already. Would you like to hear them?"

"Very much."

She recited her revisions in an eager murmur, hugging her drawn-up knees and gazing at the sky.

> Now, you sniveling hypochondriac,
>   Your sort of thing is done;
> Drop that pillbox right away
>   And get inside of one.
>
> Don't throw up your hands because
>   Your stomach's bent on bolting;

Don't turn and run because you find
The masses are revolting.

"Auden," I said.

"I yuv you!" She kissed me in a burst of gratitude for having guessed. A window slid either up or down — it makes no difference which. "It's now a much better satire on the whole ivory-tower proletarianism of that day," I said when I could speak. "What else?"

She reeled off several more, all showing the same ripening *mondanité* at work. One thing about the late-bloomer is that it usually blooms fast. I fancied I could *see* Sweetie improve the way you can see the hand of a clock move if you watch closely. I don't know how long we sat there. The melon-slice of moon paled as it climbed the sky from Persian to cranshaw; from cranshaw to casaba. The stars struck me as a handful of hot rivets precariously holding together a night threatening to burst under the strain of too much ecstasy.

Sweetie flung her arms out at an angle slightly acute to that of crucifixion and exclaimed, "The Riviera!"

"The Palm Beach of the old country," I smiled at my pupil, wiping at a stain of claret on my hatband. I shifted on my haunch, half-crazed by a night so drenched in implication.

"I had an idea about your Frost," I said. "Put back even the little you've changed of the original. Leave the title and the entire first stanza exactly as he has them —

> *Whose woods these are I think I know.*
> *His house is in the village though;*
> *He will not see me stopping here*
> *To watch his woods fill up with snow . . .*

— only capitalize 'village' to make it Greenwich Village the owner lives in — "

" — and the poem a satire on the city man dabbling in

bucolics! The whole suburbanite thing!" She gave the editorial hand a grateful squeeze as Appleyard fluttered into view around the side of the house. He made apologetically for the glider from which he plucked a magazine and as hurriedly vanished, darting us a smile of discreet excitement, a kind of deferential frenzy.

"I'll get her between covers yet," I called.

"I know."

In addition to whipping half the old poems into shape according to the agreed-on plan, Sweetie wrote several new ones for the book-length manuscript at which we now drove, all in the course of the next few weeks. She worked at the same fever pitch as that in which *A Shropshire Lad* was forged by A. E. Housman, who was, as a matter of fact, represented in the new crop:

> *Loveliest of pies, the cherry now*
> *Completes a fine repast;*
> *'Tis not the first I've ordered, lads,*
> *But it will be the last.*
>
> *For soon they'll slit my trouser-legs*
> *And shave my head, and then*
> *They'll sit me in the chair from which*
> *I'll never rise again.*
>
> *The lengthy error known as Life*
> *Began in a single cell,*
> *And that is where for luckless lads*
> *It sometimes ends as well.*
>
> *And so it's down the row I go*
> *With my eternal curse.*
> *And that's what comes of reading*
> *Pessimistic verse.*

My own favorite was one that took off from Byron's "She Walks in Beauty," probably because I relished being in the know as to its private origins (how we love to have literature reduced to gossip!). For it projected perfectly at last that fear of the Chintz Prison that haunted Sweetie, as it may well haunt every woman:

> *She walks in beauty like the night*
> *Watchman on appointed rounds,*
> *In the nursery, checking children's*
> *Winter respiratory sounds.*

> *Robed in flannel she comes hither,*
> *Shod in slippers she goes hence,*
> *Sits behind the desk and reckons*
> *Up the measure of their pence.*

> *Bedded late, she rises early,*
> *And swings before his sallow nose*
> *The coffeepot, her morning censer,*
> *Which is better than the rose.*

Before the leaves fell we had a book together, and before the snow flew, published — under the name of Beth Appleyard. I knew a Bridgeport printer of trashy comics who did occasional art books for a hobby. He brought out *The Mocking Bird* in a brochure on deckle-edged paper bound in maroon vellum, selling at two dollars. It didn't set the world on fire but it did Sweetie, who packed up and lit out for the Village, among whose espresso shops and walk-up apartments she found enough kindred spirits, liberally enough sprinkled with admirers, to make her stay on. Rumors of how the Mocking Bird Girl was carrying on down there boomed like breakers up the dull shores of Decency. And before the buds were out I was called on the carpet again at the vine-choked cottage on Beacon Street.

"What have you done to her now?"

A prostrate Appleyard put the query this time. He lay on a mound of pillows, a medicated sock of a tasteful pattern pinned around his neck, and a crick in his back. The latter was an injury sustained, according to the attendant Eve Bickerstaffe who had done the phoning in terms of asking me to tea, from too much exercise in a rowing machine he had in the basement. But basically he was a man stricken by news of a wayward daughter. The effigy of Adlai Stevenson dissolved into that of an old woman in a nightgown which I was a moment in placing. Thomas Wolfe's mother on the publication of *Look Homeward, Angel.* Had it not put her to bed, pale, the model of familial slaughter in our time? If Appleyard was going to be derivative too . . .

"You've heard about Sweetie?" he whispered, fingering the sock in a way that subtly shifted our problem onto a new plane.

"I hear from her now and again. Why?"

"Not from her — *about her*. They're not the same thing at all."

There was the groan of a bedspring followed by a human one — or perhaps the other way around — as Appleyard sat up a little on his pillows, dealing them a series of blows. An electric cord led to a heating pad under his back. The box the pad had come in was on the counterpane. On its cover was a picture of a beautiful woman lying in bed with the same product, voluptuously fingering the thermostat.

"Just what do you want of me?" I asked.

"A balance between what she once was and what she is now. Something in between. A little sense of proportion, please!"

"I'll get it right yet," I said from the foot end of the bed. "I'll get her right yet. But I think I ought to have a clearer picture of how things stand at the moment. What exactly have you heard? If you can give me some idea."

He laughed and fell back among the pillows, as if the sight

of parental collapse were description enough of the sins being committed under my auspices. Eve Bickerstaffe leaned down and touched his brow with a damp handkerchief. "He's weak," she said.

"We're none of us a tower of strength," I answered charitably. Her glare told me how I had mistaken her meaning, on which I murmured a word of apology with some despairing of the hands. "He has fever — this isn't like him. Please sit down," she said, noting my quest for a chair not too discourteously far from the sickbed. I settled on a wicker hassock shaped like an hourglass which creaked furiously under my weight. I noted among the medicine bottles the consoling presence of a pint of Four Roses, and licked my lips. Curiosity was the one bearable ingredient in my emotions, and I was resolved not to have it short-changed.

"I must know what you hear about Sweetie, in order intelligently to proceed with this thing. Can you be specific?"

"Oh." He gave a deprecatory wave, and a bit of the old Appleyard returned in the will to disapprove on intellectual rather than moral grounds. "The usual kind of Girl Cutting Loose the Minute She Gets Away from Her Family. Isn't the Jazz Age supposed to have gone out with Fitzgerald?"

"There's a new Jazz Age," I said, "and a Fitzgerald revival in full swing. This time it's all more casual, therefore probably deeper."

"Well, I'm not casual! Wait till you have daughters dancing on the table in their shift!" Appleyard summoned his polemic resources for a last heave onto his elbow as he fixed me with a sharp eye. "You realize it would kill her grandmother to hear about this. Of course we're doing our best to keep it from her. So *shh!* Here she comes now."

Mme. Piquepuss looked anything but distraught, whatever she may have overheard. Spruce in green taffeta, and only a little bent under ancestral jewelry, she nodded to me as she crossed the room to a window chair. It had been otherwise at our last meeting, when I'd reported on the poems she had stolen for me to read. When Mme. Piquepuss learned they were derivative she was fit to be tied. She thumped her cane, snatched up knickknacks and flung them to the floor, in a rage at having this bridge to the world for her grand-daughter blown up in her face. She had given the impression not of a vestigial human being so much as an incipient poltergeist. I forewent any actual exegesis of the text. Accusing her of having an heir who dealt in *double entendre* would have meant gewgaws flying in my own direction, while detailed analysis of symbolisms might have put me in receipt of more than bric-a-brac. It was enough to have to explain to *Sweetie* the sort of thing she was trying to do — where she was infusing her work with Freudian elements, where Marxist. Now, as I say, it was happily otherwise. Mme. Piquepuss laid a hand on my shoulder as she passed: blessings on a friend who, by alchemies and devices themselves of no interest to her, had set her child on the road to the world at last.

But the other two went on about getting Sweetie home. I sensed between Appleyard and La Bickerstaffe a nervous conspiracy. The latter kept depositing finger tips on the buttons of her blouse, as on the stops of a flute.

"So we were hoping you'd care to try again with Sweetie — run down to New York and look in on her in the Village," she said.

"What! Like Lambert Strether in *The Ambassadors* sent to spy on What's-his-name in Paris?" I saw the miles of relentlessly combed Jamesian syntactical fleece stretching away into a dubious future, and rejected it out of hand; unwisely perhaps, since I was groping for a literary formula that would get us all out of this mess, some *mystique* as potent to stop the spell as the Faulkner had been to start it. But I did not see this as Henry James. I saw us as long out of those drawing rooms slogging steadily across the Waste Land we had blundered into in search of the Other Side. God only knew what was on the Other Side, but we had to cross the Waste Land to see.

I was glad at any rate to hear Appleyard croak from the hill of pillows: "Oh, nothing like that, old man. Just tell her we still love her and want her to come home."

Mme. Piquepuss's voice rang unexpectedly from the window seat. "But she is having fun. Let her have her fling."

Appleyard hitched himself up again. "I don't want to have to cut her off with a penny!"

As though he were dying in a great Galsworthian bed!

Fever or no fever I sensed something fishy here. The room was swelling with hypocrisy. Then in an instant it was all clear.

It was when the old beldame, in response to that Galsworthian death rattle, coughed into her fist and said, "I send her checks enough to live on. Let her have her fling. This way she will meet some nice yunk man, n'est-ce pas?" A startled glance between Appleyard and his bride-elect as she fled for the kitchen teapot told me the story.

The old woman was living her life over again in the young. The candles had been snuffed on her parties long ago, but she remembered the waltzes in vanished gardens, the lovers swirling in the soft French nights, the champagne and the stars, the kisses and the grieving violins. Her beloved Proust reminds us that when aged people seem to sit with their dim eyes fixed at a point in space six feet in front of them, they are actually looking at something sixty years behind . . . Dream away, Mme. Piquepuss, I get the whole thing now. It is the middle-aged plotters we have on our hands now. They're scared stiff that in a burst of senility you'll cut *them* off with a penny, leaving everything to that girl who has found the road to the world at last. . . . How I had misjudged the woman, as menace! She wasn't the American Puritan at all, only the Gallic *grandmère*

bent on seeing the Dance of Life go on. Her skittishness about
any irregularities in the order of events was understandable
enough. There was a story that a sister of hers, on a long-ago
railway journey to Petrograd aimed at healing a romantic sorrow, had been ravished by Rasputin.

A silence fell among the rattle of crockery in the kitchen —
a listening silence. Why did Eve Bickerstaffe want money? Because she had some. Money mates with money. The two lie
down together and breed themselves endlessly upon one another . . .

"I don't sleep for worrying about it," Appleyard whispered.
"I want my girl home. Where a man can keep an eye on
things. I don't sleep any more."

"You slept last night," Mme. Piquepuss offered encouragingly. "I looked in a few times." She sat tranquilly, the eagle
eyes in repose, the chocolate fingers on the table-edge before
her. They looked like a row of eclairs which a butler might
presently serve us in silver tongs with our tea. But when tea
came we had sponge cake augmented by certain gray straw-
berries.

"Well, I don't rest when I sleep," Appleyard resumed. "Anyone knows that when you're worried about something you can
sleep eight hours or even ten and wake up feeling just as tired
as when you lay down."

"Or even tireder," I said, inclined to be cheerful now that
the miscreants had been unmasked and we knew where we
stood. The ass in bed had forfeited my sympathy but I felt
guilty at the rather notorious Freudianism that came to mind:
how offspring out to set the world on fire often want only to
burn the old man up. Well, he had missed the boat on her
poetry. He had thought the stuff hopeless.

I did not begrudge the losers my good offices for that one
last trip to New York they asked of me. After all, my aim was
to extricate myself from *l'affaire Appleyard* as gracefully as

possible, and a graceful exit usually means a leisurely one. My father gave me one good piece of advice in his lifetime. "Never slam a swinging door," he said. I had had too much kickback as it was. So I took the tea and ate the cake and walked out of that house with a kind of gingerly tact. Which was just how, two Saturdays later, I walked into Sweetie's.

At least into the apartment at the Bleecker Street address I had for her. I began to wonder whose it was soon after she admitted me.

"Chickie! Come in, come in."

She sang to the tune of camel bells, or some local silversmith's equivalent dangling from her wrist. The clatter of wooden sandals on the bare floor was intermittently muffled on the archipelago of small rugs we crossed to reach the living room. Her nails were a pale green now, and her lipstick seemed brown, though that may have been a trick of the light. I became aware of conversation other than ours. A young man with pink hair was sitting on a carousel horse in a corner and telling a girl parked on a rattan stool, "You can't say that about Bea Lillie. I won't let you." The girl had wheat-colored hair hanging over one eye, which made her seem to be watching you from behind a curtain. Sweetie introduced them as Bill de Chavannes and Ursula Thorpe, and hurried off to get us drinks.

I stood at an open window while Bill de Chavannes finished his findings for Bea Lillie, whom he described as a masculine Oscar Wilde. The window gave on a tiny courtyard in which more children than there are in Decency were playing at more games than I had known existed. "Sort of a Breughel effect," said Ursula, who had drifted to my side.

Sweetie returned with highballs and the remark that she still didn't know "where he keeps everything." From which provocative clue flowered the facts of her present life. "When Danny talked about his convertible," Bill laughed, "Beth thought he meant a Cadillac or at least a Lincoln, and went home with him."

"What kind of convertible did he have?" I asked.

"Castro," Bill said, indicating the davenport on which I sat.

From this and other Restoration exchanges I gathered that there was a *bon mot* circulating in the Village that went, "I have a rendezvous with Beth." It was said to have originated with Dylan Thomas — whom there was now a prolonged attempt to locate. It consisted of telephoning, asking droppers-in if they'd seen him, and even yelling out the window. "It's no use," said Bill at last, dismounting the horse. "He's reading this week end at Bennington or a Welsh workmen's local or something like that. Danny!" he finished as the master of the house strode in.

I saw a baked face with handsome features which included the diamond-shaped eyes of the Irish. Danny Dolan carried himself with a scrupulous erectness, as though he had once encountered the phrase, "the lean, clean breed," and vowed to live up to it. But he was clearly out of his element in this flat of his. His father owned a steel mill which enabled him to own some racing horses — the carousel steed wasn't the only sign of his passion in the room. He was just back from Philadelphia where a three-year-old of his had been operated on at the University of Pennsylvania School of Veterinary Medicine for the removal of a chip from one of the sesamoid bones in his right foreleg, fractured during the running of the Belmont stakes.

"He was all right in there," he told us, accepting Sweetie's own highball. "I knew he was a smart horse, but the way he cooperated when they gave him the anesthetic was wonderful."

"Sort of a Hemingway hero," Ursula murmured, lip at glass.

Danny roamed from seat to seat like a man trying out chairs in a furniture store. "Where shall we eat?" he asked with a kind of truculent hospitality, the sense of strain put on limited emotions by playing host to a constant flow of superiors.

Beth removed from the refrigerator a gory butcher's parcel which she opened for our inspection on a stack of magazines. "I bought this meat, and got to thinking I might cook it. But what *is* it? I forget what the butcher said."

We studied the bloody still life from our respective distances, without profit, yet as though it rang a bell. Ursula succeeded in identifying it.

"Sort of a Chardin quality," she said.

Danny rose and gave his belt a hitch. "We're a rotten set," he said with some smugness, or at least the wistful hope that he "belonged." He glared at the window and then around to the rest of us, his diamond eyes glittering.

"Let's go to the Aching Joint," somebody said.

"Let's go to the Onomatopoeia," somebody else said. "There's a new comedian there with a death wish, who gets his head out of a noose just in time."

Bill rose to announce his suggestion. "Let's call Mary Troiseme. I hear she's back at Rye."

Thus it was that I found myself in Danny's station wagon, which reeked provocatively of horseflesh, speeding back in the direction I had just come. In thirty minutes I would be halfway home again. My bag was in the rear.

"Sort of a Kafka nightmare," said Ursula, between whom and Bill de Chavannes I was wedged in the back seat. We sipped highballs as we twitched through traffic on Riverside Drive. "The set in Rye is even more decadent," Bill said. "They sit on the beach drinking Vichyssoise through a straw."

"The Gauls are at the gates," Danny said at the wheel. It had the ring of a phrase he had picked up somewhere, but he looked at Sweetie beside him in a kind of plea for credit for his cleverness. She was apparently queen of this crowd, arbiter of a worldliness which I tried to calibrate by dropping the name of Westport into the discussion. It aroused gales of mirth. Sweetie turned to kneel on the front seat, facing us.

"Have you ever read Kafka, Chick?" she asked. "Well, you must. Start with *The Metamorphosis*. It's about a man who turns into a cockroach."

"Oh, let him alone, Beth," Bill said. "He's read *archy and mehitabel*. I sometimes wish that's where I'd stopped."

At last we arrived in Rye. We swept up a drive whose gravel looked as though it bathed regularly and stopped before a broad stone house around whose veranda ran a balustrade capped with marble figures in reclining positions. On the porch a woman of no attributes, wearing a hat that looked like a dove put through a wringer, stood between two leashed wolfhounds.

"I'm so glad you got here before I left because I can't stay," she said, showing neither surprise nor indifference at our arrival. "You'll find food in the refrigerator, plenty of liquor in the cellarette, and Waldo in bed. I'm awfully sorry, but I have to go to New York."

An upper window slid open and a man's face mangled with sleep was thrust out. "I'm *glad* I mistook the Worcestershire sauce for Angostura bitters," he called down. "It's what we all need. And I don't take back what I said about shoofly pie. Hello, all." The window slammed shut as the woman was drawn by the hounds toward a clump of rhododendrons where a taxicab was waiting in cover. "Good-by, Mary," they all shouted. "Have fun."

"I told you the Gauls were at the gates." Danny fell in beside me as we started for the house. He was shaking his head.

"I know for a fact of people in Westport who roast marshmallows on a Roto-Broil," I offered out of a persisting chauvinism for my home state. He danced bitterly, punching the twilight.

We climbed a flight of stairs like the bed of a dried cataract and trooped through a cathedral door held open for us by a white-jacketed Negro chewing a soda cracker. He showed us to our rooms by pointing at their approximate locations through the ceiling. I alone had luggage — toted in the suspicion that I might never check into the Algonquin at all but go right on home from here.

My memory of the next twelve hours is a blur, like a spectrum spun at a rate too fast to distinguish separate colors. After a dinner of roast lamb at which Waldo appeared — a compactly portly man in a sleep-muffled rage — there was a round of parlor games and smoke-wreathed disputes through which Waldo also intermittently somnambulated. He grew more dangerously awake by the hour, however. Someone played a phonograph album given his absent wife by a previous guest, a symphony of a pioneering dissonance that made him stiffen in his chair like a convict through whom an electrical charge is being passed. Seeing this, Bill de Chavannes explained the composition's merits. "The classical composers aren't in it for tonal violence," he said. "To approximate that, you'd have to play Beethoven and Brahms at the same time." Waldo seized the album and thrust it into the annotator's lap, in which remnants of dessert still lingered. "Take it! I insist — I'm giving it to you!"

One of several newcomers was persuaded by a scrawny beauty in a sweater to read from his poems, a volume of which happened to be around. They weren't too bad. I liked particularly "Fat-Rocked My West," "Crating and Uncrating," and "Mother, Walk with Me on State Highways." "Take it," Waldo said to the scrawny beauty who had been loudest in her praise. Beads of moisture stood on his brow. It seemed he was determined to break up housekeeping; that when he had distributed the furnishings he would begin on the house proper, tearing it stone from stone and handing them to passers-by. I remembered a cartoon with the caption "Don't admire anything or he might give it to you," and decided to keep my mouth shut. All the good it did me!

In a sudden silence, Sweetie looked around and said, "Where's Danny?"

"On the veranda blowing up that rubber horse he left here last summer. He said he's going for a swim."

"He'll turn *into* a horse, like that man in Kafka who turned into a cockroach," said Ursula, who was beside me on a couch. She slipped an arm through mine and scratched the back of my wrist, "Don't feel too bad about the *archy and mehitabel*. It's never clear in the story that it's a roach the man turns into — just an insect. Waldo, don't you have a collection of Kafka's stories?"

"Take it," Waldo ordered me when he had found it. "Take it away, do you hear!" Instead of looking into it, however, Ursula and I got on the subject of sex.

"Don't you sleep with anybody beside your wife?" she asked me at last.

"No."

"Just what are you trying to prove?"

When she turned her back for a cigarette, I darted out the door and upstairs to my bedroom. I found I had the Kafka still in my hand. I lay down with my clothes on and read *The Metamorphosis* till I fell asleep. I dreamed that I was in the Hal Roach studios in Hollywood where a lot of people were throwing pie plates at me in which there were no pies. The flying tins were sharply metallic, and quite dangerous.

I awoke to a gay commotion beneath my window. Someone had turned the garden fountain on and in the moonlight Sweetie could be seen advancing toward it with soap and towel.

I strode out the front door past the balustrade on which the marble figures lay in their cool sleep and down the stairs to the lawn. I shouldered past a pair of youths who were arguing about whether Hemingway was yellow, a larger group watching the Nude Bathing with shouts of laughter, and fetched up on the other side of the fountain where there were no spectators.

"Sweetie, you're coming home with me," I stated through the splash of water. "I speak as your editor as well as your friend. You can do some fine things in the light verse field, but you've got to get down out of there and dry yourself off first."

She made a face of comic surprise as she postured among the stone dolphins and the nymphs shouldering their tilted urns, lathering one or two along with herself. I turned my back, refusing to look.

"Men are such pigs," she said. She threw some water at me, and I edged out of range, where I stood with a foot on a white wrought-iron bench, waiting stoically — Pygmalion facing revisions. The frolic was over in a moment and I heard her approaching across the grass behind me, toweling herself.

"You know something?" she said. "Ursula likes you. You can sleep with her if you want."

"No, thanks."

"Men can be such swine. Still think the human form is wicked?" she taunted laughingly, belting up her own in any case in a terrycloth robe.

I turned toward her.

"Sweetie, if you knew what this is doing to your father. It's killing him. He's taken to his bed — sick at heart."

"Sick! He's on his way to France right this very minute to see about those bauxite mines. In fact he's making Granny fly with him, just to make sure everything is in order. *He's* feeling no pain. Huh!"

We moved as by unspoken consent toward the Sound, a

hundred yards away. I followed her gaze upward. All the bees of heaven swarmed. The fountain plash faded into the gentler monody of the waves, curling like white feathers along the beach toward which we tended.

"Just what do you want of life?" I asked rather largely.

She answered so instantly she must have been going to blurt it out without being asked:

"I want a child."

We negotiated a sudden drop in the genially graded lawn that gained us the beach. The sand looked so clean it might have been packaged and sent out from town, like farina.

"Why, that's fine, Sweetie. A very normal wish," I said, helping her down. "Whom are you going to marry?"

"I didn't say I wanted a husband, I said I wanted a child. I've had enough men now, Chick, all thanks to you for getting me unknotted, to know that's not for me. Or I'm not for it — what's the difference? That's simply not an involvement I'd be good for, or at. But why *should* I go in for it? Why can't a woman satisfy her maternal instinct without undertaking the institution society attaches as a condition? Why really?"

"There's no reason I suppose, intellectually speaking," I said. "Still, a man around the house . . . "

"I'll have money enough, so that's not a factor. In fact, a man might wish to marry *me* for *mine*."

"Money, money, money! Is that all I'm to hear? Legal Tender Is the Night!"

"I can be completely free about this. I've thought about it for some time. Why run the risk of marriage if there's no economic need to? Half of them fold, and the rest aren't worth a damn either, most of them. You know that."

"Do I?"

"So why should I miss out on the one experience I want now, for conventional reasons?"

135

We strolled side by side along the beach, our feet whispering in the sand. Ephemeral liquid hands sifted the moon's casual silver.

"All right, let's accept this Free Spirit theory of yours," I said. "I know it's been respectably put in many quarters, not the least a play of Shaw's. But you'd still have to choose a father for your child. How would you go about that?"

We paused for her to light a cigarette from a match in my cupped hands. She glanced at me, drawing on it. "That is a problem. Whom would you suggest?"

"Danny Dolan's a fine sort, and seems to like you."

"Like me, he's in *love* with me. That's the trouble with that. Don't go trying to get me married, Uncle Chick, that's out. And above all get the right slant on this. I don't want a love child — I want a child I can love!"

You thought this a strange end to frivolity till, looking at her more closely, you realized it was the beginning of sobriety: the high purpose of one striking out for moral frontiers.

"I've refused to marry Danny a dozen times because I don't *want* to get *involved*, and each time he gets more depressed. The last time he threatened — well, never mind that. The thing is he's so bourgeois he'd expect me to marry him because I was the mother of his child. So I'd almost sooner it were a married man, just to keep it clean. Just to keep it objective." She gave me another sidelong glance. "I've even thought of you."

"Oh, I think not," I said. "Thanks just the same though. I'm flattered. How about Dylan?"

"I don't want anyone who'd be only too willing. Your refusing shows a kind of character I'd like my son to inherit. Or daughter."

"For the child really to have it to inherit I'd have to pass up fathering it. How do we get around that?"

"No, seriously. It's just the old *l'homme moyen sensuel,* man

136

as a sensual means, that I'm proposing. There'd be nothing personal in it."

Romance on short notice. Isadora Duncan on the beach imploring a favor of her rescuer, and a child anonymously begotten on a warm Italian night. These waves plashed on a tame Westchester shore, endless little gasps of amazement. I looked up at the stars — consulted, always, as a gauge of the emotional temperature we were running. They had been rivets and bees, oats for Pegasus and intolerably twisted tuning pegs. From a radio came the strains of *Charmaine*, like scraps of silk fluttered on the spring night. We didn't know it, but just about then a radio sputtered out on a plane winging into the tinted east over the Atlantic, the last ever seen or heard of it, and Sweetie's only living relatives disappeared between two continents. The bulletins next day gave no time, but I often wonder if it wasn't just then, as we stood together in our velvet night, that their motors plunged into the sea, churning the blood of the dawn.

Sweetie sighed, stooping to fondle a stone. "Well, if you're going to be stuffy I suppose it'll have to be Danny. Because I suddenly feel time slipping. Every birthday is like a chill draft from a door somebody's left open. Oh, Chick," she cried in a whisper like the waves', and with that high dexterity of heart that was at long last hers, "I do so want a child!"

I didn't answer. Two figures in borrowed bathing suits were stumbling toward us over the sand. The first was Bill.

"It's Danny —" he exclaimed as Ursula overtook him. They stood panting side by side. Their pallor was absolute — like that of cheesecake. "Somebody saw him go out on that damned rubber thing and then when nobody saw him again for an hour — Was he despondent?"

"What are you talking about?" Sweetie faltered.

Poor Danny. Had he been out of his depth all along with those companions? Had the impossible yearning to Belong sent him to the horizon at last? Had he been infected by the same lyric dream we were all in fear of flunking, that dream thanks to whose inherent irony it was best realized by being brought down in a heap? There had been a pneumatic horse in *Tender Is the Night*. Or had he been drunk on the vision of Gatsby bobbing, sad and laudable, on his inflated raft?

I turned toward the mansion behind one of whose uncountable windows Waldo could be seen trying to give somebody something — liquidating our dream with all speed. As exponent of a militant provincialism I had only two allies — and one was mad and the other was dead, and as for myself . . . ? Perhaps a little of both.

"What makes you think — How do you — "

Bill turned and pointed up the beach along whose receding rim the pure white plumes forever waved. "His horse came back without him," the couriers panted in unison.

My eyes turning upward sought the stars one last time. They looked to me like brass tacks.

10

HERE occurred an unexpected merger of my two problems. It was lucky or unlucky depending on how you looked at it.

I had one of my charges on her feet. I was to see the other at our usual haunt after a call on Sweetie, who, alone now in the cottage on Beacon Street, was if anything more urgent in her desire for a child, a venture on which, under the sobering elms of home, I was by contrast the firmer in my resolve not to collaborate.

"I'm going to sell this place and move to New Mexico. I can write there. You'll never see me again," she argued.

"I'm sorry," I said. "I admire your spunk, but that's as far as it goes. Good-by, Sweetie, and good luck. I'll be watching for those poems. Good-by, good-by."

At the Greek's there was the preliminary chat with Nickie before the stern periodic inventory. A book of prints he had with him prompted me to remark that a good artist can get more out of a minor subject than a poor one can get out of a major.

"You're absolutely right," Nickie said. "Sargent gives us still lifes of people. Cézanne gives us portraits of apples."

"Cowplop. When are you going to nail the Smoothie? Or

Johnny Velours, as he now calls himself? Three more jobs since the Flickendens' and you're still no closer to a solution. You realize you're on a kind of probation. Your dream was validated in the sense that there *is* an adversary, but he's making more of a fool of you than we did! Lila's cooling off too. I don't know how much longer I can keep her from Reno. *You* can, by getting a job. I've been thinking." I began my walk on eggs again. "Why don't you work for a teaching certificate and then get a post at some first-rate university?"

He was lost in that dense thought into which it was so hard to pursue him.

"I've been thinking. It may not be Pete Cheshire at all. This looks like the work of a far more brilliant criminal."

"Two crooks in a town this size? Oh, come now, isn't that asking too much of Providence? Pete's using the Johnny Velours name to throw suspicion off himself, but leaving it on a calling card with each job is clue enough. It's Pete's trade mark. Let's not change the subject. Now I've taken the liberty of getting some catalogues of normal colleges . . . Please take them. I insist!"

Nickie stirred, another hue coming to the surface like that of a turning fish. "A college professor. Why not?" he said with that ominous compliance I had learned to watch out for. He had readily agreed to "look into" real estate brokering by accompanying an agent named Mrs. Apthorpe on her tours with clients. He was supposed to be exploring the possibilities of part-time employment but all it came to was some pleasant countryside rambles with a woman he found amusing, and a chance to see some local houses about which he had always been curious. "Why not indeed? One is so many things, even at once. What is a man? What is Man? Oh, who am I!"

Camus and the problem of identity. Sartre and the blown leaves of self — the whole Existentialist express streaking through a night as black as the pit. I will try again, Lord. I will lie down between the tracks for yet this train to pass over me, its successive axles grazing the tip of my nose, no real damage let's hope . . .

I saw Nickie three days later, under the rather jolting circumstances I've intimated.

I was leaning faintly against the wall of a building, in which position I had suffered a bootblack to nudge his apparatus meekly under one foot, when I noticed two backs that looked familiar. As they got into a cab I recognized Nickie and Sweetie Appleyard.

When I swept into the vine-choked cottage the minute my work permitted it that afternoon, it was to find Sweetie under a sunlamp on the living room floor. The days were cloudy and she was trying to keep up with a tan she had begun. She lay on her stomach, gnawing a pencil, a notebook on the carpet.

"How do you like this new poem?" she said, turning over. "It's called 'Taste,' and listen, Chickie, because this is my first nonparody. Here's Beth Appleyard on her own."

I stood modestly with my back turned while she read it aloud:

> If burlap typifies the taste
>   That marks the common ilk,
> A handful of us, I'd have said,
>   Constitute the silk.
> We drink espresso, we eat snails,
>   We do not read for plot;
> Preferring music classical
>   We also like it hot.
>
> Many friends have fallen from
>   My grace, as down a well,
> By playing me recorded Strauss,
>   Or serving zinfandel.

Thus one by one they failed the test
  Of Sensibility,
Leaving, in a world of clods,
  Him and you and me.

But lately flaws in his façade
  Have sometimes made me blench;
"Intriguing" is a word of his;
  He laughs at fractured French;
His stories, though not shaggy dog,
  With subtle sickness fill me;
The temperatures at which he serves
  His vintage clarets chill me.

By gradients often so minute
  Offenders miss the bus.
Oh, spirits rare are rare indeed!
  It seems there's only us.
Together we — What's that you say?
  You're fond of Duncan Phyfe?
You can stand Post-New Orleans jazz?
  Lord, what a lonely life!

"Swell. See here," I said over my shoulder while she penciled in revisions and called me swine, "your life is your own business and I realize the amorality of the artist. But leave Nickie Sherman alone!"

"Nickie who?"

"Sherman. You know who I mean."

"I'm afraid I don't."

"Stop lying — and get up. He's a respectable married man, married to my sister is where I come in on this, and I'll not have you getting your hooks into him and mucking up their already rickety life. An involvement like this might finish it."

She had slipped into shorts and a sweater, and now bent over a table to fish a cigarette out of a box.

"I really don't know what you're talking about."

"Then who did I see you get into a cab with this afternoon?"

"Oh, *him*. Is that his name? He was rather vague about it. He's a nice chap I met in a bar. Very amusing."

"Are you going to see him again?"

"He has my number."

And I had hers. This girl's purpose was firm. All the firmer must be mine: to protect my sister from infidelity by that lout. Nickie was weak and might be unable to extricate himself. I could. Nickie was a romantic who might follow her to the sands of Taos. I wouldn't.

"All right," I said with a sigh of resignation. "I'll do what you ask. Provided one thing: *you leave Nickie alone*. Do you promise?"

"I do."

"Then I'll keep my side of the bargain. When do you want to get this show on the road, as they say?"

"Tomorrow, Chickie? There's a lawyer coming in the morning to go over some things, but I'll be home alone after two. How's two o'clock? Can we make it firm?"

"I shouldn't wonder," I said, starting for the door.

Lila asked me to stop by the next morning as she had something urgent to show me. Nickie was out and the children were at day camp. Even that wasn't enough secrecy. She bolted the door after admitting me and drew the living room blinds. She then disappeared to the rear of the apartment, returning with a small carton which she overturned on a table, spilling out a shower of jewelry.

"What is all this?" I asked, fingering some.

She disentangled one of the pieces from the snarled mass of gems and gave it to me. "Recognize this?"

It was a gold bar pin monogrammed in the letter F with tiny green stones. I had seen a photograph of it in the paper.

"Isn't that the emerald pin the Flickendens had stolen?" I said.

"And this must be that signet ring of the Babcocks', and this seed-pearl necklace fits the description of the one taken from the Mulhollands' bedroom. Everything here tallies with something in the robbery lists. We've kept clippings. There it is — all four jobs."

"Then he's caught Johnny Velours!"

Lila shook her head, her eyes closed. "Guess again."

"I simply don't understand. Where did you find all this stuff?"

"Pockets of his clothes, drawers, hidden behind things on the closet shelf. I found this necklace when I was emptying a jacket of his for the cleaners, and kept looking for more. I really got suspicious when — "

"Over how long a period?"

"Just this week."

"But I don't understand. He recovers all this loot from Johnny Velours and still doesn't turn him in, though the whole town's laughing at him. It makes no sense."

"There's one other explanation that does." Lila drew a long breath and ran her palms down the sides of her hips. "He *is* Johnny Velours."

"Oh, come now, Lila, what are you talking about?"

"Something I've been thinking over for days. It all fits. I realize now he's been going out nights more than before — afternoons were usually his time out — and acting rather mysteriously. There are gaps and discrepancies in the stories he tells me. *And* it makes sense psychologically."

"How?"

"Turning the tables for that hoax." She looked me hard in the eye. "Just think about it a minute. He's the butt of a practical joke he can't take. What better revenge than to nip back to the Flickendens' on the very same night and lift some of their jewels while the revelry's still going on downstairs? Maybe on the way to the washroom. That's not the end — making them laugh out of the other side of their mouths isn't enough. He's smelled the excitement of crime and likes it. He goes out another night — "

I turned around, running my fingers through my hair. "But the whole thing was supposed to be therapeutic — "

"— and another night, to the homes of people he knows are away in Florida and Bermuda — thanks to those pictures your paper runs of vacationing citizens — most of them cards who had the first laugh, till he's leading a career of crime. That's my husband. A jewel thief!"

"You see, his ego needed some sort of appeasement, so having failed in one life he migrates to its opposite; but not its opposite really, *since it's simply the other side of the same coin.* He had got to put on the whole show himself. That make it clear to you, Sweets?"

She turned to the window, whirling away from me with a vehemence aimed at no other. I went over and laid a hand on her shoulder.

"Now, Sis, you're all wrought up . . . "

"Wrought up! Why shouldn't I be? You've made a burglar out of my husband!"

I nodded in diagnostic thought, totting up the factors in the case, now shown to be as grave as I'd all along thought. "We have a detective *manqué* who rather than bear the shame of that becomes a crook *succès*, in a switch that bids fair to make my patient the most famous, I might say artistically tidy, case of dual personality in modern medicine."

"Yes, but you didn't cure it — you produced it!" She whirled back.

"If you mean that we purposely hastened the crisis we know to be inevitable in cases like this, yes, I accept that. But don't get panicky. We induce these things now, just as obstetricians induce labor. But it's important for you not to tell Nickie you know. Let me handle it. The utmost delicacy is required. One misstep and we're all in the bottom of the gorge."

"I can't go to Reno now, of course. This is too serious. I couldn't leave him now."

"And to that extent we've gained ground. I'm proud of you, Sis. If it'll help, Nickie's is an exaggeration of a kind of split we all have in our natures. What Van Kuykens calls the Janus complex. We're all two-*faced*. How many have the gumption to be two-headed?"

"Who is Van Kuykens?"

"A psychiatrist I'm interested in."

"Shall we call him in?"

"He lives in Amsterdam. Please don't get hysterical, but not that cold calm either. Something in between. I must find Nickie and have this out with him. Maybe he's had enough of the cream of the jest to call it quits; we'll get the jewels anonymously to the police, and the whole thing will blow over."

The sound of a car stopping and footsteps outside sent me to the table where I scooped the mass of loot back into the carton. I popped it into a sideboard. The car drove off and the footsteps in the hall continued softly past the door and on up to an apartment overhead.

"Now, sit tight till you hear from me," I said. "I'll go out and see if I can find Nickie."

This wasn't easy, since he was now roaming about under two identities. He wasn't in the Samothrace, nor any of a few bars and coffee shops I knew shared his favor. Then by chance I glanced into a barber shop I was passing and saw him sitting in the chair. I watched him from behind a newspaper kiosk outside. He had that curiously meek look men have when their hair is being cut. But when he emerged, in a neat gray pinstripe, his manner was jaunty.

"Nickie?" I said, popping from cover.

He gave me a blank look and hurried on.

"Nickie?" I said, trotting abreast of him.

"I'm afraid you've got me confused with someone else, old chap," he said amiably.

My knees melted as I recognized the look in his eyes that I remembered from the brief period when his wits had wandered before. *He didn't know he'd been committing the crimes.*

"Of course. You're Johnny Velours."

"Righto. But . . . ?"

"My name is Swallow," I said, a word which meant nothing to him. "We met in a bar near here." I indicated a tavern across the street. "How about a nooner? Or is it too early for you?"

"Not at all. Feel as though I could do with a spot of downfall."

The conviction that he was Johnny Velours set well on Nickie. The caustic turn to which his manner had increasingly tended was softened. This island off the mainland of his psycho on which he had temporarily taken refuge, so to speak, was a warm, balmy place of easy tempo and gentle conversational breezes. He was a joy to talk to, to loaf over drinks with — I'll say that for him. He was vague about what he did and where he lived, whether because he didn't know much about that, having only just assumed his alter ego, or out of intentional elusiveness, as Sweetie had implied. Needless to say I had now little stomach for the tryst with her. It was two o'clock before I remembered it, and that I was due there. I would call it off; or simply drop the whole thing from my mind. Nickie required my full attention now.

It was by way of granting it that my purposes were rudely shuttled back to the other. Nickie — or I should say Johnny Velours — fished in his pocket, and finding it barren of small change, asked, "Oh, I say, could I borrow a dime? I've a call to make."

The faintly British note was in conformity to the tradition in which his present role was, after all, cast. The touch of Raffles roguishness in the way he went to the phone booth alerted me. I slipped over and listened behind it to the dial clicks. They corresponded well enough to the Appleyard number. When he returned I was seated at our table again, sipping. "Damn," he said. "She claims she's busy this afternoon. Can you ever believe a woman?"

"Sometimes," I said, with the sigh of one called sternly back to his obligations.

For it was all now only too grimly plain. It had been obviously as Johnny Velours that he had made Sweetie's acquaintance, therefore all the more urgent that I keep it from developing. The island must be re-integrated with the mainland before it acquired a sovereignty of its own, and a temporary fugue the dimensions of a complete split. Nickie needed time to resolve his conflict, Sweetie to wind up her affairs and be off for New Mexico and whatever D. H. Lawrence existence she had in mind for herself there; meanwhile those two must be kept in strict quarantine from one another. Certainly he must be prevented from becoming a full-fledged principal in her flamboyant adventure. Nobody on earth could see to that but me. Such was the office I saw duty as squarely placing before me.

So after picking up the check and bidding Johnny Velours good-by with the hope that we might meet here for a spot of downfall on the morrow, I paid, got my hat, and with a heavy heart set off in the direction of Sweetie Appleyard's.

"Come in!" I heard her voice call from upstairs when I rapped the brass knocker. I did, closing the door quietly behind me. "Chick? Come up."

148

She awaited me on the landing with a smile. She had on black toreador pants of the sort popular with the ladies that season, and was twirling a pair of horn-rimmed glasses which she explained, as I gained the final stair, she had just got for work and reading. She looked both more iconoclastic and more than ever a woman of the world who knew exactly what she wanted. I had the sense, that is to say, of an accredited revolutionary having at last thoroughly supplanted the merely rebellious child. Only recently I could not have sworn to this certainty, seeing in her progress but the surface application of Kafka over Fitzgerald, and Proust over both; like one wallpaper over another. (She was reading avidly in the small but stellar library left her by Mme. Piqucpuss.) For our private development is all too often a matter of mechanical stages for which there is as yet no corresponding enrichment of the spiritual soil. Just as in those commercial billboards on which, on wet days, underlying previous advertisements can be seen "bleeding" through, so that mingled with representations of married couples being conversationally stimulated by their choice of morning paper can be discerned a genial grandmother pressing a chest remedy on a bedridden child, while a phantom rivetworker smoking Camels haunts them both, just so I could catch, through the surface layer of Sweetie's new sophisticated self, glimpses and echoes of that wayward girl the new self had not quite yet replaced but merely overlaid; while closer scrutiny revealed that first avatar in which our odyssey in time had begun: the moppet tearing among the summer trees. Now all that was different. I saw a mature woman whose work was going well and who had a firm grasp of her purposes. So molecular, however, are the processes of growth that no word or gesture of a friend whose evolution we may prize is too slight to bear its print. Just as the enamored hero of *The Guermantes Way* could trace Albertine's transformation since last seen by the most trivial additions to her vocabulary, so that her mere use of the phrase "to my mind" — in an observation itself of no moment — was sufficiently a gauge of burgeoning womanhood for him to assure us that on hearing it "I drew Albertine towards me, and at 'I regard' made her sit on the side of my bed," so I detected in Sweetie's laughing allusion to herself as "Constant Writer" an aspect of balanced self-derision, and in her "Bet you like me behind this windshield, yuk, yuk," the grain of true worldliness. Through an open door I saw a bed strewn with writing materials, under a burning sunlamp.

"You look as though you need a drink."

I followed her downstairs, swinging my still undisposed of hat.

"Before we begin, there are a few things I'd like to say," I said. "I'm not sure whether you've thought this thing through from every angle. Supposing — "

"Oh, stop supposing," she laughed, taking my hat, which she hooked insecurely on a hall peg, so that I had to stoop and recover it. "The lawyer just left and the financial picture is even better than I'd thought. And guess what — Father named you my guardian in his will."

"In that case," I said, stiffening in a sudden access of opinion, "I must advise you against this whole business and withdraw from any further participation in it."

"Oh, don't be childish. The whole guardian idea is senseless anyway since I'm of age. It was just a gesture on his part. Pour us drinks. Give me any old thing. I want you to listen to a poem I've been sweating over."

"Ah. Let's hear it."

She dropped into a chair with a page of manuscript. "It's something I've been working at off and on, as well as thinking about for a long time. It's the theme of the artist versus society. Talent in conflict with the conventional mold. I only have the first stanza finished, but here it is:

Coleridge caused his wife unrest,
Liking other company best.
Dickens, never quite enthralled,
Sent his packing when she palled.
Gauguin broke the marriage vow
In quest of Paradise enow.
These things attest in monochrome:
Genius is the scourge of home.

"I'll go on from there to other examples, you see. Byron, Wagner, Shelley, all impossible. Then to get around to the women: George Sand, Isadora Duncan, Edith Wharton, and so on. I thought maybe you could help me with some. Who are some other geniuses whose dish of tea home life wasn't?"

"Well, I was just thinking about Bach," I said, handing her a highball. "Loyal not only to one wife but two, with twenty children all told. Not just an ideal husband but a loving paterfamilias. Then there's Mark Twain, Thomas Mann, Conan Doyle who adored his family . . . "

"You're pulling my leg."

"No, you're pulling your own. I think it's wishful thinking, this idea you artistic types hug, that you can't be one of the folks. It's a self-justification, a kind of goofing off. Why take pride in being a lousy human being, for Christ's sake?" She watched me owlishly over her glass as I gestured with mine. "Take Camus. He lives quietly with his wife in Paris. They seem to be making a go of it. Lovely daughter — "

"Oh, for Pete's sake, Chick, stop talking like an idiot. 'Making a go of it'! Really!"

"The E. E. Cummings' are making a go of it."

"If you say that one more time I'll scream. Of course there are exceptions. I'm talking about by and large. Joyce wanted his Nora always by his side, but I'd hate to have been her . . ."

151

We went at it hammer and tongs for half an hour or more, drinking steadily. The debate raged as we disrobed upstairs. "Hold on there, this average man you keep talking about," I said, gesturing with a shoe, "I want him defined."

"Oh, defined! You talk like somebody on a high-school debating team."

"Thank you."

An absurd domesticity enveloped the scene as we quarreled together in the upstairs bedroom.

"Eliot is a churchwarden," I said, my voice hoarse with passion.

"So?"

"He married his secretary. It's straight out of Hollywood, woman!"

I had to check my desire for Sweetie as I climbed, yelling, into the bed she had cleared of writing junk. This must be kept objective, a purely functional passion.

"I still think you're making a mistake," I said, slipping between the sheets. "I want to go on record as saying that this whole thing is ill-advised. However."

She switched off the sunlamp and a reading light over her pillow. "How pale you are," she said, settling beside me. "You ought to try one of these ultra-violet lamps. Do you realize I even feel better after using it? Probably psychological, but what's the difference."

"You're quite right. Tell me, how much do they cost?"

She looked up at it. "I really couldn't say. We seem to always have had one around. Anyhoo." She remolded her pillow somewhat. "You know, Chick, you have nice shoulders."

"So do you. And your skin. It's that soft brown in which French provincial furniture is, for the most part, finished."

I was aware in a drowsy haze of Sweetie rising and drawing on her blouse and toreador pants. I had dropped off. I watched with one eye as she buttoned her clothing and combed her hair. When she turned to glance down at me I shut it. She came quietly back to the bed.

"Take forty winks for yourself while I fix us some coffee," she said, a faint smile discernible in her murmur. "Here, get yourself a load of the sunlamp if you'd like." She switched it on and adjusted it over my head, tucking the sheet down off my shoulder. "Feel good? Not more than a few minutes the first time, mind, or him will burn. Did you hear Sweetie?" I nodded, smiling as I snoozed away again. The warmth of the lamp did feel good. I had a sense of delicious lassitude as I sank into oblivion with the sound of her footsteps fading down the carpeted stair . . .

I awoke from a dream of being quizzed at police head-quarters. Blinking, I pushed the glaring light away and sat up.

One side of my face itched quite a bit. When I pressed a palm to it my hand felt hot. A dresser clock said twenty to four. I sprang out of bed and into my clothes, hearing Sweetie's voice downstairs. It was the drone of someone on the telephone. Twisting into my shirt I caught a glimpse of myself in a mirror. My right cheek and shoulder were a glowing pink.

Sweetie hung up and met me as I hurried into the living room.

"That was Valerie Lewis. Trying to get *her* to sign off — Lord, Chick, look at you."

"I already have." I stood buttoning a shirt cuff. "What's the idea, leaving a man under there like a chicken under a broiler while you gab away with your women friends?"

"I'm sorry, darling, but I *told* you only a few minutes at first — "

"How am I going to explain this at home? Or the office for that matter? Come on, help me think of an alibi. Where could a working man spend an afternoon that would also reasonably explain his face being cooked to a crisp?"

153

"Oh, dear," she grieved, wringing her hands. "First let's put something on it." She flew to the bathroom, returning with a jar of vaseline as I was getting into my coat. "It's too late for that now," I said. "And what good will it do to look sautéed on top of it?"

"But, darling, it could be serious. Who was that actor who fell asleep under one and had to be rushed to the — "

"I told you this would lead to no good. But no, you needed a man to assert your independence of men with, big deal. I'm not denying the intellectual validity of varied and possibly interlocking causes — " I could not make out what else I said as the door slammed behind me and I ran down the porch stairs to my car.

I shot up Beacon for four blocks and turned left on Chestnut, one side of me red hot and the other stone cold. I slammed to a stop before a corner drugstore, having by this time worked out a plan of action, or, more accurately, analyzed the logical imperatives under which I labored. The only account of my appearance that would hold water would be for *me* to have a sunlamp too. I would have to take the sunlamp up.

The drugstore was Hickett's. I was surprised to find Mr. Hickett still alive and in there, years having elapsed since we had plagued him with superb dialogue and learned allusions at the soda fountain. I was at least grateful no one else was.

Keeping in stern profile, like a figure in a Babylonian frieze, I said with some urgency, "Have you got a sunlamp?

"Sunlamp?"

"Yes, you know — those ultraviolet things. I need one right away."

Out of the tail of my eye I was aware of him appraising my own radiation. His mustache had whitened, his hair thinned, his general appearance grown more motheaten; he had on the same gray suit he had worn for perhaps half a century and would no doubt commence eternity in. His blue eyes were as misaligned as ever, so that when he kept circling to get a view of my incandescent side and I swiveled as steadily to keep it hidden, the choreography was weird indeed.

"No, we don't," he said. "But we have those sun *bulbs*. Just the bulb, that you can stick in any ordinary socket."

"Will they do the trick?"

"Trick?"

"Yes. Give you a sunburn. Or tan, rather."

Mr. Hickett had edged out from behind the counter in his determination to get a look at the fried side of my face, and his elbow brushed a display card of combs, knocking it down. I turned involuntarily toward it as it tumbled to the floor, giving him a fleeting but decisive glimpse of what he wanted to see. "Do you need it right away?" he asked, paling slightly himself.

"That's what I said. The bulb, please."

"But — " He began a gesture at the scarlet jowl, but it died in midair as his hand fell away.

"*Will you please give me one of those things? I'm in a hurry!*"

He swallowed his eyeballs. I had not witnessed this agonized rigmarole for a decade or more — indeed I had forgotten that feature of my student days — and its enactment struck me with fresh impact. Mr. Hickett's pupils seemed to bulge as they disappeared from view under his fluttering lids, while his mouth worked in a grimace of their own. He plucked a cube-shaped carton from under the counter while with the other hand he drew a yard of wrapping paper from a roll.

"Never mind that," I said, taking the box from him. "How much is it?"

"Nine fifty."

Standing laterally, I fished a ten-dollar bill from my wallet and gave it to him. He turned to the cash register to make change in a deliberate manner. "Do you want to match the other side of your face with it?" he asked. "Is that what you want to do?"

"I don't see that that's any concern of yours. I asked whether this bulb would do the trick and you haven't answered my question."

"It's not as good as a regular sunlamp but it's ultraviolet. It's five hundred watts. I had a woman get third-degree burns with one the other day. Will that do?"

"That will be fine," I said, taking the fifty-cent piece, and hurried sideways out of the store.

So far so good. I sped toward the *Pick* office in a sudden shower, perfecting my plan of action and occasionally glancing at myself in the rear-view mirror. There was no doubt I had sustained a severe burn. Its color was deepening momentarily; by evening I would resemble a boiled lobster.

Halfway to the office I suddenly stopped at the curb. I tapped the steering wheel in thought. My wife was attending a committee meeting for some kind of women's club symposium that afternoon. Did that change the picture? Yes, and in my favor. Now would be the time to sneak into the house with my purchase, so that when she returned I might be found lying under it, home from the office early with a cold, which I was doctoring in this fashion, and with an imprudent first exposure, etc. It was foolproof. I phoned the office from a street booth, and over Miss McConkey's spluttered spate of messages and queries about where the devil had I *been*, most of them in the name of Bulwinkle, said, "I'm sick. Put off my appointments till tomorrow or the next day," and hurried home.

My heart sank at the sight of ten cars in my driveway. The women were meeting at *our* house. Well, no matter. I must go on with the plan, feeling my way and extemporizing around any possible obstacles. If I was seen entering with my purchase under my arm I would say that I had overdosed myself with it on my office couch, which had been my original idea anyway.

I parked the car as quietly as I could behind the garage, then stole round in the rain to the back yard. The damnable Blitzstein set up a loud barking, which I squelched by pausing to pet him and to enact the march around the pole which freed his tie-out chain. Shifting the parcel under my arm, I tiptoed to the house and listened under a dining room window. A gabble of voices mingled with the clatter of tea crockery told me the women were hard at it. This would be a cinch. I crept unheard into the front door and up the inside stairs to our bedroom. Working quietly as a thief, I unscrewed the bulb from the reading lamp over my side of the bed and screwed in the ultra-violet, which I snapped on. Then I removed my shoes and coat and stretched out on the bed, at peace, except for the urge to scratch my now fiercely itching face. I kept that well out of the rays of the lamp, until such time as Crystal walked into the bedroom. When I heard her footsteps, I would have but to shift my head on the pillow to be in the clear.

After about ten minutes the buzz of voices rose to the shrill clamor of adjournment. Five more and they were all out. Presently Crystal's tread was heard approaching up the hall. I put my head, cooked side up, under the light. She entered.

"Well, where on *earth* — "

"Oh, hello, dear." I stirred as from a sleep, blinking. "What time is it? Oh, my goodness, how long have I been lying here under this — My face — look at it!"

Crystal came round the foot of the bed. There were six or seven different expressions on her face.

"When in God's name did you get home? What are you — When — The office has been calling since ten o'clock this morning."

"Oh, I've been here for some time. Hour maybe. I was feel-

157

ing punk but I didn't want to disturb you, so I went quietly to bed. Sinuses acting up again, one thing and another, and this character at the office has been talking up sunlamps so long that I thought I'd give it a whirl. Well so. How did the meeting go?"

"But I came up here for something just a while ago and I didn't see you."

"Well, perhaps I was asleep."

"God, *look* at you!"

"I know. Shall we call the doctor?" I said, my anxiety shifting to that quarter. Flaming pain and unappeasable prurience mingled in my cheek, which I now clawed in a voluptuous frenzy. "Is there something we can do till he comes?"

"Wait a minute. Agnes Howe had that and there was only one simple thing of any use. What was it?" Crystal snapped her fingers in the effort to recall. "Cold cream." She darted into the bathroom from which she instantly emerged with a jar of it.

A bell rang as she twisted off its cap.

Round that pot of pomade hovered a nagging coincidence of the kind that often appear in cycles of passion or distress, and that satisfy the taste for cheap symbolism. It is said to hound lunatics and criminals, as well as those in comparable extremities. Or perhaps these repetitions occur constantly in daily life but are only noticed in the heightened awareness that accompanies emotional strain. At any rate, I recognized the blue crock of skin cream for which Crystal had come into the bathroom on the evening when, sitting in the tub, I had heard the name of the sitter which touched off all these events.

"Where were you earlier though?" she asked as she spread it gently on my cheek. "Miss McConkey phoned before lunch and then after, in a perfect — "

"I was busy with Nickie. You haven't been in touch with Lila, I take it. Well then, I'd better tell you what's going on. I think that'll do. Thanks, darling. Here, sit down on the bed

158

while we forget about me and talk about somebody else. I'm afraid it isn't a very pretty story."

"Just let me get this part here. It seems to go down your neck and —"

"She call me Dr. Swallow? Hey? Miss McConkey call me that? I have to laugh at her."

"Loosen your collar . . . That's better. It seems to go clear down — For heaven's *sake*, your whole shoulder and *back* are burned. I thought you had your shirt on when I came in just now."

11

NICKIE'S intervals on the island — to continue viewing him in that light — became more frequent and prolonged. Not, fortunately, that each assumption of the Johnny Velours identity entailed a fresh theft. There was only one new burglary in the next few weeks, that of a Jackson Pollock from the twenty-room Burwash place, thought impregnable by virtue of an alarm system which the police had considered foolproof. That, perhaps more than the literate nature of the heist, was the clincher to me that it was Nickie. Having worked on the local force he must have been familiar with the installation. Which in no way lessened the wonder of his beating it. How had he brought the *coup* off?

And he was a joy as a person. An errant charm, with no more Continental hand-munching than you could stand, made him quite the ladies' man. Lila fell in love with him all over again, if I shouldn't rather put it that she was now tempted to her first disloyalty to her husband on his account. I took her into a bar to meet him one day. Because when his vagueness about placing her became at last a total blank, I suggested she accept the challenge innate in the situation and cultivate him in his new guise. She looked pretty in a blue tweed and matching hat over cropped curls, and when I left them hitting it off in a twilit booth I sensed that I had made a fine match. My mother was luckily still on hand to take the children in this crisis as she had the last, leaving Lila free to pursue the alternate romance. That was my plan of procedure. With her entrenched on both island and mainland, we stood a much better chance of integrating Nickums. Of pulling Nickums together. And by George if he didn't fall in love with her.

"He's asked me to marry him," Lila told me.

"I'm so happy for you."

"He's promised to go straight."

A development like this becomes more credible when it is remembered that the separate elements in a split are subterraneously linked. Somewhere underwater the island is connected with the mainland, if only unconsciously. There was a further bond, that between Nickie and me in a mutual past. Johnny Velours had his roots deep in a character in a play Nickie and I had written years before. I recognized some of the mannerisms and even a phrase or two thrown out by a nimble *persifleur* drawing freely on the old days. Our county, for instance, abounds in authors of novels suitable for conversion into movies. Johnny Velours called them writers *marquee*. "Swell," I said. I found him wholly delightful. He listened too. Nor did he seize proprietorship of your ideas in mid-statement for more adroit dilation than your own, like that awful Nickie Sherman.

"By all means marry him," I told Lila. "I certainly prefer him as a brother-in-law. The thing has my blessing."

"Wouldn't that be bigamy?"

"I doubt it in this case, but I'll look it up. I know there are problems. There's the children. But I'll bet one thing. When you spring them on Johnny, he won't back out. There's that gallantry about him. Another hunch I have is that the thefts are over, or at least tapering off. They've satisfied what in his emotions had to be satisfied. And your marrying him will arrest

Johnny Velours, so to speak, before the cops can. For Pete's sake don't let him get away!"

All this — the plan to reverse our thinking and absorb the mainland into the island, to reform Johnny Velours rather than organize Nickie Sherman — might have worked, had it not been for a development from a totally unexpected quarter.

Pete Cheshire had been all this time the chief suspect, of course, and was periodically hauled in for grilling. Each time he managed to clear himself — no surprise to us under the circumstances. Then when the papers were full of the Jackson Pollock job and its sparkling execution, Pete suddenly changed his tune. He stepped forward and claimed authorship of it. There he was in the morning paper, grinning vainly between two cops. I dashed over to my sister's the minute I saw it.

"Did you see the paper?" I said.

"Yes. What do you make of it?"

"It's hard to tell. But it's obviously one of those 'crank confessions.' He couldn't resist getting out there to take those bows." I could hear someone moving about in the rear of the house, a man's footsteps. I sank wearily into a chair. "Who's in back?"

"We'll see when he comes in." Seated, Lila pruned a window fern of dead leaves. "He ferries between that island of yours and the mainland so often that I never know from one minute to the next who I'm up against. Did you know they're now calling you King Solomon?"

The acceleration and contraction of the cycles indicated a struggle, perhaps an approaching climax. They were fighting for the mastery, that pair. Nickie knew it better than Johnny; he had finally discussed it freely with me in his more limpid hours as himself. Here was a battle of wits for you: a man trying to catch and elude himself simultaneously, sleuth and male-

162

factor in one. Oh, he had got to put on the whole show himself, all right. Well might he ask as he had, "Who am I!"

"Either way, I can't lose," Nickie had observed to me the day before, when pride in the Burwash caper had made him suddenly put the cards on the table. "Or win," I'd added, and he had nodded. "Yes, we shall see who's the cleverer. I — or Me."

The footsteps in the kitchen came down the hall, through the dining room and into the living room where we sat waiting. There was no doubt who strolled in, the way our faces fell. Prud'homme waddled in his wake.

"Hello, Nickie."

"Hello, Chick." He stood there buttoning a shirt cuff. "You look a bit chewed up. What's the matter?"

"Maybe it's the worries I take to bed with me." I made a few remarks polished in advance on the subject, as a safeguard against being topped. It was actually a Proustian fragment left over from the Mme. Piquepuss days, which seemed halcyon by comparison now. "Slumber, as everyone who has suffered nervous ordeals knows, is no guarantee of refreshment. His henchman, bad dreams, can produce an exhaustion greater than wakefulness might have left us with. Eight hours of oblivion may be devoted by good spirits to the renewal of vitality, or by bad to a depletion compatible with, or even desired by, our subconscious."

"Yes. Nature gives us the gift of sleep. The rest is up to us."

"Cowplop. Well, have you heard about Cheshire?"

"Yes. I was just on my way down to headquarters. I can't let him take the rap for those burglaries, you know. It would be comic if it weren't so pathetic. The poor fool doesn't even know who Jackson Pollock *is*."

It was the credit, of course, not the rap he couldn't let Cheshire take. The whole thing came to focus in a flash — a flash as instantaneous as those with which the photographer's bulbs were exploding down at the headquarters to which Nickie must now hurry.

The pleasures of retaliation had been, though massive, secret. Hence, self-defeating. No one knew it was Nickie who had been setting the town on its ear, so each addition to the cream of the jest was purchased with a corresponding loss of prestige — a vicious circle if I ever saw one. He was building up, under cover of night, a criminal whom by day he could not catch. A public laughingstock had been the price of his private relish. Hard as it was on the ego when there had been only the *suspicion* that it was Pete who was outsmarting him with the thefts, their public attribution to the goon was intolerable. The terrible psychic balance in which things had so long hung was broken when the goon stepped forward to claim authorship. His motive for doing so was presently learned. He had been jilted by a girl with the taunt that he was just that, and would "never amount to anything, even as a crook." Lashed by the need to show her, and possibly sick of the whole scramble for status that life has become, he had cut his own Gordian knot by "confessing" the burglaries esteemed to be the work of a criminal genius, now capped by a malefaction with cultural overtones. For the Jackson Pollock job had made page one of the second section of the *New York Times*, where crimes of an intellectual nature are sometimes noted. The parallel of two men equally torn between the demands of vanity and respectability — and each choosing for the Ego — was to me an instructive one. Jail was the only place where either could hold his head up, now.

The battle of wits, though, was far from over.

"How can you prove you took the Jackson Pollock?" I asked Nickie. "Only yesterday you told me you didn't know where you'd hid it."

"I don't. Only Johnny Velours knows that, and he apparently isn't telling."

"Then how can you solve it?" I asked with my head in my hands and the feeling that I was bleeding internally at several specifiable points. "Tell us that, Nickie."

"It hinges on the burglar alarm," he said. "The fact that it never went off means only one thing: the power was disconnected. I knew that it would be, and when."

"What are you talking about?"

"Going around with Mabel Apthorpe gave me a lot of inside dope about houses, what was for sale or rent, who got what for a song from the Thruway condemnations. She's a regular chatterbox. Lots of people are getting those old Colonial houses for next to nothing from the state; the only expense is hauling them away from the highway route to sites of their own. Moving a house is a complicated business. Among other things you need a permit for special crews to take down power lines over intersections that you cross. Well, I knew from a remark Mabel Apthorpe dropped that a house the Barretts were moving to Taunton would cross Minute Man Road about five o'clock in the afternoon. By the way, they still haven't arrived in Taunton. Halfway there, they turned a corner and by God if there wasn't the Second Presbyterian Church coming up the road. *That's* being moved. They're probably still arguing about who's going to back up."

"Never mind that. What about the Pollock?"

"Yes. I also knew the Burwashes were in the Caribbean. Those crews work fast, but the lines are down long enough for a man to break into a basement and shut off a burglar alarm, so it won't ring at central headquarters."

"I see. But one thing puzzles me. You knew all this, but how did Johnny Velours know it? He did the job."

"The two personalities overlap at different points. They acquire new impressions together, accumulate certain memories in common, and so on," he said, getting his hat from the hall closet. He stood a moment in thought. "I believe the two identities are beginning to fuse."

"Swell." I rose, my voice shrill with apprehension. "Which will be dominant?"

He shrugged, not as though he hadn't his suspicions, but as though the subject were for the moment best put by. "I've got to get down to headquarters. I really feel I must do this. It's the only honest thing I can do in the circumstances."

And off he went to recover the thunder a boob was trying to steal from him. This involved his being questioned, booked on suspicion, and held for observation. I was almost grateful for a call from Sweetie and its summons to my other problem.

"I wanted to tell you," she said, shining at me across the room. "I'm going to have a child."

"Really?" I said. "I'm so happy for you. Well, well, a child. How long have you known?"

"Just today." She smiled tremulously, standing in a corner, and rather shyly picked up a plate of food she'd been lunching on there in the living room. "Can I give you something to eat?"

"No, thanks," I said, upright in another corner. "I'm not hungry."

"Are you blushing? It's hard to tell, your face is still pink."

"It's peeling. Another week or two and I hope to look human again. Well, well, so it's under way. Well, that's that." I glanced toward the door.

She nibbled a sandwich, then thrust a fork into a heap of something on the plate. "I suppose everything will go all right?"

"Of course. Why shouldn't it?"

"There's nothing to be scared of."

"What's there to be scared of? You'd think you were the

first woman to have a child," I laughed reassuringly. I shifted my weight from one foot to the other. "It's perfectly natural. Woman is the Custodian of Life. Only by merging herself in its Continuity can she fully realize herself. That's why you're doing this. Remember?"

"I hope you'll stop by once in a while. Just to look in on Sweetie, who's all alone, till she's used to it." There was about her a touch of dependency that was new, while at the same time her eyelids fluttered in an old way.

"When will you be leaving for New Mexico?"

She frowned into her plate, chewing. "Ik, I hate potato salad." She returned the plate to the table and sat down in a deep chair, tucking her feet under her. "Well, I'm having a little trouble with the house, actually. I need a better agent. I gave Wood and Apthorpe an exclusive on it, you know, but they're not getting anywhere for me. The thing to do is list it with the whole Real Estate Board. Then everybody'll be in here poking into corners, won't they?"

"Haven't you had any offers?"

"Not a nibble."

"Oh?"

"And now there aren't even any lookers any more. Sweetie doesn't understand it."

"I do. It's that damned Thruway. I was against it from the beginning. It's knocked the bottom out of the market in two ways. First, people don't want to buy around here because of it; second, it's flooding the market with houses you can pick up for nothing anyway, just haul them out of the way of the bulldozers! That's progress?"

"Don't slice the air so. You make me nervous." She clutched a strand of beads, some trinket of anthropological import from the Village days. "You mustn't upset a woman at a time like this. Be nice to Sweetie. She's not building the old Thruway. *She's* bearing your *child*."

"I'm sorry. Everything is such a mess in this state. Well, I didn't vote for that bunch in office."

She sat appraising the house with fresh affection, her eye clear and bright, like that of a nesting bird. "Ish kabibble if I don't sell the house. It's so snug in here."

I set down my briefcase which I had been holding all this time, and which was bursting with work, and took a stance squarely in front of her chair.

"You must go to New Mexico," I said quite calmly. "The climate is ideal, perfect for expectant mothers. Artists colonies there offer a milieu tolerant of the sort of thing you're trying to do. Oh, the Southwest is wonderful! Now, you go there, do you hear? I'll look after the house for you. I'll sell it if I have to — if I have to buy it!"

She came over and put a hand on my shoulder. "You're so strong. You give a woman courage. The kind she needs at a time like this."

"This isn't like you. I thought you set such great store by your independenre."

"Oh, I do. I do. But this is a new feeling along with it. A kind of dreamy sense of being a complete woman at last. *I'm so alive.*"

I had a sense of something rather to the contrary, the slightest regression into the girlhood from which we had at such cost only just rescued her, but I said nothing. I had, for example, not heard her refer to herself in the third person since the intermediate Fitzgerald period of half-girl half-woman affectations that preceded her emergence into the adult world. I laid its revival to the first tremors of discovery, and trusted she would steady down in time. Every woman had qualms at first.

"I must run along now," I said, getting my briefcase. "Remember the owner of a house doesn't have to be around to sell it, in fact I've heard it helps to be away. Just turn it all over to your agent and go. Free as a bird. The best of luck with it, and with the baby," I said, backing toward the door, "*and your new life in New Mexico.* Good-by, Sweetie. Good-by, good-by, good-by."

"Hello, Chick?"

"Why do you phone me here at the office? You know you mustn't."

"I just wanted you to know. I've had an offer on the house."

"Wonderful! Getting your price?"

"Twenty-five hundred less, but I've instructed my agent to take it."

"That Miss Apthorpe?"

"Well, Mr. Wood is handling it."

"That's great. I'm delighted for you."

"I wanted you to know. Will you drop by and celebrate before I go?"

"Oh, sure. Little drink on it, before you're off to the great Southwest — for good. Good luck with the closing and all."

It was an evening bathed, for me, in that relief from anxiety which I sometimes think must be the keenest of human joys. I rough-housed with the children, joshed with my wife, ate like a horse. I picknicked in bed with crackers and cheese, then a poppyseed Danish and a second glass of milk. Books to catch up on strewed the counterpane. Fillmore walked in wearing a ten-gallon hat tipped slightly forward, like a stranger entering a saloon in a manner calculated to arouse curiosity.

"Why do you follow me wherever I go?" I said. "Can't you see I've made a new life for myself out here? Why do you hound me?"

"Harry wants to know about the Wells, Fargo money. He's coming on the noon train tomorrow, Murton."

I laughed at the ceiling, wriggling among the bedclothes. Fillmore went out, passing his mother coming in. I smiled innocently over as she regarded the Danish I was eating. "Just having a roll in the hay," I said.

She sat on her side of the bed, with a book of her own in which she was underlining passages heavily with a pencil. I drew her skirt up and pressed a cheek to her thighs, murmuring a declaration in her favor.

"That whinnying noise," she said. "And how about putting your shoes in the closet? You've got five pairs lined up in the corner there. . . . Chick, I think it would be nice too, but I've got to go out tonight."

"Lambswool, where?"

"Mabel Apthorpe's. We've got to prepare for this panel discussion we're giving at the Club. She won't be home till ten, but it shouldn't be more than an hour. Maybe when I come back if you're awake . . . "

"What's the panel discussion about?"

"The Ordeal of Modern Woman is the subject."

"You mean those two cars, automatic dishwasher, beautiful house in the suburbs but Something's Missing? That ordeal?"

"The fact that she has all that after being educated for something else — ignoring your sarcasm." Crystal tapped the open page with her pencil. "There's some statistics in here that would raise your hair. The number of women who have all you say — who are supposed to Have it Made — and who end up in nervous breakdowns, alcoholism, affairs they don't want and what not. There's a case a thousand feet up your own road. Have you heard about Alice Drury? She's turned Lesbian. It's a fact. She's left Frank and is living with that woman who opened up the boutique. Why do things like that happen?"

"Why do they? I was only being facetious a minute ago. Of course it's a problem we all worry about. Why is it?"

"There's no simple answer, but one thing is that the whole *lifeline* of woman today is ridiculous, in an awful sort of way. A woman today is educated to be an intellectual companion for a man, a creative mother to her children, and a cultural force in the community," Crystal said, rising and thoughtfully lighting a cigarette, "and after getting her degree, or even degrees, wakes up one morning and finds herself a housemaid to a stockbroker and a chauffeur for three kids. She spends four years at Bennington in a leotard, and there she is, stuck in a — a — "

"Chintz Prison?" I said, going over for my glass of milk.

"Say, that's good. I like that. 'The Chintz Prison.'" She gave me a smack. "Thanks. That'll make a wonderful title for the symposium."

I was glad in any case that my darling was out of her own Chintz Prison when the phone rang, because it was Sweetie's voice at the other end, "Chick? Can you talk?"

"You're damn right I can, and this is what I have to say," I answered in low tones. "If you telephone me here one more time I'll come and strangle you to death with the cord. Is that clear?"

"I'm sorry, and I wouldn't have spoken up if it weren't O.K. But look, have you any idea where I can get some rasp berries?"

"Raspberries! At the store of course. Can't you just go to the store and get some? Is oo completely helpless? Why do you bother me?"

"It isn't just that. Chick, something's happened. Could you possibly stop over for a second? Don't if you can't, but oh, I wish you could. I'm frightened."

"What about the deal? Did you get a binder?"

"What's a blinder? Tell Sweetie what a blinder is. Oh, hurry."

"A *binder*. That's a down payment on a house. Did you get yours?"

"That all fell through. They withdrew their offer. But that isn't what I have to see you about. This is something serious."

"I'll look in tomorrow."

"Tonight?"

"All right. It just happens to be convenient. But I've no sitter so I'll only be in and out."

"And as long as you're coming, would you pick up those raspberries on the way? You're so sweet."

Because I knew of no grocery store on the way that would be open, and to save time, I got a package out of our own freezer. It was of course still frozen when I arrived at Sweetie's. I dropped it on the table with a graceless clunk. "Now this terminates my connection with this matter. Is that clear? All right. Now what's your news?"

"I think you'd better have a drink first. How about a beef bouillon and vodka?"

"A *what?*"

"You mean you've never heard of beef bouillon and vodka?" she said, indicating her own drink, which I had thought a very stiff whisky. "Where have you been? It was all the rage in the Village. It's called a bullshot."

"I'll just have some Scotch. Go on talk while I mix myself one."

"After I thaw these raspberries." By the time I had poured my drink she had set the package in a pan of hot water, and returned from the kitchen chafing her folded arms through the sleeves of a feathered silk robe.

"Chick, there's no money."

"What are you talking about?"

"Just that. Father's will is meaningless. A later one's turned up leaving everything to Eve Bickerstaffe. Or Mrs. Appleyard rather. Chick, they were married all along. They kept it a secret because they thought Granny would disapprove. I suppose that's why they did."

"And maybe to keep a couple of other husbands she's col-

172

lecting alimony from from hearing about it. Where is she?" I demanded.

Eve had instantly flown to France after the mishap, to be on hand for identifications when the victims were brought into Le Havre, and had stayed on to help resolve the family's financial affairs, which still revolved around those bauxite mines in southern France. After the success of his own little flyer in them, Appleyard had persuaded Mme. Piquepuss to repose her fortune there. Eve was being helpful for good reasons! Next there had been a letter from her saying she was going to settle down in her native London, to forget. So my "Where is she?" was rhetorical. I knew very well she was out of the country or I'd never have lent myself to Sweetie's personal scheme. My question had been an angry outburst at Eve's own programs, now seen in their perspective. God knew she was the last woman I wanted around, but I resented her snug position as contrasted with Sweetie's (and my) dire one.

"She's bought a house in the Chelsea section," Sweetie said. "That's where she wants to live."

"The ——!" I didn't let fly with the epithet, which was legible enough on my pursed mouth. "The grasping, scheming little —"

"I know." Sweetie circled the room, nursing her arms. "Still what's she done worse than marry a man for his money? It happens every day. Anyhow, most of the money went from Granny to Daddy to Daddy's widow, before Granny could settle any on me. You see, she postponed doing that because she had this idea I wasn't ready for it. She gave it to Daddy to handle for me. Then when she saw me on my own two feet, she decided to go ahead with the settlement. Only it never got on paper. That's what she was going to Europe for. To get a look at everything before final arrangements."

"Can't you break the will?"

"We'll try, of course."

"Have you been in touch with the Lady of Chelsea?"

"Our lawyers have been on the transatlantic phone. My Feldkamp and her London solicitor."

"Tchach!"

"Please don't huff and puff so. You're no C. Aubrey Smith."

"And you're no Isadora Duncan," I said, turning on her. "All that Free Spirits stuff! Children Without Official Permission. Well, you're free now — free to show what you're made of backed into a corner. You'll have to get a job — "

"Job?" she quavered.

"For one thing. How do you expect to support a child? You're going to have a child, you know. Oh, what a fool I was to let you talk me into it. I thought you were in the clear, financially and all. Why the hell didn't you look into that side of it more thoroughly?"

"I *did.* Is it my fault if I had the rug pulled out from under me? Oh, we mustn't quarrel — *now*," she said with an excruciating little implication.

I was thinking about something else. She was so impractical that maybe she didn't even have the facts of her own physical situation straight. Maybe it was all a false alarm. It might be only a straw, but it was worth grasping at.

"Are you sure about your condition?" I asked, hoping against hope. "Did the doctor tell you definitely?"

She gestured impatiently. "Oh, yes. I passed the rabbit test."

"You mean you flunked it. I passed it!"

We paced the room independently for a time. We passed one another without speaking, like strangers promenading in severely stratified quarters. Suddenly she dropped into a chair in panic.

"A child on the way and no money. Oh, Chick, what'll we do?"

" 'We'?" I said in an unexpected treble. I stopped and fixed

174

her with a level eye. "Now, look. Get this straight, once and for all. I mean very, very straight. This is your doing. Leave me out of it. I'm having no part of it. I can't afford to get mixed up in this."

"We're both in it up to our necks."

"No, we're not! Not me. No, no. Include me out."

"To think this could happen to me. *Me*."

"That's better. Because it's not my responsibility. But I'll tell you what I'll do," I said, relenting when I saw the distraction with which she drew a handkerchief through her fist, a warning signal that she was slipping farther back into her old self. The feathered *peignoir* was another, an echo of the Ophelia-like abstractions and the air of slightly disheveled classicism that went with being an Isadora Duncan *manquée*. Both echo and premonition now? And would the latter be worse than the former? "I'll tell you what I'll do. I'll pay your railroad fare to New Mexico. Once in Taos, your artist friends will take care of you."

She didn't answer. She stared at the carpet. I wished I had used some other phrase than "take care of you."

"So far away," she said. "And how will the hospitals be there? Hospitals! I've never liked them."

"They're just like anywhere else, Sweetie. All modern improvements. There's nothing to it any more. And the spirit of D. H. Lawrence brooding over all. You're sailing under lucky stars, Sweetie. And so good-by. Good-by, good-by, good-by . . ."

She smiled and got hold of herself. "You're sweet, Chick," she said, rising and narrowing between us the distance I was trying to expand. "A tower of strength, too. I'm glad it's you."

I backed off from that extended hand, that nesting eye. "You mustn't get too attached to me. I'm going to be firm about this."

"I don't think that's precisely the tone to take to a girl in a condition like mine."

"You're not a girl — you're a woman."

"Doesn't it mean anything to you that I'm carrying your child under my heart?"

"Not a damn thing," I said, wincing under the deliberate words.

She turned and went to the window, gnawing a corner of the handkerchief. I was at least grateful for the theatrics.

"I'll kill myself," she said.

I drifted to the piano, where I stood looking down at a stack of sheet music. I riffled the frayed edges with my thumb, thoughtfully. "I wouldn't do that," I said mildly.

"Yes, I am. The whole thing's falling through. It's no use." She turned back again and plowed the floor with unsteady tread. "I'm going to kill myself."

"Well, I've done all I can to talk you out of it." I turned around, raising my arms and letting them fall. "When would you do it?"

"When?"

"Kill yourself. How soon?"

"I don't understand how it all could have turned out this way. I only wanted to realize myself as a human being, and as a woman." She no doubt fancied these to be words of a highly radical order, unaware how absurd they would have sounded on the stage.

"I imagine many a nonconformist has run into this surprise. Bohemian and artistic types think of themselves as too impractical for conventional life, whereas it's precisely the unconventional situations that call for the utmost in being businesslike," I said. "But to get back to the suicide thing, I know many people think of that as being 'the easy way out' and so on, but I have never been of that opinion. *I* think it takes courage. And *I'll* give you *credit*. Sweetie, I'll praise you everywhere."

I had ample occasion to ponder in the next few days what I

saw with sudden clarity that night: that people are often not emotionally up to things they may condone intellectually; that a course of professed independence is often steered out of weakness, the dull daily round entailed by attachment being the one calling for strength. Likewise, finding it imperative to look in on Sweetie on evenings when I should otherwise have had a choice of attending a Little League dinner, playing with Blitzstein and the children or bowling with the bunch at the office, I was able bitterly to reflect that conformity is after all the broad highway — it's the way of the transgressor that's strait and narrow.

Sweetie was barefoot next time she let me in. That and a white dress with more fluttering fringes than I had seen since the days we played grownup with garb unearthed from attic trunks hinted a further slipping back. She must have been in the brook, because her hair was wet as a Rhine Maiden's. We were losing ground steadily. She was folding on me, all right.

"Chick!" she exclaimed, her voice gay now, no anxiety on her face as she took my hand and drew me in. "How do you do?"

"Peak, like John-a-dreams, unpregnant of my cause."

"Come into the garden. It's wonderfully cool out there, and you can hear the water racing over the stones. The rain makes the brook allegro."

I followed her along corridors through which she slipped with the ballet grace that always characterized her but which was more flamboyant than ever now. It was pleasant in the garden, though I had a splitting headache. I saw in the light those delicately bloody and lividly violet hues painters find it to contain. "What's new, Sweetie?" I asked, sitting down on the glider. "Any house hunters? Has Feldkamp pried any of that money loose for you?"

"The market is still dead as a doornail. And Feldkamp is trying, but he says it'll take months and months to contest a will. Maybe years. But the most thrilling thing happened. I just had a telephone call from Eve Bickerstaffe. All the way from London." She touched my knee for emphasis, and her voice was excited, like a small girl's. "Guess what! I explained I needed money and she said she didn't realize I was so badly off. She said she's going to send some right away and will make all the concessions in the will business that seem right, but all that will have to be done through lawyers. She's not coming, but she's going to have her brother call on me. He lives in Pennsylvania. Colonel Bickerstaffe. She's instructed him to look into this whole matter."

"Have you told anybody what you need the money for? You haven't done that, have you?"

"Oh, no. That's our little secret," she said with another coy gesture, and a chilling inflection that put Fitzgerald in dead storage.

"I thought you were going to kill yourself. What ever happened to that plan?"

"Let's go for a walk in the orchard. It's heavenly now."

As she wandered off among the trees, I stood before the glider drawing a magazine from my pocket. It contained an article by a Japanese explaining the Oriental view of self-elimination as being, not a craven resignation, but a ceremonial declaration of great dignity, a form of communication. "I think you might be interested in this," I called. But when she didn't answer, but continued into the green grove, I shoved it back into my pocket, as something known to have been all along intended for my own perusal. As I overtook her, I said quite tersely:

"You've got to stop this nonsense. You realize what's going on and that the time is passing, don't you?"

She turned around and said in one of her moments of sharp sobriety, "Yes, I do. And I can tell you one thing. If I ever get out of this mess, I'm going to teach Sunday School."

"I'll be in the front row."

The next time she was in the treehouse. I followed her shouts round to the rear but couldn't find her. Another call brought me to the foot of the maple. Looking up through the dense foliage, I saw her face hanging from the old eyrie.

"Come on up," she said, "and have lunch. I've fixed you some lunch. See?" She held up a bag of bananas and a box of Crackerjack.

"No, thanks," I said, "I'm not hungry. And I've got to get back to the office."

So there we were. What had been intended as the final step in her maturation began its reversal. The arch at which we had so long labored crumbled under its keystone, leaving our work in ruins at our feet. So Beth Appleyard was not, when the chips were down, up to it. Layer by layer the accumulated husk was stripped away, veil by veil the literary stuffs out of which her salvation had been woven were torn asunder and abandoned to the wind. Her history was being re-enacted in violent retrograde, like those movie films spun hindwise at top speed. We were back where we started. Worse. At least we had never played *house* up there, in the old days!

"Do you understand what's going on, Sweetie?" I asked, squinting up into the checkered boughs.

"On?"

"Yes. Inside of you."

"Sure."

"What else?"

"I'm going to get all round in front, like a music cabinet."

"That is correct," I said, my flesh creeping under my shirt. "And do you know why?"

The head hung in space, a round blank of interrogation.

"Do you know what caused the way you are?"

"Yes. We went to bed all bare."

She had recovered the crystal wonder of childhood. She was

clean out of this. I knew she would be no damn help to me in having this baby; I would have to see it through alone, and that with the added nuisance of her tagging along because of the technicality of its being in her belly.

Why couldn't I go mad? Everybody else was. They were dividing like amoeba all around me, taking refuge in fantasy and make-believe, snug in their retreats. Must I stand alone in the chill blasts? Apparently.

Sweetie's head had vanished from the treehouse doorway. Now it reappeared wearing a straw bonnet with flowers on it, while a bunch of bent stems in her fist completed that air of trampled innocence that had always been her *pathétique* with me. She tossed a few blooms down to me. Daisies, dandelions, and kiss-me-at-the-gate fluttered toward me among the wavering leaves.

I stood watching like a man truly, horribly, utterly up a tree.

12

IN the days that followed, days that tramped heavily by like the feet of some huge beast that threatened to trample him — oh, how he wished they would, to death! — Charles felt something weigh on his conscience. It was an uncommitted act — that he might commit. It seemed to be connected in his fevered mind with some kind of heavy literature that he had once read, not Russian but even worse, that lumbered its way over you with those bone crushing elephantlike feet of the days that Time went by like — yet with what snail's pace!! — that the memory of was as onerous as the fear that he might commit the act it portrayed was acute. Even when he said, "Sweetie, let's go down in the basement," and she said, "Why?" and he said, "Oh, I don't know. We haven't been down there in a long time. I'd kind of like to see the old place again," even then he didn't dare admit to himself what his thoughts were luring him toward. He pretended they were early Thurber. "I want to kill you. There ought to be a piece of iron down there I can do it with — come on," he said, leading the way downstairs — "or coal."

When they reached the basement he saw that one end of it had been converted into a gymnasium. He remembered Appleyard's obsession with keeping fit. There were bar bells of varying weights, parallel bars, tumbling mats, and, of course, the rowing machine that had put him, Appleyard, to bed. He paused over a dumbbell lying on the floor, and stood looking down at it with a thoughtful air, trying to guess its weight. It appeared to be about fifty pounds.

"You going to hit me over the head with that?" she giggled.

"If I can lift it." He stooped over to heft it. It was too heavy to raise with any degree of ease, let alone wield with murderous intent. He looked around some more. His eye fell on a set of chest pulleys attached to the wall. "I'll have to build myself up with that first," he said.

"Well, all right. How long will it take?"

"Not too long. I'm a little out of trim. It shouldn't take too long."

"I have other things to do, you know."

"So have I."

She stood hesitantly, watching him. "You want to kill me, don't you?"

"It's one possible arrangement, that has a lot to recommend it. Do you see any bugs in it?"

"Are you going crazy?"

"If I can arrange it." He backed against the wall and gripped the handles of the chest pulleys. He experimented with the stretchers, pulling them a few times. "This is a cinch. It shouldn't take much of this to tone me up. I'll be right with you."

She watched him a moment longer, then ran her own eye around the basement. She hadn't been down there herself for some time. "What will you do with the body?" she asked.

He finished his workout, breathing a little heavily, but not too much so. He was glad to see he could do that much without winding himself. He was what is called a good insurance risk, and proud of it.

"The body?" he said, coming back. "Bury it in the woods

182

behind the house, probably. Or I may dismember it and leave it in sections at the checking rooms of different railway stations."

"Are you trying to scare me?"

"No — why would I do that? It would only make it harder to do. You'd get skittish, panic, and then I might panic. It'll take enough doing as it is. Don't be so impatient. Women always want everything right away. They're always nagging you to get things done."

"Well, I wish you'd hurry. I'm getting nervous down here. I have some marketing to do. To market, to market, to buy a fat pig. Then home again, home again, jiggety jig," she said. She paused in the light capers that had accompanied this snatch of song, and regarded him narrowly. "What will your wife think when she finds out about it?"

"Finds out about what?" he asked, looking nervously away.

"That you've done me in."

"She'll be proud. Every woman secretly likes to think of her husband as a lady-killer."

He didn't like her expression, which always preceded her attempt to broach the subject of "us" — which was what she had been doing in a roundabout way now. He knew he couldn't keep up the pretense that this was Thurber very much longer; that any second the whole thing would shift gears into that other he dared not name even to himself. It was all too grimly embodied in the rowing machine, off which he had all the while been unable to keep his eyes. When she began a fidgety movement toward him, he gestured at it impulsively and said, "Get in. I'll row you across the lake."

She laughed as she sat down in the seat at his elephantine fancy, her cheeks as flushed as the dawn. When he tried to "get in" beside her he saw there was only room for one, so he said, "I'll sit on this box over here. You row me across."

"The girl do the work?" she said.

"It will do you good. The exercise is what you need." He shook his head at the whole situation. "How to keep fit to be tied," he muttered.

"All right," she answered trustingly, "if you say so," and going along with the playful mood she bent to the oars with a will, even saying, "Heave ho, my hearties." He gnashed his teeth.

They "rowed along" for a while, Charles watching her tug obediently, trustingly at the oars. Oh, God, where would it all end? The Thurber was only a stall, a finger in a dike against which the heavy seas of that other monstrously pounded. Better to withdraw the finger and get the inevitable over with.

"Have you ever read Dreiser?" he asked.

"A little. I managed to avoid it in high school, even the *American Tragedy*. That's the classic, isn't it?"

"That's the one."

"I did see the last movie version of it. I believe it was Montgomery Clift who went to the chair that time. Chick — "

"Row."

Now it swept over him in a rushing billow of raw emotion that caused him to thrash on his seat what he wanted to do. He pretended to be gazing across the water, even shading his eyes to sustain the fiction, but it was mainly to shield his face from her, because in suddenly placing the style that had been weighing so heavily on his spirit — it hit him like a ton of bricks! — he also apprehended the temptation its recognition was whispering to him — thoughts so diabolic he was sure she must read them in his face, which was fulvous. Yet how innocently she sat there! So suffused with the dawn tints of her maidenhood, that he continued to see her in the light of, for hadn't she her purity still as far as he was concerned? He had not possessed her in the orthodoxly carnal sense, only lent his flesh objectively to her special purpose. How he longed to be free of her! He would do anything to end this nightmare.

184

Anything?

No!

And yet . . .

God!

"My arms are getting tired," she said.

"We're almost there." He pointed behind him while with the other hand still shading his eyes, almost believing chimerically the pretense he was trying to sustain. "Head for that island. We'll have a picnic in a secluded spot there I know about."

"But my arms are coming out of their sockets," she protested. "Here, you take the oars. You need the exercise more than I do. You look awful. Are you worried about something?"

He uttered a hollow laugh, more like an animal cry that was torn from him. "Of course not. What would I have to be worried about?"

She paused to rest on the oars a moment. They drifted as among water lilies, into which she smiled faintly, her long lashes tending downward in an expression of maidenly modesty. "Chick, is it true you're having marital troubles? I hear rumors to that effect."

He leaned forward, and there was again the rain of blows on his knees which he presently discovered to be himself like a lunatic rapping for order in a dream.

"You're not getting me, cookie, even if I am junked by my wife over this. So get it through your head once and for all, and if you can't I'll have to drive it through with a hammer and chisel: *I'm not available.* I'm not getting a divorce, and even if I did I wouldn't marry you. So put it out of your mind. If you think there's the remotest chance of it, you're wrong — *dead wrong.*"

The insinuation in his tone appalled him. Was it *her* he was trying to scare or himself? Could he really go ahead with this black thing? No! The incredible thoughts in his mind were unbelievable.

And yet . . .

God!

"It's so cozy, together down here, just you and I, talking about books. We have a lot in common." She let her hand down, trailing it in the imaginary water. "We could make a go of it."

Oh, how he longed to go mad. To be clean out of it on some island all his own. Some delusive refuge on which he could sink to peace, his mind a blessed blank, knowing from nothing, as they said these days, remembering from nothing. Rocked in that Lethean rest, not tossed on these detestable waters into which he had inexplicably, weirdly, blundered, thanks to the writers to whom he had gone for inspiration. Well, maybe this one could get him out of it — maybe this idiom would see him through . . . somehow . . . he knew not how. Not much style, to be sure, but that was not important. It was after all the fashionable romantics, the masters of preciosity, who had got him into the mess; maybe the grim realists could get him out.

How?

Something lit inside him like a flare — a red flame ignited in his solar plexus — his very gut. The memory of something Sweetie herself had once said when he was grooming her to be a Scott Fitzgerald character: "Oh, Chick, I'm going to live if it kills me!"

Why was he recalling that just then? As a cue to what he himself was secretly . . . ? No!

And yet . . .

God!

"Why are we doing this?" she was asking rather plaintively.

Not aware, or only half aware, that he had risen, trembling, to his feet, he sat down again. Not aware that he had sat down,

186

he rose again. He kept this up, as if in a dream, as if now quite insanely engaged in the setting up exercises for which they had descended to these quarters. At last he settled himself, and frowned thoughtfully into the water, on which they might now be considered bobbing momentarily at anchor.

"The whole thing is a social document," he said, puzzling his way through it as he went along. "Yes, that's what it must be, what we've blundered into — a social document. We're the product of cultural forces molding us without our knowledge, and often against our will."

"We are?" she asked delightedly, as though they were being distributed roles to play in a game.

"Of course. You know that. Civilization — that is to say, a world we never made — has held up shibboleths for us to pattern our lives after: bugbears for us to avoid as well as ideals for us to strive after. Being products of our environment, we are pawns in the hands of fate. Is that clear?"

She nodded a little too readily. "Yes, but — "

"*Row.* Goddam it, row, pull as though your life depended on it."

Now she rose to her feet, with that expression of vague inquiry that he had hated always. "I know why you want me to overexert myself," she said. "I see it all now."

"Don't be so damned winsome. The alternative would be a miscarriage of justice, and that's a hell of a lot worse. Life is too full of it, as our best writers have been telling us. There's no rational explanation to any of it, we're all puppets of a blind fate, chips bobbing on a meaningless sea. So what difference does it make if we prevent another cipher in the human swarm . . . ? Sweetie, what is the matter with you? What's the trouble?" he said, the horror of the suspicion of his guilt dissolving in the bliss of the realization of his own worth implied again in the chivalrous solicitude with which he took her shoulders and pressed her back down on the seat.

187

"Sit down. Are you all right? You've got to be careful at a time like this, girl. Shall I get you a glass of water?"

"No, I —" He had been startled by the way her eyes had fluttered upward in their sweet shutters, almost like Mr. Hickett's whom they had tormented in the old days.

"Then what . . . ?"

She pointed up. "I thought I heard someone in the house. Yes," she whispered, "there is somebody."

He stood listening and, sure enough, the floorboards creaked under a cautious tread as a muffled voice was heard, "Is anybody home?"

"I *thought* I heard the knocker," Sweetie whispered. "Who can it be?"

"I don't know, but I know one thing — I can't be seen here," he whispered back, in that ferocious generation not of panic so much as outrage, in which in one instant he not only heard the footsteps moving toward and then down the stairs and turning saw the coalbin door suggestively ajar but also, whispering, "Shh!" half-helped, half-hauled her out of the rowing machine toward it, the door; hearing also in that split second the old weary shifting of gears again; thinking as they shot on tiptoe to and then through the door *Here we go again back to Yoknapatawpha County.*

When he had drawn the door softly shut again, the latch chuckling softly into place, they stood in total darkness, one which was not only the absence of light but the obliteration of the twenty years and more since which they had last stood here, now as then, then as now, waiting in the still unblasted dark while the footsteps came down the stair in trancelike recapitulation of those other footsteps linked forever in his mind with the smell of anthracite; that anthracite of which there were now only a few lumps left, the furnace having been converted to oil, as he either knew from hearsay or maybe sensed in some quantitive modification of the probably thirty cubic feet of blackness in which they stood — always had stood and maybe always quintessentially would, locked in some eternal obfuscation which neither reason nor morality could unlock. So it isn't just being flipped back into that other literary key, he thought with clenched teeth (the teeth doing the clenching (yes, that too)) it's being flipped back in Time itself. Thinking while the teeth transposed themselves into a smile, "This is it. At last I'm going mad, thank God." Not resisting but welcoming the hallucination that it was Granny coming once again as in that other time whose very seconds were impacted in his bones; greeting with a foretaste apparitionlike and serene the conviction that he could even hear commingled with the footsteps the light tap of the cane. Well, he thought, this does it: I am about to see a ghost. This is where it all started and this is where it will end: in a phantom come to avenge that seed which the unlawful conjuncture of mine and this girl's has dishonored, whose outrage to that ancestral pride and principality of blood from which at least heis has flowed is enough to wake from its Atlantic sleep this ghost astride the very apotheosis of Pride, like a witch astride a broom. It is here to take issue with issue still unborn. More. To deny with some Authority wombed and suckled out of the very Absolute itself — the ultimate and unassailable Du Sollst — this tampering with the ancient pomp-entrusted taboo-hedged tribe-hallowed immemorial mammalian meat. She has come from a watery grave to police that seed. "Thou shalt not go hence till thou hast paid the last farthing," will say that voice which is no voice, with a last imperial gesture of a hand that is no hand though it is at this moment fumbling at the latch, scaweed draping the whilom bones, the whilom eyes adream with that old philoprogenitive reproach, all come to ask account for this ancestral blood they at least — the whilom eyes hands bones voice — had for *their* allotted years held in sacred usufruct. Thinking, too, who thought all this, *maybe now I can get this bastard out of my own system,* him with his apotheosis and usufruct and God knows what all. Maybe this will do it. Because I am going to crawl out of Yoknapatawpha County if I have to do it on my belly, and make my peace in bedlam rather than New England. Maybe if instead of apotheosis and usufruct I say usutheosis and apofruct it will all go away. "Usutheosis and apofruct."

The footsteps whispered closer, stopped. In an instant of suspended outrage he felt, sensed, dreamed, the seachanged arm and the whilom bones lifted to the latch; saw, felt, smelt and tasted the chuckling latch pressed and the door swing open.

The upraised arm didn't remember the bulb in the bin, but only poised apparitionlike and bemused in the pale broth of light falling from behind it through the soiled window and frayed lace curtain. The figure stood like ectoplasm, the two pairs of eyes in the coalbin blinking out at it, its own eyes blinking in. The voice that attached itself to the figure was firmer and more masculine than his thoughts had led him to expect.

"Is there anybody in there?" it said. "I'm Colonel Bickerstaffe. Miss Appleyard? Don't be afraid. I believe my sister-in-law told you I would look in on you. . . . No one answered, and I mean when I heard noises down here — Hello! What in God's name have we *here?*"

13

THE Colonel and I were sitting on the sidewalk at the Samothrace having a *fine*. It was warm outside and even more pleasant and warm inside where the brandy trickled down our throats. The Colonel smacked appreciatively, holding the glass up to the light.

"This is good brandy. How come he serves it instead of Metaxas? He's Greek."

"He's *a* Greek but he's not Greek. He doesn't care. It's an oversight when he gets good stuff. We used to tell him what to get in the old days when we sat out here like this a lot. He doesn't know anything about brandy. He just sleeps over the cash register, like an old hound dog told to stay there."

"This is just like the real old days. That chestnut tree across the street with the high school kids walking under it holding hands, and the way the light strikes the briefcases. It reminds me of a little section in Montparnasse." We watched a couple of couples cross the street and become lost in the swirling crowds.

"I know what you're thinking," I said.

"What?"

"What's in the briefcases. Who they read nowadays. Who's surviving. And whether he'll still be read when you get through with your thesis."

"Cut it out about the thesis. I wish I hadn't told you about it. I'll finish it when I get out of this —— Army, and he'll still be read, or if he isn't the books'll be mellowing on the shelves till people get around to him again, like wine in the bin. It'll be down there getting better and better, like a Chambertin '37, or maybe even a Lafite '28, at least the war books and the Spain." The Colonel laughed, showing an octave of good teeth. "You don't like to talk about bins, do you?"

"Cut it out about bins all the time," I said, only half kidding. "I've told you the whole story, I've spilled as many guts about it as you have about the thesis, and I was just thinking how nice it is to get it off my chest with somebody who understands. So let's lay off the bins." Then I grinned, and said, "You were very brave to go down there. You were all right in there. How did you know what you'd find? There might have been a rat."

"Wasn't there?"

"Cut it out."

"It was nothing," the Colonel shrugged, doing it well, a thing not really usually done well at all, but a thing easy to do with a pair of shoulders like those, I thought. The Colonel was looking at something else across the street, watching the way the light fell on it or appreciating the way a pair of legs moved rhythmically under a skirt. I myself took the opportunity to note again the Colonel's scrupulously pressed uniform, polished shoes and gleaming silver leaf. I was going to ask something about the Army when I was asked instead, "Did she hang around here too? The girl who got you in trouble? Did she hang around here with you punks then reading Dowson and Wilde, for Chrissake?"

I shook my head. "She was not of our generation. I don't mean that chronologically, I mean spiritually."

"Jesus, what a word."

"Forgive me for offending you with such a —— word as that.

But here's something for you. What generation were we? I mean if yours was the Lost and the one coming up is the Beat."

"What do you mean, Lost? How old do I look?"

"Again I mean spiritually, to use the word that offends you. You're obviously in your thirties," I said, lying by maybe a decade, "just like me. So what generation was ours?"

"The Spontaneous Generation," the Colonel laughed, "judging by that girl's condition."

"Cut it out about her. There'll be time enough to get down to the brass tacks when we've finished this *fine*, but while there's a little in the glass let's talk about style some more. Who else do you like? What do you think about Faulkner?"

"He has a style which is a dust-catcher."

"Proust."

"A swell trip if you like detours."

"What about Wolfe? Do you think he'll live?"

"I didn't know he was sick."

"Let's talk about some poets," I said, wanting it to be staccato but not that staccato. "Where would you place E. E. Cummings?"

"Somewhere between the Elizabethan lyric and bubble gum. He's fun — an important element in art. Hamlet is fun, so are two, no three, Goyas, and most of Ecclesiastes."

"Now there's Dylan Thomas. Are you familiar with his work?"

"It's nice work if you can get it. But I don't get it."

We sat with our brandies, keeping talking about style. The whole high school let out nearby, not just a few kids at a time, and as the boys and girls poured by across the street we watched the way they walked, recalling how Havelock Ellis defined walking as regulated error, a kind of systematic falling forward and catching yourself, and seeing if the definition held up against the data going by over there. We watched the way the light fell on the figures in motion and on the flanks of a fire engine rushing by on its way to a house which eventually burned down, wiping out a family of five. I turned my head and snuck another look at the Colonel, watching the way she watched these things.

After a minute I said, "How long have you been in the WACs?"

"It's actually the WAC, since the 'C' stands for 'Corps.' Two years during the war, then a few years at Columbia, then when the thesis wasn't going well, back into the WAC for another hitch. I expected to be in New York again, on this public relations job they've given me, but instead they shot me out to Philadelphia. What a town. But I'm getting a little research done even there. I expect to finish the thesis in another year, and hope it's good enough to become a book."

"It will," I said, "and I'll look forward to reading it."

The Colonel seemed to lose interest in the subject, or at least in talking about it any more, and turned to look up the street. I saw the well-molded back of her head, and the brown hair gathered there like a coiled bullwhip.

"I can see where this girl is something of a pain in the ass," she said.

"You sure like understatement," I said. I didn't want to get around to that quite yet, but to finish in peace the *fine* left in my glass. "Who else has got it? Who else is good?"

"Some authors lay it on with a trowel, and that is not a good thing to do with understatement," she said.

"No, it is not. Does Compton-Burnett do that with hers? Lay it on with a trowel?"

"Yes. She is an example of the dangers of that. It looks bone-bare on the printed page, but when you get to reading it you see it's as drawn out as Henry James. Throwing it away is as difficult an art on the printed page as it is in the theater. Who else can throw it all away?"

194

"Hemingway, for my money."

"Of course," the Colonel said, with an expression I cannot report on as I looked away just then to avoid her seeing mine. "Flaubert threw just enough of it away to make what remains last, and the authors of the Gospels did it just right too, and that's true of all of *Huckleberry Finn* but not of Twain, and you find it in some O'Hara and the best of Pogo. Nowhere else."

"Throwing it away wrong can be just as bad as chewing the scenery," I said. I looked at my watch — three-thirty. I put back the *fine*. I let its warm glow spread around through my insides a minute, then I twitched my chair around to the table. "What'll we do? About the kid I mean."

"You mean the one you've got in your hair or the one she's got in her stomach?"

"Cut it out. Both. You've taught me to be hardboiled about the thing, to take it all on a plane of pure physical sensation and phenomenon, which I have every right to since it's a web I'm caught in, not one I spun. But I'm still human and want to do what's right. Everything I can, within reason, and without throwing my private life up for grabs. I don't want the pool of blood in my own house because it wouldn't be fair to my wife. It was good of your sister-in-law to turn over the five thousand pending the probate of the will, when she learned about the circumstances. But what'll we *do* with Sweetie? I make it plural as you so kindly invited me to while you're here. But your three-day pass has already run for two. When will you go back to Philadelphia?"

"Tomorrow."

"All right. So what would you do if you were me? She won't be any help, as you can see. She didn't even get you right. I could tell right away you weren't Eve's brother, and now you're not even her sister, but an in-law. Let's see again, you're Eve's second husband's sister. Right? Well then, what would you do?"

"Turn her over to a good case worker. What else? What the hell are you bleeding and dying for. You were only the best available substitute for artificial insemination."

"Where's a good case worker?"

"There's supposed to be a good new agency in Chickenfoot for what they used to call fallen girls. I remember it now because my superior officer had a friend who got in trouble. She held her hand going through there. You take this girl there, who's had her way with you and got you in such a jam."

"Now let's lay off that," I laughed, "and about the reversal of the sexes in our time, too. And especially about the Decline of the Male. All that. Tell me some more about this agency. Will she be able to stay there too? I mean later?"

"I think they have rooms. Go and find out. Lay it on the line to them. They're human, if I'm not mistaken."

"Would you come along? I don't think I could face it alone? Will you run over to Chickenfoot with me, if I made it, say, tomorrow morning?"

"Why not?" the Colonel said firmly, taking a compact out of her shoulder bag and powdering her nose with a series of violent slaps that left her in a white cloud. "The thing looks to me as though it needs a woman's touch."

We went out the next morning about ten o'clock. The Colonel had phoned Philadelphia the night before and got the dope about the agency from her superior officer, a General Winrod. Sweetie sat in the back seat eating chocolate-covered peanuts and reciting poetry. She had come willingly enough and was in good spirits. That's all there was to say about her, except that her color was fine and her skin seemed to fit tighter over her flesh than usual.

"What about Willa Cather?" I asked the Colonel, resuming a discussion we had going in the front seat, when there was a lull in the recitations from Sweetie, whom of course we had to humor. "What do you give her?"

"B-plus," the Colonel said, doing it like a schoolteacher giving out grades — doing it that way this time. We made a game of it all the way to Chickenfoot, driving in a steady drizzle. "Her style was pure. I mean pure. And the stuff is still there."

"Fitzgerald," I said, steering around a small crater in the Post Road.

"A-minus, the minus for the touch of elegance you can't get away from. But one book has lasted and will last, and maybe two."

We drove along in the drizzle, keeping discussing good writing. When we got on the subject of the lyric note, where it had been missing and why in modern letters, and where it had been and was struck, I couldn't help reciting a pastiche of Millay Sweetie had done. I did it because it was apropos, but also to show that the girl I had let myself get involved with had been a person of some parts, not what the Colonel saw eating Goobers in the back seat; to give her an idea of the iconoclast before she had folded on me, so the Colonel wouldn't think I was a complete knucklehead.

This is the way the sonnet went:

> I'm sick, my Lord, of doing things by halves.
>> Let's either be completely good and moral
> Or frankly bend the knee to golden calves.
>> Let's pick a fight, but not another quarrel!
> I will not perch again upon this hassock
>> While you in half-length silken smoking coat
> Sit down and play me one more semiclassic.
>> Instead let's seize each other by the throat.
>
> Death hot or cold, but not this tepid life!
>> Half-measures, hemi-quavers, pseudo-urges —

> *I was not meant to be that kind of wife!*
> *I am by nature meant to live in splurges.*
> *Cup running over, when will you come to pass?*
> *Oh, Christ, here comes another demitasse.*

"Pretty good," said the Colonel, whom I had given a copy of *The Mocking Bird* with the aim of building myself up as noted, which she had apparently not read. "Do you know any others?"

I recited one of Cummings which we had finally included:

> *Poets have their ear to the ground more than most people*
> *If only because more than most they are beating their heads*
> *against it*
> *Thus, Mad*
>   *ame,*
> *Every true artist is a p*
>   *i*
>   *o*
>   *neer*
> *Eliot was streamlining in 1912*
> *Dali's limp watches ant*
>   *icipated cheeseburgers*
>   *And I burr*
>   *o*
>   *k*
>   *e the ground for S*
>   *c*
>   *r*
>   *a*
>   *b*
>   *b*
>   *l*
>   *e*

The agency when we got to it was in a pretentiously simple building, modern and new on a square of lawn on the outskirts of town. It looked endowed. It was near a motel, in the parking lot of which we had to leave the car, the street being crowded.

The woman at the desk was a brunette with blue eyes who interviewed Sweetie first, in another room. She let the Colonel and me cool our heels in the waiting room, though as she went out the door she and the Colonel exchanged a glance that I didn't have much trouble identifying. The Colonel touched the coiled bullwhip in a way she hadn't for me and dug the compact out of her shoulder bag.

I sat there hearing a faint murmur beyond the door which presently swelled to an extent requiring more than two people to make it. Sweetie's audience was widening. I tried to wait faster, as it were, trying not to look at the clock and not to listen. I heard the term "boiled in oil" bandied out there anyhow. When the brunette came back I saw Sweetie in the distance behind her, sitting on a chair and eating a box of Crackerjack which she must have had in her handbag all the time, though it looked given to her, two or three agency people standing around her like policemen around a lost child in a precinct station. The handbag was one of those wicker cases out of which when opened you expect to see a carrier pigeon fly. I tried to work up some resentment, which somehow fell flat inside me like an omelet all the time, and was trying to get it up, saying "Hey, get your dander up," to myself, when I again saw the look pass between the brunette and the Colonel, and then I just laughed and lay down, mentally speaking. They seemed to have come to an understanding.

"I have nothing to do with this, you understand," the Colonel said to her. "I'm just along."

"I understand," said the brunette, like someone reassuring

another that they knew the other was "finer" than that, and wouldn't knock a poor kid like that up. Then the brunette looked me over. "Would you step inside, please? Miss Appleyard will wait with your friend here."

I went in and sat down on a straightback chair beside a desk that the brunette sat behind. It was like asking for a loan at a bank.

"Now, then, you are the putative father?" she said, pen poised over a fresh blank, or a fresh side of the same one she had put Sweetie's information on.

"I don't know what that means, but if it'll make you feel any better to put it down, by all means do so," I said. "I just want to make it clear that I am not — "

"We don't ask questions here," she answered with cool charity. "Not about the emotional aspects of the case, just a short formal questionnaire. First, can you contribute anything to her care?"

"I'm willing to give a little, though only as a fr — "

"Just how much?"

"I don't know yet. I'll think of a number in a minute. You see, this must be made plain. The whole thing was an iconoclastic experiment, somewhat derivative of Isadora Duncan, while leaning heavily on Shaw, that misfired — "

"What is your name?"

"Nick Steele."

She wrote down something that seemed to take a couple more letters than that. She had probably profited enormously from her interview with Sweetie, at any rate writing without hesitation.

"We'd like to know something about both parents, for the sake of the adopting parents. They like to know something about the nature of the father and mother, though of course we never disclose identities. May I ask what your profession is?"

"Bricklayer," I said, making a mental association with the object I longed most to have in my hand at that moment. "A good solid profession, wouldn't you say?"

"I'm sorry you feel a tone of sarcasm is necessary."

"This is as good a time for it as any. The whole thing was just a gesture on the side of feminine independence, a blow struck for freedom, you understand," I said looking at her hard.

"You didn't seem to have much trouble gaining her confidence," she answered. "I suppose you gave her the impression you were of a wealthy family —"

"I didn't tell her any such thing. I said I had a rich background. That's something else altogether. She knew me well enough, and this was all her doing. She's made free with the facts if she left you with any other impression, because I wanted, and want, no part of it. I'm sure I've left her in capable hands as far as carrying on the noble Experiment is concerned. I'll leave you a thousand dollars in unmarked bills under any tree you name, but for the rest, include me out."

There were more dirty looks as I went out, though they were clean, antiseptic looks, and I could feel them behind my head. When I got to the outer office the Colonel greeted me with a smile, though it went over my left shoulder to the brunette it was intended for. Sweetie had disappeared into some farther recesses of this institution. The brunette must have made some sign to the Colonel, who went in to see her, only briefly, returning to call me to the doorway and say, "I think I'll stay a bit. You just go on back. I'll stay, and don't worry about Sweetie. They'll look after her here. I'll phone you when I get back to Decency and tell you about anything of Sweetie's they may want sent out. Forget about it. I mean put your mind at ease. I'll arrange the whole thing as best I can. I'll probably take this young lady out to lunch, so don't worry."

I walked past the motel to a nearby bar to have a drink on

it, but it was no good. I tried to curry favor with myself but I didn't want any part of me. I wasn't going to give myself house room. My disapproval wasn't moral, since I hadn't done anything Wrong in the technically ethical sense, but intellectual — call it that. I mean now that the relief was here I saw myself in perspective as a goddam fool. Not just with this but with other things. I reviewed my life, as from a mountaintop, and every dramatic peak (or valley, whichever way you want to look at it) was the action of a goddam fool. For a man not to be able to abide himself in the essentials is a sorry thing — not sad, which has dignity, but sorry, which hasn't. I wanted to kick myself. I couldn't stand me. It's been like that all along. I'm just not my sort.

So I sat there *thinking* the relief as I nursed my beer in the bar but not being able to taste it. It was like a check I couldn't cash. A check for a million bucks too, I told myself, because here you're off the hook you ninny but not able to enjoy it because you don't deserve it. I sat there so long it got to be lunchtime, the bar turning out to be a grill filling up with local businessmen and office girls. Two of the girls coming in together looked familiar. They were the Colonel and the brunette of the Inquisition. They had made even more progress with one another than I had suspected. They were quarreling.

Christ but the war between the sexes is complex, I said to myself. I finished my beer and left my table to some people who felt like eating. Then I paid and went out and walked back to the motel in the rain.

14

I AWOKE from a curious dream in which I was incompetent. With that odd unreality we experience in dreams, I seemed unable to do anything right, but bungled whatever I put my hand to.

I had been demoted to the composing room where with a pair of tweezers I was trying to pick the apostrophe out of Prud'homme's name. Bulwinkle entered and the tweezers became a mallet which I seized and began to thump his backside, no doubt inspired by his pictorial frontage to think of him as a bass drum.

I lay awake for some time after in full daylight. Blitzstein barked under the window. My head shook a demurrer on the pillow: I could not, this morning, march around the post. Rising itself seemed a feat too Herculean to ask. My skin would fall off my face under human gazes; their eyes would melt mine into soft rosin blisters. As often when in need of encouragement to vacate the placental warmth of bedclothes, I selected some stirring instance of human accomplishment, of obstacles overcome, and by this means hauled myself out of bed as by a system of moral weights and pulleys. This morning I chose Walter Gieseking's hands. "Those thick German fingers playing Debussy," I said to myself. "Opalescent impossibilities like *Reflets dans L'Eau* and the second *Arabesque*. If he can do that, the least you can do is get up!"

Inside of an hour I had come to a running stop on that island of coagulated stockings we know to be the hooked rug in front of Bulwinkle's desk.

"Sir," I squeaked with that high derision that would never be seen through by those mindless eyes, "I'm ready to take on Today's Chuckle, as you asked. I believe you said it paid fifty dollars extra a week, was it? And since it so happens I can use the money just now, why, here are some samples I've done . . ."

I set on his desk a page of typewritten specimens of the genre which I had stolen from the fronts of gas stations, dredged up out of memory or manufactured on my own. One went:

"Aunt Hilda, make a noise like a frog."
"Why do you want me to make a noise like a frog, Willie?"
"Because Daddy says we'll all be rich when you croak."

I relaxed my at-attention stance to one more or less at ease.
"Are you still planning to run them boxed on the lower front page, Mr. Bulwinkle?" I asked.

He emitted a sound that may have been a grunt of affirmation or an unwilled digestive adjustment. He was reading the second Chuckle. It ran:

She: "Am I the first girl you ever kissed?"
He: "You do look familiar."

As Bulwinkle read these and companion specimens, I absorbed the art matter on Today's Tie. It showed an Indian brave, in the prime of life, spearing fish from a canoe in primeval woodland. I'm sure it was an Indian though his face was

204

obscured by one of my employer's chins. The scene was the sort often depicted on barbershop calendars with a caption like "Many Moons Ago." There were never any captions on Bulwinkle's ties, though. His taste was too restrained for that.

He had finished perusing the samples. He picked up a cigar that had been smoldering on the rim of an ashtray.

"I'm glad you came in to see me, Swallow," he said, "because I was just going to call you in. Not only can we not give you Today's Chuckle, I'm afraid — we'll have to ask for your resignation as the Lamplighter too."

"Oh?" I said. "How is that?"

"You've been practicing psychiatry again, against my express orders. I've explained to you, you don't have a license to practice it, and the first thing we know we won't have any to publish a paper if we don't let you go."

"May I ask for a fuller explanation?"

"Fuller! You know what I mean. Your brother-in-law again. I've kept it all out of the Pick because you're mixed up in it, but now that he's coming up for trial it's getting into other papers and even on the AP wire. The thing will be a national subject any day now."

"Not just national. International," I said, dropping something else on his desk. It was a cable from Van Kuykens, my hero, and read: EXCITED HEAR BONA FIDE DUAL PERSONALITY UNDER YOUR CARE STOP MOST RARE OF COURSE STOP WANT VERY MUCH SEE HIM AND YOU IF I MAY STOP BUSY ROTTERDAM CONVENTION NOW BUT HOPE FLY AMERICA THE TWENTIETH PLEASE WIRE REPLY.

Bulwinkle read that over twice, and was a good deal longer in coming to a conclusion than on the Chuckle thing.

"Who is this Van Kuykens?" he asked.

"An eminent Dutch psychiatrist of whom I happen to be a disciple. I've been modeling some of my therapies on his discoveries," I went on, feeling the moment had come to shoot the works and strike out boldly. Pussyfooting was a thing of the past, and even a tone of apology would hinder rather than aid my cause.

"What we have is a full-fledged Jekyll-and-Hyde case," I continued impressively. "You can take a timid approach and fire me like a scared rabbit, or you can back me up with the full force of the paper and see me through, with possible eventual honors for everybody."

"Or the hoosegow."

"Which reminds me that I must visit my patient," I said glancing at the clock. "My first duty is to him. It always was and always will be."

"When is the trial coming up?"

"A week from Thursday, and I can tell you what'll happen. He'll prove to the court's satisfaction that he committed the thefts, be exonerated on grounds of temporary insanity, sent to a state institution and in fifteen minutes be seen to be so completely sane they'll have to release him, as the law requires."

"How do you know?"

"Because the thefts will have resolved the personality problems that led to their execution. Problems of ego, the will to power and to excel — other drives I can't explain to the layman just like that. Van Kuykens will know what I mean, and I rather feel he'll back me up. If you want meanwhile to have put the paper in the position of having thrown me down, that's your risk. But the publicity will, I think, be far *more* than you expect once Van Kuykens gets here. Because here is one Dutchman who isn't peddling cocoa."

Bulwinkle swung wretchedly back and forth in his swivel chair. He frowned to the top of his skull, which he rubbed with a palm, as though by friction he might generate the thought necessary to cope with this thing.

"I don't know why you're taking bows for the Jekyll and

Hyde since you didn't cure it the way I hear tell — you brought it on."

"I don't see what's to be gained by splitting hairs. If by that you mean precipitated the inevitable and thus shortened the subject's cycle, yes — we do that nowadays. Like induced labor in childbirth. Or to put it another way, we don't hesitate to break bones that must be reset. I acted on Van Kuykens's theories — new concepts of shock which, again, I'm afraid I can't go into here. But I think you're right in suspecting that this case may become a classic of its kind." I glanced at the clock again, somewhat more impatiently. "Well, what do you say? Want to let things ride as they are for a bit? If you don't you may live to regret it."

"Not the way my blood pressure's been lately, I won't!" he said, and exclaiming, "O.K., O.K.," waved me frantically out.

As part of his professional defense I was allowed to visit Nickie in his cell. Which was pleasantly cool after the rather muggy summer streets. He was lying on his cot writing on a writing board propped against his drawn-up knee. Some of the college catalogues I had got him were scattered on the blanket. Nickie was very popular with the guards and allowed special privileges and kept under very relaxed watch, so it was no trick for me to slip him the bottle of good brandy I had brought in my briefcase, for which he had asked. He took a drink, smacked his lips appreciatively, and when I declined one, corked the bottle and tucked it under his mattress.

"I've also brought you a banana," I said, extracting it from my briefcase. "You expressed the hope of one last week."

"The urge has waned," he said, pocketing the fruit, "but thanks just the same."

"What are you writing?"

"Nothing."

"Something in the manner of the *Ballad of Reading Gaol?*"

207

I asked, trying to get a look at the manuscript which he shoved out of sight in the bedclothes.

"You certainly have a great sense of humor. It's not poetry."

"No muse is good muse."

I crossed my legs and smiled.

"Well, things are looking up," I said. "You'll be judged criminally insane, of that there can hardly be any doubt. A great psychiatrist named Van Kuykens is flying over. He'll be in our corner. Much better than that droopy alienist the court's assigned. Of course you're straightened around now, so they'll have to release you instantly. So things are sorting themselves out. Soon we'll have everything tidied up. Lila and I got all the jewels back to the police, so there'll be complete restitution — that'll be in your favor. No loose ends. The Jackson Pollock we found behind the tapestry in the city museum where you told us you'd hid it. Thank God for that last recurrence as Johnny Velours or we'd be still looking for it. Have there been any others? Lapses as him I mean?"

He shook his head, staring rather wistfully up at the ceiling.

"Then we've got you coalesced." I closed the snaps on my briefcase. "I regret to see his passing too, in a way. But he served his purpose — that of a poultice draining off the infection, so to speak — and truth to tell, some of his charm and sweetness have rubbed off on you. They really have, Nickie. You're a pleasanter fellow. Mellower, somehow. Now let's talk of other things."

I tried to make conversation that would cheer him up, to chat of things that would get his mind off himself — pleasant, healthy things going on in the outside world.

"It stood in the paper that the nose might fall off the Statue of Liberty," I said.

"Good." Nickie got out the bottle and took another swig of the brandy, which he then again secreted in his pallet. I hoped sincerely that we were at last, here in this cell, going to have a relaxed little talk, unmarred by any of that vying for superiority in phrasing that had so grievously bedeviled our communion hitherto. My reasons were more urgent than usual. In my present, and mountingly tense, condition it was imperative that I not be upset. I had been experiencing tingling sensations in my left arm accompanied by slight chest constrictions, which the doctor had diagnosed as "false angina," nothing to worry about, except that I should not deliberately and needlessly court vascular strain. Therefore when we got on the subject of marital problems, branching out into generalizations from remarks on the vast improvement in Nickie's own that had resulted from the crisis, I trusted he would let a man speak without interruption on a subject that was, after all, a man's own field, and not indulge this beastly habit of summing up in a brilliant phrase or two what a man was trying to say.

"What people call disillusionment is usually a rather unsophisticated dismay with the discovery that the wine of romance has lost its sparkle," I began in any case. "It need not, for that reason, lose its flavor. The two ought not to be confused, and the avoidance of this confusion is maturity. Indeed, when the sparkle has left is the time to begin to appreciate the flavor, and any poor wine can be made tolerable with it. If a wine has soured, that is one thing — throw it out. But do not throw it out just because it is flat."

This may not be the peak of human wisdom but it is reasonable counsel. I had thought it out along those lines and worked it up into a series of columns, which accounted for the polish of my disquisition, for I was quoting myself verbatim. Any extemporaneous improvement on its statement would therefore be doubly galling. If he attempted it now with what was, as I have said, my own line of goods, then I would wash my hands of him. Let him rot in jail. He was lying on the cot with his hands under his head, nodding in a familiarly ruminant way as he toyed with the ideas I threw out. I cleared my throat to indicate that I wasn't through by a damn sight, and hurried on.

"As for the notion that marriage is dull, let the cynics who to prove it point out the frequency with which it 'ends in disaster' realize what they are saying when they say that. For Fitzgerald was never wronger than in that oft-repeated and trenchant-sounding but really meaningless epigram of his that there are no second acts in American lives. The second acts go on in bedrooms, without audiences," I said, watching him like a hawk. "Of the two ways of making love, adultery must seem the safer, as the aerialist engaged in it swings to an eventual stop, or else lands in marriage itself which is strung out protectively under the highwire. Whereas a man failing in marriage has nothing to break his tumble. Except to find another mate as fast as he can, which is exactly what most divorced people do."

Nickie, who had been nodding more eagerly, now sat up.

"Truer words were never spoken," he said. "Marriage is like turning somersaults on a net, with a trapeze to catch you if you fall."

"Oh, horse manure!" I fairly screamed, bringing both hands down on the briefcase in my lap, which then slid to the floor as I rose clutching at my chest. "Why *must* you always talk such rot, *must* you always talk this kind of smart talk in this childish need to create an effect? When *will* you grow up?" My words came out between gasps for breath, which went in and out with a kind of dense, baying sound. I walked around the chair, trying to get my wind back and my pulse down. "I just want to get you squared away. I don't want a heart attack. I just want some peace."

"Sit down," Nickie said, forcing me back onto the chair, "and put your head between your knees. Away down, even lower than that — as close to the floor as you can get. That's right," he said when I had arrived at a completely doubled-up position. "Now sit there quietly for some minutes. Don't move. And above all *don't talk*."

He soaked his handkerchief from a tap at the washbasin and applied the cold water to the back of my neck, while I loosened my sopping collar and tie.

"I've warned you of this before," I said in the inverted position. "I don't know what's going to become of you if you insist on cow — cow — " I paused till another fit of spluttering had subsided. "If you insist on couching everything in paradox."

"Easy does it. . . . Don't talk. . . . Shall I call a doctor?"

"You mean you have a doctor in the jail here?"

"Yes. He's in for malpractice, but I'm sure the guard — "

"No, thanks."

"Still now, and away down with the head." He forced it nearly to the floor, causing me to topple out of the seat. I righted myself, and continued:

"The reason I think no on the doctor is that ministrations are often disturbing since they certify the gravity of the condition for which they are sought. It's the William James principle, that we don't run because we're scared but are scared because we run. The blood's all rushing to my head."

"That's where it's needed."

My nose began to bleed. I dug out a handkerchief of my own from a hind pocket which I had no little difficulty in reaching, and put it to my nose, so that I had handkerchiefs wadded at both ends of my head. I held it there till a good deal of blood had soaked into it, then held it out for his inspection. "See? Hypertension."

"Easy does it."

"Blood is a funny thing," I said, putting it back. "It stood in the *Reader's Digest* — "

"Please. No popular medicine, please, and above all no mention of that magazine, which makes my own blood boil. It's the nadir of taste. The *Reader's Digest!* Television scripts!

Movies! If there's any one major cause for the spread of mass illiteracy it's the fact that everybody can read and write."

"At it again, are we?"

"Sorry."

The spell passed, and I think bore fruit. I sat up again, taking a sip of the brandy. Nickie watched, sitting on the edge of the cot, his expression sobered, his whole manner chastened, and in his eyes the promise to be less exquisite in future.

But the incident upset me, and I felt it my duty to report it to Crystal in the hope that I might be spared any unnecessary strain at home as well, for her and the children's sake, toward whom I had responsibilities which I wanted to be around for some years yet to shoulder. I didn't volunteer details of my recent medical history, exactly, but rather had them drawn out of me. It began when Crystal came into the bedroom and found me in bed reading a book actually addressed to women, entitled, *How to Keep Your Husband Alive*, and aimed at showing them how to achieve this by generally relieving strain. There were chapters on "Misunderstandings," on "Tensions in the Home," "Nagging," and so on. I happened to be reading passages dealing with the heart, which brought on her rather alarmed queries.

"Oh, come now, tut, tut," I said, putting the book down on the table where she could find it later. "It's nothing serious. Just using the old bean is all. Come sit by me." I patted the bed. "How's your speech going?"

She picked up the book worriedly. "Are you sure . . . ?" I took it from her and set it farther aside, out of reach.

"None of that now. You can dip into it later, when you have time. It's obviously been prompted by so many husbands' pre-deceasing their spouses, to the, we know, dismay of the latter. This is a rational, impartial word to the wives, as it were, about how to meet the problem by reducing tension-producing situations and generally keeping off a man's back."

"Who wrote it?"

"The author is a John Charles Freemantle."

"I'll bet."

My hand crept to my chest and shoulder, as I smiled with a pointed tolerance. "You see? How we're at it again? Without realizing it, without even trying? *These are the things that must be avoided.*" I patted the bedclothes again, and this time she sat down. "Now let's talk about your speech, because I've had some ideas for it. Not mine, really, but yours. I was thinking today about the female need to be independent, to realize her own individuality above all else."

"I don't believe I . . . As I remember it, you said that."

"No, I'm sure it was you who said it, and very well, too. That's why I want to be sure you get them into your speech. Your notions reminded me so much of that play of Shaw's, *Getting Married,* that I got it out of the library today. There it is, over there on the dresser. Anyhow, there's a character in it you must quote, in your remarks on female emancipation, including the right to have a child without benefit of a husband, if she so desires."

"*What?* Wait a minute. I didn't say that."

"You believe it, don't you? Think about it a minute. Why, just because a woman wants a child, should she take on this snoring, shaving beast known as a husband if she doesn't want to? Hasn't she a right to do it by herself if she so desires?"

"Well . . . I suppose so . . . "

"Well then say it!"

"But it would be a little outside the scope of the panel — "

"Oh, scope! Give it scope. And a little resonance and dimension."

"But the clubwomen — "

"Oh, bother the clubwomen! This is no time to pussyfoot! We're in a time of ferment, an exciting time with new ideas in the air, which should be examined in the court of public opinion. Go on, set the ladies on their ears. Get some pizazz into your old forum!"

Crystal laughed nervously.

"Dare I? After all it *is* the debating team idea, of giving all extremes a hearing . . . "

"That's the stuff! And I'll bet there won't be a woman in the audience who doesn't respond to your tocsin call. Every female secretly hates the slavery of her lot, and any man worth the name appreciates the fact. How they dress you in little aprons and put you in the Chintz Prison. I feel awful. So even if you don't come right out and endorse the position, state it anyway as something that very much needs saying. You've got Shaw behind you, and me too. I'll back you up. So have no fears whatever." I got out of bed and into my slippers. "Come on down in the kitchen and let's have some beer and cheese while you take notes. I'll find the scene in the play where Lesbia makes this ringing plea for the bachelor mother. Gives the ringing defense for that."

We had a wonderfully companionable evening, there in the kitchen, working on Crystal's speech and drinking beer while we discussed it. I wheeled the typewriter in from my study and wrote most of it out for her. We didn't get to bed till long after midnight, when, tired as we were, we collided in the dark bedroom while undressing.

"Ought we to in your condition?" she said.

I slid to my knees, whinnying, my hands lapping her cool curves. I called what they sought "a fringed exclamation held in a sweet parentheses of loins." The quality of the poetry injected a note of shame into the skirmish that curiously quickened our passion. When it was spent, we lay staring up at the ceiling, our bodies like balloons that had floated back to earth, though I refrained from stating as much this time. Crystal's head was on my breast, my arm around her, as we murmured of this and that.

214

"Lambswool, I've been wondering," I said, "if we shouldn't invest in some property. Decency is growing, and real estate's the thing to put your money in — not leave it lying around in the bank or in low-rate government bonds."

"Who's doing that?"

"I was thinking if we bought another house and rented it at the prices they're getting these days, we could clean up."

"We don't have any money lying around."

"I could borrow some."

"I see. Borrow some spare cash."

"I could take a mortgage on this house — that is, spread it over the two. Lots of people do that. Plow it back into improvements or into other property."

"What house did you have in mind?"

"Not so fast," I laughed. "Don't rush me into this thing. None in particular, but I'd be perfectly willing to keep an eye open for a good bargain, if you feel that's what you want. I mean for that much more security, for your and the children's sake. There are always sacrifice sales, as they call them, one thing and another, that you can pick up cheap. Because the people have to get out of town for one reason or another. I'll keep an eye peeled, then."

"So you'll have two houses to maintain, when I can't even get you to fix a plug in this one."

"I don't think it's that bad. The thing is, Decency is growing by leaps and bounds as a city of families, and I think a man should own a part of the growth of his community. Oh well, we'll talk about it later. Don't bother me with it now."

We settled down for sleep, relaxing a little away from one another and bouncing into new positions. Presently we lay on our sides. The dog's chain clanked faintly under the open window. In the distance could be heard the thrum of trucks going to Boston and New York on the Thruway.

I raised my head. I said, "Come to think of it, I do know

of one house that's for sale, now that you ask. The old Apple-yard place. I understand you can pick it up for a song."

Crystal mumbled something indistinguishable. Then the bed-spring creaked sharply as she awakened momentarily, and I could sense her leaning on her elbow behind me.

"By the way," she said, "have you heard about Sweetie Appleyard?"

"No. What?"

"She's going to have a child. Some man's got her in trouble. Can you imagine that?"

the MADHOUSE

To write is always to rave a little —
even if one did once know what one meant.

ELIZABETH BOWEN: *The Death of the Heart*

❖ ❖ ❖

15

"CALL that copy! Call that a story!" The Boss's voice was like sailcloth ripping. His laugh was like canvas snapping in the wind, while his mouth itself was like a rent in the same fabric, or, when shut tight, like a seam in it. He didn't have laughter in the sense of human mirth — he just had a laugh. It came across the desk now and stung Swallow's cheek like a whip — which was where the simile fell down, as all similes, at some point, do. "I thought that approach rather a good one for my story," Swallow said, standing at attention on the hooked rug. "The whole problem of sexual victimization from the male's point of view, for once. It's in the title itself: 'I Was An Unwed Father.' I thought it might make a good title for the whole series, and since I need the money right — "

"Series!" the Boss laughed. His words were like a gust of sleet. "You think for a minute I'd run a whole *series* of these? 'I Was An Unwed Father'! What a ridiculous business. Confession magazine stuff!" Swallow looked at the Boss's tie. It depicted a mermaid of indeterminate age, sitting on a rock surf casting, or doing what looked like surf casting within the physical limitations of the art form. "You're fired."

Swallow was aware, over the breakfast table of which he was oblivious, of his wife snapping her fingers under his nose, like a hypnotist bringing a subject out of a trance. "Hey, wake up. Some more coffee? Wake *up*. What kind of a Walter Mitty are you?"

One who, instead of indulging in dreams of glory that offered escape from the harsh world, spun fantasies so nerve-wracking that it was a relief to get *back* to reality. They were supposed to make the facts of his existence, momentarily at least, more palatable by contrast. And indeed the kitchen seemed friendly now by contrast with the office from whose merciless imaginary developments he had been recalled; the sun streaming through the dotted Swiss curtains made everything seem all right again, the sleepless night and its tortured apprehensions an unreal dream. His wife, crisp and neat in the flowered housecoat, sat across from him, snapping her napkin out on her lap.

"I was trying to tell you that Sweetie Appleyard is going to have this baby," she said. "Somebody evidently has her in trouble. Imagine it! Taking advantage of a girl like that. What do you think of a man who'd do a thing like that?" Swallow was "fletcherizing" his food, as they had used to call it, after the nutritional expert who had advocated prolonged mastication, chewing it long past the point where there seemed to be any need, then chewing it some more, as he could remember his parents doing at the dining room table when the health measure had been in vogue. Swallow was fletcherizing his toast not out of partisan design but to postpone passing it along to a stomach at which he was already extremely sick. "Chick, for Pete's sake, I'm talking to you. I said what do you think of a man who would do a thing like that?" "I'd like to wring somebody's neck," he muttered.

. . . " . . . is too good for him," the attorney for the defense said in conclusion, and turned from the jury box and sat down. A stir ran through the spectators, many of whom glared at

Swallow. He was sitting on a bench with an infant in his lap. He was feeding it a bottle, which, when the child had finished, Swallow handed to a bailiff. Now his own lawyer rose and called for Beth Appleyard. There was a stir of quite another sort as she twitched on high heels up to the witness stand. She was dressed in a fashionable suit of dark tweed and a cloche hat, and smoked a cigarette in a long holder. Swallow's lawyer, a portly man in gray pinstripe, sauntered up in a leisurely way and said, "Ladies and gentlemen of the jury, we shall prove to you that my client is *not* amiss in naming the woman on the stand in this maternity suit. She is not, at the moment, wearing what could precisely be called a 'maternity suit,' being one more adapted to the stylish literary bars and restaurants which she prefers to that Home which has been traditionally regarded as a woman's place." There was a courteous titter at the labored joke, whose author shot his cuffs and added, "Which she prefers, I might say more bluntly, to shouldering her share of the responsibility for bringing a new human being into the world. I will now ask my client to rise." Swallow got to his feet, shifting the infant on his arm. "Miss Appleyard, will you now rise." She did, drawing the collective gaze from the more pathetic pair. The lawyer then pointed to her and, turning to Swallow, said: "Charles Swallow, take a good look at the lady in the witness box. Now tell the court, is she or is she not the mother of your child?" Swallow declared in a clear and ringing voice: "She is." The lawyer sat down and the counsel for the defense rose again. He was evidently very skilled at conducting bastardy cases, for he now cross-questioned his own client with devilish ingenuity. By a series of adroit leading questions and subtle time manipulations he made it appear that the accused could not be the mother of the child because she had spent the years in question on the French Riviera and touring Europe with Nicole and Dick Diver, Abe North and other friends of hers from the Fitzgerald era. Impressed, the judge rose and began to excoriate Swallow. His words were drowned in a roar from the spectators as they surged forward and flung themselves on Swallow in a welter of flying fists.

. . . "Good morning, Dr. Swallow. Dr. Swallow, I said good *morning.*" "Oh, good morning, Miss McConkey." He gave her his hat to hang up, and stood contemplating the stack of letters on his desk. "The decline of the American male may be discerned in the increase in the American mail." He seemed about to gather it all up in a lunge and hurl it out the window.

"Dr. Swallow, I wish you'd tell a person what the matter was. You look just awful, and you're a thousand miles away. Do you worry about your patients so? Is that it?"

"I worry about them, yes. For instance I have a young lady who's in trouble, as they used to say," Swallow said, suddenly feeling he had to talk about it, treat it as an objective reality rather than something festering to twice its size in his mind. "Do they still use that expression, Miss McConkey? You're of a later generation than I. Are they still treated as fallen women, or are they excused in our more liberal outlook?"

"Not by me, they're not! It's just *because* of modern enlightenment that they have no business getting into such scrapes. I don't know what gets into girls like that." "You don't?" he said, wearily. He dropped the subject. Miss McConkey would be no help. He sat down at his desk. "Any Urgents or Specials in these?"

"Yes. There's one from a woman in Brooklyn who's hysterical. I'll read it to you."

Swallow listened with elbow on chair-arm and knuckles to mouth, a pose which he unconsciously struck in her presence because it gave him professional substance, and justified the term Doctor with which she persisted in greeting him. Seated herself, she cleared her throat and read the letter:

222

DEAR LAMPLIGHTER:

I have just found out my husband is heterosexual — whatever that means. The way I found out about it, I happened to overhear some people talking at a cocktail party, and from a name they dropped I knew it was about my husband. One man laughed and said in a low voice, "There's no doubt *he's* heterosexual."

That was all, but oh the blow of finding it out this way. Everywhere you turn these days you hear of some new kind of perversion or abnormality. How can a person keep up with all these big words, the curse of our time? Homosexual, asexual, bisexual — now heterosexual. That's a new one on me. What does it mean? It's not in my dictionary. How serious is it, can anything be done for these people? What do they like to do? My husband never gave me any inkling, living a regular sex life with me to all intents and purposes, maybe a little more than average actually, but they say that's often a cover-up, to hide something. Oh my God, that this could happen to me, could strike without warning, my whole life in ruins. Can you answer me about this, also tell me how best to handle the situation in the home. We have eight children.

Miss McConkey put the letter on the desk. "That's all," she said. "It's signed Mrs. Rausch. Do you want to dictate a reply?"

"Not now. I want to think about it a while," I said. "There's something else I have to attend to first. Would you go out and get me Mrs. Swallow on the phone?"

"Okie doke." She rose and walked to the door. "What is heterosexual, Doctor? Is it bad?"

"It can be hell. Get me Mrs. Swallow."

My reasoning was that I was taking my predicament altogether too subjectively. In the objective environment of the office, I realized how undiplomatic I had been in avoiding the subject of Sweetie at breakfast. As with Bulwinkle, the thing to do was wade in, answer questions freely and ask them freely. I knew in my own mind I hadn't done wrong — I had *been* wronged. All right then, get the aggressive before it's too late. To appear on the defensive now might make impossible later that interpretation of events that should be the very least I ought to aim for: that I had been a boob, not a rat. Play the mouse now and I would be hanged for a rat. It was with the ideal of being thought a sap firmly in mind, therefore, that I spoke out clearly when I heard my wife's voice on the wire and said, "Angel, I'm afraid I was purposefully vague about this Sweetie thing, because her father had sort of deputized me to play the, well, the Dutch uncle to her before he died. So I feel in a way responsible. I had her under my wing, you see, and that's why I feel somewhat accountable now. It seems I made a botch of my job."

"I didn't know you'd been seeing the Appleyards."

"I know how you hate it when I take on people that I know personally, or that we do. No lectures, please — you were right and this proves it. But there's no use calling myself a damn fool. The thing is, what can I do now? How did you find out about it, by the way? That's what I was curious about."

"Mabel Apthorpe told me."

"Ah, the news behind the news?"

"She's been in and out of the Appleyard house trying to sell it, you know. Nobody told her in so many words, but she caught on. You know how sharp Mabel is."

"Sharp as a tack." I twisted the telephone cord in two fingers. "She say who the man is?"

"No, but she does happen to know that he tried to put her away."

"Put who away?"

"Sweetie. He clapped her into an institution of some kind in Chickenfoot. It's a shelter that uses them to further some kind of psychological survey they're making. Sort of guinea pig idea. Which is all right in itself, of course, except that they keep them under lock and key and pick their brains day and night, like the Communists in *Darkness at Noon* to hear her tell it — "

"Wai—hait a minute! Hold on there. I happen to know about this place. They're doing a bang-up job of work there in research. This shows you the evil of rumors. I took her there myself, to tell you the truth."

"You *what*? You knew about Sweetie all the time?"

"I was the first to learn."

"Why didn't you tell me?"

"I've told you why. You'd have lit into me, and right you'd have been, hon, but look. You say 'to hear her tell it.' To hear who tell what? If Sweetie's under lock and key."

"She got away and ran home. She broke out the second-story window and slid down a rainpipe."

"Where is she now?"

"Home. That's how Mabel learned the whole thing."

"I see. . . . Well, that's the sort of thing I wanted to find out. I'll go call at the Appleyards'. I suppose I ought to follow it up."

"You'll no such thing. You stick to your work at the office. Now I mean it, Chick. I'm sick of these briefcases full of work you bring home. I'll look in on her myself."

"Don't. It's my place to. I want to see the house anyway. It's for sale. Remember I told you about that."

"Yes, I do."

There was a silence.

"So let me go."

"No. You look enough like something the cat dragged in. Do your work and that's that. This calls for another woman anyhow, the way the poor thing sounds. Maybe I can worm the name of the man out of her. It seems to me he should be made to help. I'd like to get my hands on that swine anyway."

"You would?"

"Yes I would."

"Is this the liberal I hear talking? The stormy petrel of the women's club? Or do my ears deceive me? Let's not forget what our friend Spinoza says — 'neither to weep nor to laugh, but to understand.' "

"I understand plenty without Spinoza telling me. Anybody who'd do a thing like that to a girl like her." Crystal's words became deliberately spaced, as they often did when she was making a particularly portentous judgment, so that each one had the value of a separate sentence. "He's an absolute. Utter. Unmitigated. Swine."

After throwing up (do you think the stomach will not mind what the mind will not stomach?) I clapped my hat on and hurried out through Miss McConkey's again baffled importunities into the street. Crossing which I was narrowly missed by two honking motorists. I bought a pocket tin of aspirin in a drugstore and took two at the soda fountain. I headed on in the general direction of Beacon Street and then up that toward the Appleyard place, with no actually clear idea whether I would go in or not. I was riding a new busline to work these days, leaving Crystal the car, so its presence in front of the house would tell me if she was inside. It wasn't there now, in any case. I stood looking at the house from across the street half a block down. The door was shut and the curtains drawn. I went to Mr. Hickett's drugstore and asked him

226

for a sleeping pill, which he refused without a prescription. I reminded him that I had got some about a year before with a prescription that could be renewed once. I remembered the date closely enough for him to be able to look it up, which he did, and which satisfied him.

"I'm going to deliver a lecture this afternoon, and I like to take one to calm my nerves before I go on," I said. His eyes went, and were not clearly seen again till he made change for my five-dollar bill. While waiting for it, my eye fell on a stack of display pistols in the toy section and I bought one, moved by an impulse obscure to me. While he waited at the cash register for the financial fluctuations to subside, I browsed further. Humming, I reached up to a row of Frankenstein monsters on an upper shelf and wound one up. I smiled as it marched across the counter for me, swinging from side to side with that mechanical lope made familiar by horror movies. I returned it to the shelf, though, and went back to the cash register. As Mr. Hickett was counting the change into my hand, a whirring sound drew our attention back to the toy section. Some evidently unused tension in the windup spring of the monster sent it marching to the edge of the shelf, where it toppled over and landed on something fragile on the floor, judging from the tinkle of broken glass that followed its plunge.

"How much does that make it?" I asked, extending the money back in my outstretched palm for him to take more of. He shook his head, growing rigid, as if pleading the speedy curtailment of this unendurable moment in human relations. I gathered up the sleeping pills and the revolver with the change and fled.

I went down the street in an aimless frenzy, hoping for some program of action to emerge. I walked under a ladder propped against a building; another honking motorist met my crossing on a red light; I fondled the phial of sedatives in my pocket, realizing also the idea I was toying with. Mightn't it be the best way out, for myself and those dependent on me?

But before such resorts were reached perhaps I could frighten Sweetie into keeping her mouth shut, or even scare her out of town. I had been walking in the direction of her house again. This time I would go in, thrust the pistol at her and say point-blank, "Look. One word out of you and it'll be your last. This is what you'll get." Such a threat should by all means be tried. But as I approached the house, my blood froze at the sight of my car parked in front of it. I wheeled abruptly around and started back.

I wandered into a small school supply store with a candy and soda counter. There I ordered a Coke, to take a sleeping pill with. I realized that I could never eat a fistful of those capsules without some previous sedation, but one or two taken first might calm my nerves enough for me to go on with the rest. The owner, a shuffling old woman in a soiled Mother Hubbard, said she was out of Coke, so I settled for a grape soda pop which she served in the bottle. When she had shuffled off again to resume unpacking merchandise at the back of the store, I took a capsule, washing it down with a gulp of the grape pop. I sat for a bit, loitering over the bottle.

Of all the pleasures of the dentist's chair the best, I think, is that little nozzled hose that squirts a thin stream of liquid over your teeth between more basic procedures. An adequate substitute is to shake a bottle of soda pop you might be drinking, holding your thumb over the top to build up a head of pressure, then aim it into your mouth and move your thumb, or let an edge of it up, just enough to release the charge of soda, which will come out in a jet as fine as any dentist's. The charge will be even stronger than his, due to the carbonation. I often drink a good part of a bottle this way, playing the stream around my teeth and gums and even down my throat.

228

I suppose it's a rather special, even decadent, pleasure, but a pleasure nevertheless.

I had agitated the grape soda a few times and fired it into my mouth in this way when I became aware of a pungent silence back where the old woman was stacking things away. Moving my eye to the left, I saw her watching me from behind the toppling ramparts of educational supplies. I swung away, and sat gazing idly out the window. "Getting hot," I said. The silence continued. I tipped back what there was in the bottle and got up. "How much is that?" "Seven cents." I had even change, and, dropping it on the counter, went out.

How I got through that day I'll never know. I wandered about with that bemused indifference to traffic, to people, to falling timbers at demolition jobs that characterizes a certain stage of intoxication. Shunning the Appleyard house now that I knew what die had been cast there, I returned to the office, where I plunged into work for the rest of the day. At six o'clock I took another capsule and girded my loins for the return home, striding into the house head high, like a doomed arrival entering perdition.

"Where's Mother?" I asked the boys, who seemed alone inside.

"Building a fire in the barbecue pit," Fillmore said. "We're cooking out tonight." The touch of routine restored a measure of sanity to the nightmare in which I groped. I thrust my head out of the bedroom window and called down "Hi," to Crystal. She looked up from the pit, into which she was dumping charcoal from a bag. "Hello." She turned back to her chores. I kneeled at the window while she soaked the charcoal with lighter fluid, grinning aimlessly into the empty air. "I'll do that."

I was waiting to take the things from her in the garage.

"Well, did you look in on Sweetie?" I asked, putting the lighter fluid on a shelf.

"Yes. I did." She walked into the kitchen while I held the door open for her. We were like two people observing the forms of courtesy during a tour of hell.

"How is she?"

"She was sitting on the floor playing records, so I had to shout at her. She's obviously feeling no pain, which is something to envy in itself. She's dotty. And one thing about the insane — they have no nervous breakdowns."

"Terrific. No nervous breakdowns among the insane. What a revelation. Like an apocalypse. What perception. Almost Nietzschean in its sweep."

"She looks good. She even has a fine tan. As though she just got back from Florida rather than Chickenfoot."

"Swell."

"Where on earth would she get a coat of tan like that?" Crystal asked, her head in the icebox now. She rummaged in a drawer of greens. "It's been cloudy all summer except for this last week."

"Search me," I said. "Well, that's that. You've done your good deed for the day. Heck, I don't see why you should bother yourself about it any more. Ah, these pork chops look beautiful." I had unwrapped the meat on the table. I remembered the Village days when Sweetie and her set had identified cuts of flesh according to what painter they recalled.

How could I explain to Crystal the woman of the world Sweetie had been then? "Guess the charcoal's soaked enough now, so I'll go light the fire before I take my bath. We'll need a good bed of coals for these babies. They must be two inches thick."

Sitting in my bath, I couldn't keep my eyes off the wall switch. Staring at it, I remembered something about a Kansas farmer who had electrocuted himself listening to a radio in

230

the tub. When I had finished washing, I rose and stood dripping a moment in the water. I started to reach for a towel, but instead my hand extended itself toward the light switch. Raising my eyes heavenward, I felt across the metal plate till my finger found the switch, and snapped it. The room became flooded with light. Drying myself on the mat, my glance tended toward the open medicine chest at the slot for used razor blades. I reminded myself that I must get some new ones. I stretched out on the bed where I lay naked in the breeze from a fan. It was one of those powerful fans set in the window, designed to suck the cooling night air into a still warm house, during hot spells. It was powerful enough also to suck in the gnats that would otherwise not have made it through the screen mesh, and I soon found myself in a cloud of them, and of the smoke from a cigarette on which I mournfully drew, all violently whipped about in currents of air. Half of the midges were damaged in entry, and lay dead or dying on the bedclothes or on my bare body. Crystal entered. "That's how to get a good case of double pneumonia," she said. I nodded, staring at the whirling blades. I rarely smoked. The cigarette was one of hers, and she noted its consumption with interest. "Better get the chops on," she said. "They'll need at least half an hour. They're thick."

I slipped on Bermuda shorts and a T-shirt and went into the bathroom. I took two more aspirin, swallowing both at once. They went down abreast and became stuck in my throat. There was some "after you" nonsense between them while I waited. "Goddam you, get on with it," I said to them. Crystal heard me from an adjacent bedroom and said, "Who were you talking to?" "Nobody." She gave me another look before going down the hall to the kitchen, where she proceeded to assemble a green salad with great abstraction.

I laid the chops on the grill — eight of them, two apiece. The fire was far from having settled down to the bed of coals outdoor cooking really wants, and, after fifteen or twenty minutes, when I began to take them off, I heard Crystal behind me.

"Oh, I don't think they're nearly done. Let's see." She had a knife in her hand, with which she sliced one open. It was crisp enough outside, but pink inside. "That's how to get trichinosis."

I nodded, setting two of them well to the side of the grill when I put them back, where it was unlikely the heat would adequately reach them. "I'm going to kill myself before something happens to me," was the way I seemed to be summarizing the situation to myself.

16

W ELL, thank God that's over." Crystal dropped into a chair and put her stocking feet on another. "No more speechifying for me. Oh, the bliss of not having it to worry about." She rubbed her feet together with pleasure. "Oh, the bliss."

"How'd it go off?" I asked, carrying a Martini to her. "How'd it go down with the ladies?"

"They loved it. They laughed and applauded the stuff from the Shaw play. A kind of nervous laugh, but they applauded."

"I told you they would."

"But it isn't Shaw speaking," she noted argumentatively to me. "It's just Shaw giving a character his head, as one point of view. He doesn't advocate it himself, as you led me to believe." I shrugged. She watched me, sipping the drink. "It seems to me you're awfully eager to plug the emancipated woman these days. Why is that?" She set the glass down and dug a cigarette out of her bag, for which I was ready with a lighted match. "What more can you tell me about this whole Sweetie business? It grows more confusing by the day. Now Mabel Apthorpe says she's willing to go to another agency, or give one a try anyway. Are you ready to talk about it?"

"Aren't you going to ask me what kind of a day *I* had? I spent it in court, you know."

"Oh, my God," she said, with a gasp at her own forgetfulness. "How wound up we can get in our own affairs. Poor Nickie. How did it go?"

"Never mind the poor Nickies. *He* wasn't feeling any pain. It went off just about as expected. Nickie proved to the court's satisfaction that he committed the robberies, and without help. He was very amusing, almost like Oscar Wilde in the dock at Old Bailey. He tied his *own* lawyer up in knots when the lawyer tried to suggest he'd had a collaborator, and asked the D.A. to take him as a client. He said to have no fears about the fee. He's going to claim the reward money for catching himself. Two alienists said he was quite batty — using other words of course. Van Kuykens hasn't showed up, damn him, but we didn't need him. Nickie was exonerated and remanded to Round Hill for observation. He'll be out of there by the week end if things go according to plan." I sighed with relief, stretching my own legs out. "We'll have an intact Nickums coming home to us, so we'd better have a plan of action ready. Of course it's almost certain now he'll study for a teaching certificate. He's raring to go back to school. Thinking about his wardrobe and all already. He'll make an amusing teacher somewhere. Perhaps Bennington could use him, or Sarah Lawrence. He wants to offer a course in Listening."

"Listening?"

"Yes. He claims nobody knows how to do that any more. Just all public speaking. We hear but we don't listen. The General Semantics idea."

"Well, I'm glad to hear it's all coming out in the wash this way." Crystal sighed and shook her head soberly. "It's something to give a prayer of thanks for." She drained her glass and held it out for another, which I promptly poured from the shaker. "Now let's talk about Sweetie. Who's the man?"

"Professional ethics — " I began, knocking at the buttons of my shirt.

Crystal jerked her feet off the chair. "Oh, damn your professional ethics! Why do you keep pulling that every time I ask for a simple piece of information? I really do insist on being treated as your wife."

I looked over at her from my chair, after sinking back into it. My hand was under my shirt. "Ought we to rile me in this way?"

She rose and padded into the kitchen with her drink. I followed after a minute, to find her tying on an apron. She went to the sink to scrape some carrots. I sat down.

"My idea about all that is as follows," I said. "She'll snap out of it once it's over and they, as we say, lay the child in her arms. It's just pregnancy that's got her jittery — motherhood will make her get hold of herself again. It often happens. She'll be all right. And in the end she'll up and take the child to New Mexico with her as planned."

"As *planned?* You mean she wanted this child?"

"Of course. That's the whole point."

"*Planned?*" Crystal wheeled slowly from the sink till she faced me, a half-pared carrot in one hand and the vegetable scraper in the other. "Like the woman in the Shaw play? The model self-sufficient modern woman I was up there touting for you this afternoon? Is that what you had me up there doing? Taking up the cudgels for your cause?"

"It's the principle of the thing — the other is only incidental. Anyhow, is it a bad thing to see that a child so bred enters a world congenial to it?"

" 'So bred'? How deeply are you mixed up in this thing?"

"I gave it my blessing, yes. Not without protest, I assure you! I approved of the experiment on intellectual grounds, of course, as any civilized person must, but I warned her it was too much to bite off. I really did try to discourage it, and to bring Sweetie down to earth generally. Remember that trip I made to New York, just after the shopping one you made there? It was to fetch her home when poor old Appleyard asked me."

"Now for the sixty-four-thousand-dollar question, if such an old-fashioned thing as a traditional housewife may presume to pry into the intellectual life of her husband. Did she get her tan from the same sunlamp that burned you?"

I bent over in the chair and put my head well down between my knees. I loosened my tie and collar, also the buckle of my trouser belt. "It stands in the book that this is one of the cozier forms of domestic murder, in our time."

"Did you — "

"I feel I must warn you . . . I can't answer for the — "

She dropped the carrot and the knife both in the sink, wiped her hands on a towel and went out, closing the door with satirical care. After sitting in the silence for ten minutes staring with a leaden stupor out the kitchen window at nothing, I rose and went to the bedroom. She was stretched out on the bed, her head propped on a wadded pillow, staring out the window at nothing.

"To think I was up there pulling your chestnuts out of the fire for you. Publicly spouting the rationalizations you put in my mouth. Up there on the platform of the Decency Women's Club making your filthy defense for you! Don't touch me! How could you do such a thing? I'm too curious to be furious. How could you?"

"Maybe to provide *you* with a cushion against outrage, in case it ever all came out. To remind you that you have a tolerant point of view about such things, a mind hospitable to experiment, and thus to spare you the pain that comes when we let the emotions rush in and overwhelm that fortress." I tapped my skull to emphasize the point. "It's a long story, but to keep it to the bare essentials — "

"Bare essentials, yes. By all means let's have those. Those are the ones we want."

236

"Don't say things unworthy of you."

"The bare essentials and the naked truth."

"Don't. To begin with, your correspondent refused flatly to have any part of it. Period. Then one day I saw Nickie with her, and I knew damn well if I didn't consent to father her child — " I flinched as Crystal jerked her head on the pillow, her eyes shut, as under a lash laid on her. "If I didn't, he would. And he's weak. There seemed to be no doubt that he'd get emotionally involved, which would mean curtains for his marriage. Which, as you know, we've been trying to save. Whereas I wouldn't — I mean get emotionally involved. So, weird as it may sound, I thought it best that I consent precisely because I'm the kind of man with more sense than to get mixed up in a thing like that. Sweetie even wanted me for that reason — to give her child that sort of heritage."

Crystal threshed on the bed with her back arched, like a tormented fish. I felt as though hot wires were being drawn through my flesh. I had never wanted more to take her in my arms, now when it had never been more out of the question.

"But a girl like that, Chick. How could you?"

"She wasn't like that then, don't you see?" I moved to the side of the bed, my arms outspread. "That's the thing. She was a sophisticated woman of the world then. The woman who wrote that book of poems. You've read them. You must know the girl you saw the other day isn't that one. I saw a child as probably just the thing to complete her maturity, seeing she didn't want a husband and marriage. But when the chips were down she wasn't up to it. She folded in the stretch. Or call it a sort of backsliding. Anyhow there you have the cards on the table at last. On the table and face up."

She shook her head, not in denial but in disbelief. "It's still impossible to take in."

"Can't you see how completely *impersonal* my part in it was?" I pleaded. "Lots of women have children by men not their husbands, and I don't mean only the mixed parentages of all these divorces. I mean artificial insemination. All right. Think of it as just a case of that. Of artificial insemination, only using me as the test tube. There. Isn't it beginning to seem a lot better already?"

"Oh!" she gasped, bringing her fists to the sides of her head as she rose. "Don't make it sound any more like trash than you have to. Don't stand there jabbering like somebody out of *Tobacco Road*, or as though we're talking about cattle!"

"*Tobacco Road!*" I exclaimed resentfully. "*Tobacco Road!*"

In my gropings for a literary formula that would get us all out of this with a whole hide, I had certainly never thought of *that*. And yet was it as far-fetched as I liked to imagine? If what had begun as Marquand could deflect into Faulkner, why couldn't what had proceeded as Fitzgerald end in Erskine Caldwell?

"Oh, my God," I said, smiting my own brow now. "This is the end." I banged my head on the wall. I suppose this was the point at which I went to pieces. "I can't handle it any more. You take it from here if you want. Try to make head nor tail out of it. I can't. You see her through from here, you and Mabel Apthorpe — she's your sex, not mine. See her into a new agency, get a good lawyer to break the will, sell the house, bundle her off to New Mexico with her brat. There she can carry on in the spirit of D. H. Lawrence. Lady Loverly's Chatter. Oh, my God. I'm glad I won't be around to hear it, there or anywhere probably. Because I'm finished. I've had it. Oh, my God, my God." I slid down along the wall onto a hassock, dropping from there to the floor, where I sat among some pairs of shoes laid in a row along the wainscoting. I pulled a bookcase over with me, spilling the contents in all directions.

Crystal had stopped in the middle of the room, and now watched me writhing among the reading matter and the footwear. "What's the matter with you?" she said in a shocked tone. "Pull yourself *together*."

It was then the idea of lunacy returned, as an alternative avenue to self-removal. Yes, it would be better for all concerned if I took leave of my senses. Was I already doing so? My behavior just now seemed to indicate as much, and the expression on Crystal's face as she helped me to my feet seemed to confirm it. My conduct that had led to this pass was suddenly illuminated in the light of it. Of *course* — only a man not responsible for his actions would have gotten himself into such a muddle.

"Are you saying that just because you heard me talking to myself?" I said as she hauled me up by the armpits. "I always do that."

"Steady. Come over to the bed." My legs shot out from under me, like a beginning ice skater's.

"Don't you think the floor is beginning to buckle?" I babbled as we started toward the bed. "What kind of a summer will it be? Will the Dodgers beat Yale?"

She got me to lie down and felt my forehead.

"Do you feel sick? You seem hot."

"Your hand feels cool. Ye ministering angels — "

"*Shh*. Our thermometer's broken, too. I think I'll just call Dr. Bradshaw. I told you you'd catch your death lying around in drafts the way you do."

"Oh, what rubbish . . . Well, if it'll make you feel better."

Dr. Bradshaw didn't arrive till nine o'clock. He sat on the bed and quizzed me in a manner he had that was both expansive and distrustful.

"How do you feel?" he asked.

"Not so hot. He's burning up."

The doctor poked a thermometer into my mouth, and as I lay there waiting for it to register and for him to finish taking my pulse, I wondered if it mightn't be pneumonia taking hold,

239

and became apprehensive. My temperature was between ninety-nine and a hundred — just about the degree a certain percentage of the medical profession think can be emotionally induced. He asked whether I had any aches and pains, and I said no. "Are you worried about anything?" he said, a little too readily I thought.

"No."

"Yes, you are. Tell Dr. Bradshaw about your angina."

"He already has," the doctor said, raking the gray hair that made him seem so distinguished (except for its being crew-cut). "I've explained it's what we call false angina. Rather common. Muscular spasm that sets in when a person is under strain."

"I didn't know you'd been in to see the doctor," Crystal said. "Why . . . ?"

"I didn't want to worry you," I said.

Dr. Bradshaw coughed into his fist and said, "Let me just test your reflexes." He drew the bedclothes back and tapped my drawn-up knee, with results that seemed to satisfy him, though he wielded his mallet at length to obtain them. He flicked the point of a pencil across the soles of my feet, causing my toes to flex. "Babinskis seem all right. Now, look. I'm going to hand you a coin with your eyes closed. I want you to hold it in your fist and tell me what it is."

He pressed a half-dollar into my palm, which I clutched a moment and said, "This is a dime, Canadian, dated 1915," with a little wan humor. He pocketed the coin and then instructed me to close my eyes and bring the tips of my two fore-fingers together in front of my face. My fingers sought one another in vain, passing repeatedly without making contact. "Now bring one of the fingers to the tip of your nose — slowly, from way out front, like this. With your eyes closed. No cheating." I crooked my arm, and brought my hand carefully toward my face, poking myself in the eye.

240

He turned away to cough again, and said, "That's enough. Are you sure nothing's worrying you?"

"Not that I know of."

"Well, anyhow." He sat down on the bed and wrote out a prescription on his knee. "Give him a few days' rest," he said. "This is a sedative so he can get a good night's sleep." Then he did something unexpected, which I alone saw, as Crystal just then turned to set the prescription on the dresser. Grasping my leg through the bedclothes he looked me rather archly in the eye and said, "I'm sure things'll clear up in time. Sorry I have to run along so soon, but I have another call to make and it's away at the other end of town. Over there on Beacon Street, you know. Miles to go before I sleep." He winked and said, "You take it easy now, skipper. Everything will come out all right, I think, do you hear?"

17

CHARLES SWALLOW awoke from troubled dreams one morning to find that he had been transformed in his sleep into a great pig. It dawned first on him in the inkling that his posture, he was lying on his back, was for him not quite the comfortable one, it was eased somewhat by tumbling over onto his side. Resting in this position a moment he noted that his limbs themselves were not in any case at ease, but stiff and sore, as though from the strain of the mutation that had occurred during the night. Yet a more cogent source of apprehension lurked in the memory, still fresh in his ears, of the sound that had awakened him; not his usual snoring, instead it had a peculiar timbre, both more nasal and more guttural. It was all too renderable in the experimental noise which he now in waking gingerly made: "Oink, oink." He fell back with a sense of grief.

This was certainly not what he had expected. Of all the hopes and aspirations they had as schoolboys traded about what they would be when they grew up this was the last he would have chosen — and his poor parents likewise. He suspected in his first resentment that he was the victim of Symbolism, that crashing vogue of the writers in whom he had for a generation put his trust, though if they could see him now, their product, they would instead of standing by their mysticism turn tail and chatter a little about "auto-suggestion" and "somatically realized guilt delusion" and other such scientific terms. So much for them, the swine! He would have to see it through alone. Swine. There was the key to it! He had been called that by two women, one whose prey he was and one whom he had wronged, and it seemed fitting to be turned into such an animal for punishment. Ah, but in that very feeling that he deserved it, that he "had it coming to him," lingered there not maybe a spark of evidence that he was not quite one yet? He had so far only the data of his ears and the sense of touch. He must make further tests.

Opening his eyes cautiously he ran his gaze down the length of his body to observe its surface texture. The color that greeted him was not alas his normally pasty pale one but the loathsome faint pink of the species in question, no doubt about it, while kneading his flesh with his hands he found it to be of undue solidity. A memory drifted back to him of how the time on his uncle's farm, "Gesundheit," he had lifted into his arms a suckling pig and been amazed at the repulsive muscularity of the wriggling beast which he had expected to find fat and flabby. There seemed to be that heaviness in his members now, no two ways about it, coupled with that stiffness of the joints before noted. He kicked back altogether the bedclothes, which looked markedly more wallowed in than usual even after the most disturbed dreams. Henceforth his name must be S. Wallow, he could see it on a card over the little teat of a doorbell. He appraised the disgusting pinkness and hardness of his constituent parts in the light of this fine morning. The straight hairs upon them seemed to have become more dense and numerous toward the development of a true hide. He turned his head in sadness to the pillow against which he snuffled and grunted "Oink, oink," once again. He remem-

243

bered boyhood hours at "Gesundheit," to whose green acres and sweet summer winds they had repaired every June. But he must not torture himself with nostalgia, rather examine if this was not a further vestige of the human condition. All the precincts had not been heard from. His face — that was the crucial test. He must obtain a glimpse of that with all haste.

In the urgent need to do so he dropped himself out of bed so that he landed on all fours on the rug with its pattern of forest creatures by a river with a dull thud. The thud was dull but the pattern was interesting. But he could not linger over it in artistic appreciation; in his impatience to learn the worst he trotted on all fours to the dresser, to find that locomotion natural, alas! Indeed the painful thing was to stand on his hind legs, as he now must proceed to do to reach the mirror of the highboy. He had to haul himself knob for drawer-knob up the façade of the highboy, like a mountain climber in a difficult portion of his ascent, finally clutching the bureau top, then securing his position with his elbows, on which he rested a moment. Now for the peep over the ledge to see his face.

He had fancied that his vision had not been too clear, and now the reason was plain. His eyes had shrunk to half their former size or less. They had never been very large, little more than slits, but now they were mere beads. Yet the lids themselves and the surrounding flesh had swelled into reddish puffs, almost closing them — but not quite. Little blue swine's eyes gazed at him. As for his nose, it had always been sizable, but now it had expanded into a fine snout of which the nostrils were somewhat splayed and straightforward. It rested on the bureau ledge as he contemplated the spectacle of himself. One more precinct remained to be heard from — his round bottom. Had it a tail?

Fearfully he turned away, preserving this last moment of doubt. He tried to nurture his hope by walking on his hind legs to the window. See? He could do it still, there was a ray of encouragement. And he would keep his pajama trousers on even though it was all he wore, to declare that the metamorphosis was not complete and never would be — there was some resistance in him yet. Then his hand stole down the inside silk seat of his pajamas and felt — was it a crude appendage? No more than a twist of lemon peel but a beginning? Or was it a tangled strand of the garment's drawstring? Such explorations would never be satisfactory by themselves anyway, he must see with his own eyes that too. Also the ache in his arms rendered them difficult. Yes, he must have a look.

The bathroom medicine chest had a glass, but mounting the washbasin to avail himself of it was out of the question. The small Dresden wall mirror was of an altitude requiring that he pull the bed over to it and stand on that, too much monkey business in his present state, besides he would rather not have his backside wreathed in that mocking circle of pink Cupids around the glass. The dresser mirror did not tilt; the only means that remained, therefore, was to climb up on the chiffonier itself.

Making sure the bedroom door was closed as far as it would go, which was not all the way because in the damp weather half the doors were swollen and would not shut, he wriggled out of his pajama trousers. He pushed across the rug a chair up to the chiffonier, and by standing first on that, then hoisting himself up on one leg, then painfully, slowly the other, he achieved at last a kneeling position on the dresser top, pushing aside hairbrushes and pintrays, some of which spilled to the floor. What a pigsty the room was getting to be! Now he was on all fours, but parallel to the mirror. To obtain a clear view of his rump, he must edge that around. The area of the dresser surface was limited for such a movement, however, nevertheless by inching with his forepaws as closely as possible to the corner edge and swinging his back thus, while at the same time straining his head to look over his shoulder, he managed a satisfactory clear view of the mirror. What met his gaze in the glass was the bedroom door thrust cautiously open and his wife's face appearing in the crack, just a split moment before the door was clapped shut again on her soundless gasp.

In his confusion Swallow tumbled off the edge of the dresser. Luckily he caught at the arm of the chair, which broke his fall to the floor, where he sat a moment grieving by the broadloom river taking stock. "Stock" was the word for it now all right! He was grateful he yet merited the adjective "live." As he caught his wind and recovered his composure somewhat, a marked shift in his thinking occurred. How selfish he had been in dwelling on the problem only from his own narrow point of view. It was time to think of it from that of his loved ones, yes more than time. He blushed from top to bottom, in fact all the way up, at his self-absorption, and seated in the chair he put his mind to the crisis as a family one of accommodating the father they now had. It pleased him to retain these vestiges of human affection and sensibility despite the humble form in which his spirit was now immured. Even sitting in the chair itself was another point of satisfaction, being an anthropomorphic gift which his metamorphosis had yet left him. What were some others? He remembered an amusing pig he had once seen in a tent show near "Gesundheit." It had been dressed in a bow tie. That was the sort of thing that must by all means for his dear family's sake be cultivated, so they could see what a cunning member of the domestic circle he might yet be, sitting at table with a bow tie on as he raised a teacup to his snout. That was the direction in which to strike, without delay. He trotted on his hind legs to his tie rack, from which he selected a blue and white polka-dot bow tie, which he tied at the bathroom mirror on his bare neck. He minced about with it on, swinging gaily through the bedroom. He was waltzing across the carpet when the door opened again and another figure stood beside his wife — Dr. Bradshaw, looking rather pale this morning. "Oink, oink," he said, bowing a little. His wife fled in full rout down the hall while the doctor entered, blenching, and closed the door behind him.

"What seems to be the trouble?" the doctor said. Swallow tried to talk, to say it was nothing to worry about, but his voice was nothing but the hoarse gutturals that he had uttered up to now. By painful effort and much clearing of the throat, he forced out a few articulate enough words. "I'm all right," he said. The doctor nodded, but his black bag was shaking so the contents rattled.

Urging Swallow back onto the bed, he drew stethoscope and other implements from it. With a tender thumb he raised each of Swallow's eyelids. Swallow was perfectly familiar with this method of studying the pupils for signs of hysteria. He knew his own were anything but distended. The doctor gave off physical examinations and in keeping with his known determination to practice psychosomatic medicine wherever called for, as most family physicians now feel they must, asked, "Do you have any feelings of guilt about something you've recently done that might make you feel you *deserve* to become . . . ?" Swallow shrugged, and was about to answer further when the doctor asked, "Have you had any nourishment this morning?"

This was the signal for Swallow to assume once more a kneeling position on the floor. Where by dint of shoving his snout around the carpet like a rooting boar, emitting the while grunts in keeping with the pantomime, he succeeded in conveying to the kindly doctor that he must have thrown to him a pan of slops. He would have added for a joke to lighten the dark moment a little, "Nobody knows the truffles I've seen."

But the doctor was shaking his head in horror, striving to deny that his patient was what he fancied himself to be, that it was all a product of his overwrought imagination. He spoke of contrition syndromes and symbolic self-punishment. "I am a pig," Swallow persisted with a certain mulishness. The sound of his voice caused the doctor to fall back a step, perhaps more than the words themselves. In stumbling toward the dresser he brought to Swallow's notice a banana that had also fallen off the bureau, where it had been left the night before. To assure the doctor that he must and could eat in the fashion indicated, he worried the peel down by hacking it about on the carpet with his snout and paws, at last succeeding in snapping off a portion of the white fruit. Seeing the doctor reel back yet another step convinced Swallow of the need to show further that his plight was not as tragic as might be thought, and therefore to strike again the note of whimsicality from which the bow tie had been the first resolve not to exile himself, he turned his face upward to the doctor with his lips curled back in a fetching grin, while with a forward thrust of his tongue he extruded banana through the crevices of his clamped teeth, to make the other feel better. This time the doctor fled in the direction Swallow's wife had gone — to the kitchen, where together the two were heard in a whispered consultation, and then the doctor on the telephone booking accommodations at some establishment of which Swallow could not quite catch the name.

Swallow lay down on the bed again in a tired but at the same time satisfied state, relieved that the first shock had been absorbed by his loved ones, to whom would remain now the task of "adjustments" and "arrangements," luckily always themselves something of a diversion from an ordeal. The bedroom door was now open as well as a window, and through these a faint breeze circulated about the room. Its cool caress was welcome to Swallow's face, which suddenly seemed hot, no doubt from all the exertions. The poor doctor had not told him what the thermometer had said, or perhaps even paused to read it himself in his consternation.

Over the summer sill, and above the urgent low murmur of kitchen voices, came the sound of Blitzstein barking — not his annoying loud baying but rather a gentle, questioning bark which seemed to establish in Swallow a gentle sense of kinship with him and with all dumb beasts. Swallow was gratified to note again this solicitude of which his spirit was capable despite the lowly house in which it was now lodged, and it was this happiness — mingled somehow with contrition, yes, and restitution — which Swallow cherished as, just as the tide of sleep carried him off, he called to the kitchen: "And don't forget. Throw the dog out of the window a bone."

He awoke in a strange bed. Not awoke exactly, but felt it penetrate his consciousness that it was a strange bed in a strange place, before sinking into even deeper slumber . . .

. . . Then for some reason he could not explain, except within the logic of dreams where no explanations are required but oddity itself imposes its kind of clarity, he was in one of those places where people take their laundry to wash it in automatic machines. The public Laundromat. It would be a mistake to say he was there in person: he was rather there in spirit, to witness the two old women who were the only customers as they drew the soiled family clothes from their bags and chucked them into the washers. The machines were side by side, the center pair in a glistening white row of perhaps ten. The women sat side by side on a bench to gossip, and as the machines simultaneously commenced the first of the cycles, the drone of their words mingled with the hum of the motors and the wash and splash of the water and the clothes, while all of it seemed to be going on in Swallow's head itself, where it merged in an endlessly flowing river of dialogue.

It was a literary friendship. (*Laughter from the tooth-less crones.*) Can't you see them in their trysting shanty, talking about books. Well, it's the sterne realities they'll be facing now.

SECOND WOMAN

What he minds most they say is the being a laughing stock. It's his *rire* end to be seen sticking through the britches he was too big for.

FIRST WOMAN

And hers out front. They must have known it would illicit comment.

SECOND WOMAN

That sort's not practical, the artistic — and when it comes to the poets! I understand he could be treacly in his tastes for all that. Not even above a little Tennyson.

FIRST WOMAN

Chacun à son goo. And that's not all. Think o' them fancy composers they must have cuddled up listening to. Everything was fine and d'indy then, but I de falla now to see a bright side to the situation. Now don't fly off the handel about the modern stuff, Molly, that's not what the subject is about. Let's stick to it for once, for a luscious one it is, my duck.

SECOND WOMAN

I'm not shootin' me mouth off about that aspect of it

either. There ought to be a law against all these illicit relations. What's needed is some good plain penal reform.

Beginning with his. Cut it off without a pity — and
don't stop there either. Let him die intestate, him on his
Castro convertible.

SECOND WOMAN

So he'll never go whole hog again? (*Laughter*) But he
won't soon again anyway, I'll be bound. Still, it'd be a
stop in the right direction.

(*There is a pause and they suddenly turn silent and
thoughtful, even sad. There is a transition in the
machine and a change of tempo in the wash*)

FIRST WOMAN

(*Half humming*) Ha hee ha ho a low . . . It's keening the sound of these machines makes me feel like doing. A mournful ancient oondark sound it is, this in the
Laundromat, as of all the waters washing all the shores
in the weary world. The splash and swish of the suds reminds me of all the rivers running into the sea, yet the
sea not full. There, the pre-rinse is over, and now it's
the water frothing and swirling in the seacove, lonely
beyond knowing, my Molly, the last outlet of Time
. . . the wash everything comes out in as they do be
sayin'.

SECOND WOMAN

Stop your lip, woman, and leave the poetry to them as
can moan it proper. Poets are born, not made.

Aye, but we know one was made, don't we now? And proper too she was. She priapubly had them lined up waiting their turn. Had I the queue for passion she has I wouldn't be doin' meown washin', let alone others'. There's food for thought there — intravenus injection. Still 'twas she, not I, met with a foetal accident.

Ah, you're a foul-mouthed sweet old soul. Yes, made she was I must admit — and made once, maid no more.

Stop grinning with them two remaining teeth. They remind me of cloves, which reminds me I've got to get home and fix a ham for the poor old clod I've remaining to me. An incurable rheumatic. Ah well I love him just the same, the same. He's persona non Groton, but he's mine, and he wouldn't go cheatin' on me even if he had the opportunity, like that other blatherskite.

Oh, let's not blacken the lad to the point of using him as a sinonim for all ruttin' off the reservation. I've heard rumors *he* was the one prevailed upon. The soft sell and then the hard sell, and him so young and rubicund. It's the company he kept.

Kept is it now? *He* keep anyone, that cheapskate, at least to hear tell? He'd never get in that deep — he'd never get fiscally involved if he could help. Furs and flowers, and then Christmas coming round and she up there in the flat waiting over the eggnog, in hopes that St. Necklace soon would be there. And him with his Santa Claustrophobia. No, not him. Just once he slipped and now he's slapped and that's the long and the short of it. Slapped around just like that clothes behind the glass there. Did you ever hear the one about the woman who looked at one of these and said, 'Well, if that's television . . . '?

Oh, woman, if you can't tell jokes at least no older than yourself, button up. Here comes the Spin-dry. Then you can spread your washin' proper and get home to cook that ham. How do you cook a ham?

(*Growing absent*) So little thyme. Sanctuary much, he'll say ironiclike. He was good for the jests he was, once and many a spare quid for a case of bottles. Remembrance of Things Pabst, that's the story of our life, and ah, how we lay dreaming on the grass. Him reading to me books with plots. How Greene Was My Valley of Decision then. Yes right off, and him with the wherewithal to hitch us up straight off. Legal Tender Is the Night. Him laying in bed drunk singing as I dropped my shift on the cold hotel room floor, Sister Carrie Me Back to old Virginibus Puerisque. It's all a welter mitty in my head, thinkin' back so fondly. For the lad it's Beth In the Afternoon. As I went walking down the street I metamorphosis. It's like that Spin-dry in my head as it must be in his too. I hear he's mental now, aw, let's have a kind thought for the chap. This is the end for him:

delirium: tear-a-lira-lirium: stream of conscience: you pays your money and you takes your joyce.

(His head spins furiously at top speed. Then something mercifully clicks the end of the cycle and the whirling slows. The spectral blur sorts itself out in a circle of faces wreathing the bed, into which he looks up. Dr. Bradshaw is there, then another physician, a nurse, and Crystal too, wiping his brow.)

DR. BRADSHAW

(*Raking his boyish gray hair*) It's the most amazing case of auto-suggestion I've ever encountered in my thirty years as a family doctor in these parts. To think so strongly you're a swine as to turn into one! *Look* at it. I mean the eyes. Like beads.

UNIDENTIFIED MAN

And the red along the face — not just around the eyes. If it isn't arrested the whole skin surface will be covered with it, which might be fatal. The only case on record like it that I recall is in *Tender Is the Night*. The woman in Diver's sanatorium there, remember? [Then this man isn't a doctor but a critic, and the consultations are literary, not medical. Could it be Blackmur? Or Burke? One of the giants? One of the Symbol Simons of literature?] It was related to the blush. When guilt is so strong it *has* to be organically realized —

SWALLOW

(*Resentfully*) You mean this is derivative too? I tell you I won't —

(Hands press him firmly back onto the bed)

254

He seems to take it so personally. But there, he's dropped off again. He must be exhausted. But now to get back to what we were saying, there's another way of analyzing this particular hysteria. The need to convert himself into a swine may be an indirect way of blaming the woman.

DR. BRADSHAW

You mean the Biblical legend — ?

PROBABLE CRITIC

I was thinking mainly of the Circe scene in *The Odyssey*, where she changes them all into pigs, remember? Thus it becomes, you see, the woman's work, the woman who's responsible.

(Swallow sits bolt upright, profoundly elated)

SWALLOW

We've done it! A Homeric parallel. This is it! We've made it! We're in! Tell Cowley, tell Warren, get everybody on the wire, we're in, do you hear! A Homeric parallel! At last! Get Wilson on the wire, get Hyman and Daiches and Jarrell! Shoot it to the newspapers and magazines. Wire Prescott and Rolo and Gissen and Hobson and Hutchens and Hicks —

VOICE

He's really delirious now.

(The two washerwomen briefly reappear, keening and chanting "Dear a lear and leerious . . .")

255

FIRST WOMAN

You need to cut it both ways now, with hidden mean-
ings I'm afreud. You Rahv Pater to play ball, and a little
Levin levineth the whole ump. Ah well, they were boobs
in the wood, those two, like us all, beside this babbling
book that has no end. My years ache with the melan-
choly plaint of footnotes, and my poor head rumbles
when the Kazins go rolling along. And that other bunch
washing their Lenin in public. Who will resolve all this
and bring White peace again? Look look, the desk is
groaning, and my poor chair's gone ashen. What's left
for the likes of us but to draw up our chair to the fire of a
night, and munch the tried old crusts again. What ails
the new loaf I can tell you straight. It's too inbread and
lax —

SECOND WOMAN

Lacks what?

FIRST WOMAN

That good old William Butler Yeast.

SECOND WOMAN

That does it! I'm going home to Maugham.

(*The two women fade, gently moaning
"Tear a leer a lirium . . . He's a merewolf."*)

SWALLOW

Phone Fadiman —

VOICE

Shh . . .

256

*(Another voice is heard offstage, growing louder. It is
a Dutch accent of somebody obviously shouldering his
way forward)*

DR. BRADSHAW

Dr. Van Kuykens, thank God you've come. (*There is
a stir of handshaking all around, while a hand with a cool
cloth continually soothes Swallow's brow*) This thing
has gotten a little beyond me. I mean while we doctors
like to keep abreast of psychosomatic medicine as the
situation calls for these days, we're not geared for anything like this. It's an amazing case. Organically realized
delusion. I'm sure you can tell by one look what he
fancies himself to be.

*(Dr. Van Kuykens wedges a round, smooth-shaven face into
the circle. He looks Swallow over, feeling his forehead
and taking his pulse. He lifts Swallow's left eyelid and
lets it drop.)*

DOCTOR VAN KUYKENS

I can certainly see what dis is at a glance. Dis man has
got trichinosis!

OTHERS

Trichinosis! (*They back sheepishly off*) I never gave
that a . . .

DR. VAN KUYKENS

Severe edema of the eyes. Bad enough to make dem
almost disappear. Soreness of de muscles I'm sure from de
vay he moofs on de bed . . . (*He breaks off, open-
mouthed a moment.*) You mean I have come all de way

257

from Rotterdam to diagnose an case of trichinosis? Och, God in hemel, wat is me dit? *Ezels!* (*Going away*) Give him aspirin, a mustard bath to bring de fever down, absolute rest and quiet. Plenty of nourishing food as soon as he can take it, and in a few days maybe a little light readink.

(*Blackout*)

18

I LAY back in the bath with my eyes closed, both to savor its warmth and to blot from view the humorous wallpaper, depicting children poring over textbooks while their parents sat slumped before television sets and reading comics, with which the room had been invested in my absence. As I paddled the lush suds, my senses flowering in the scented steam and my mind lolling among memories of corrupt aristocratic courts, I heard my wife call from the bedroom, "Don't poke. You've a new sitter to pick up and she lives way over there in that new Hampton Common section. A Miss —" There was a pause while she deciphered her own handwriting on the telephone pad. "A Miss Charpentier. You may have trouble finding it, so allow for that."

J. B. Priestley. The aria da capo, or repeat, ending, where everything starts all over again to see if we have learned anything. No. Not in my present condition. I was old and tired and resembled a wirephoto of myself. So please: include me out. No need to waltz me around again anyway, not on my first day home from Round Hill and the two of us only wanting to go out for a quiet bite of dinner together. Rather let me just savor my narrow squeak by calling Crystal in to sit on the laundry hamper to file her nails instead of on the edge of the bed.

"I see you can scratch your nose without any trouble," she said, entering. "Your nervous reflexes were so bad you couldn't find the tip of it and so on with your eyes closed. I noticed you didn't have any trouble just now, and your eyes are closed."

"Maybe I'm some better."

I watched her perch on the laundry hamper and, crossing her legs, bend intently over the emery stick as it rasped across her nails.

"Tell me about it again," I said. "Go through it just once more, step for step, from where you took over. You say you got suspicious about Dr. Bradshaw knowing so much about the situation, just as I did, so you went to him point-blank and said, 'Look, are you taking care of Miss Appleyard too? Is that it?' And he finally broke down and said yes — "

"Chick, I don't want to go over this any more. It's too painful. He did say, 'I know your husband well enough to know he wouldn't do what this appears to be on the surface, so there must be more to it than meets the eye. More than Miss Appleyard is telling me.' That's what you want me to say again, isn't it?"

"For your sake as much as mine. Didn't he say about your husband, 'He's made of finer stuff'? Wasn't that the phrase he used?"

She sighed. "He said he decided to dig for the facts it was obvious Sweetie wasn't volunteering, till she finally broke down and admitted there had been more than one man. She didn't *want* to know for absolute certain who the father was — that was part of the anonymity idea. She chose the candidates carefully, yes, letting each think he was the sole man, but there were more than one. The child's father was to be the masculine sex as such, not any specific individual that she herself knew it to be. Doctor Bradshaw finally got her to show him a diary she'd been keeping, which was more articulate about the whole thing than she was at that frightened stage of the game."

260

"Well, and then when she did panic, she had to do exactly what she had been trying to safeguard herself against — cling to one individual man after all. And to make him feel responsible, so he'd stick, and see her through. Also the shoulder to lean on must be that of someone she might begin to think of as a husband after all, which she now saw wasn't such a bad idea at that. So she chose me because I was more the sucker type and, what's more, because she had somehow picked up the notion that we had marital troubles. Which is a laugh in itself."

"Don't be too sure of yourself too soon," Crystal said. "Because I haven't told you everything. There's one more thing I found out — that I don't like."

She blew on her nails and studied them rather unhappily. I plunged briskly about for the sponge and soap.

"What was that, sweets?"

"The sacrificial lamb part of your story. I asked Nickie about Beth Appleyard and he said he'd never met her. He knew about her from you, but they had never met."

"He's a liar."

"No, he is not. He absolutely and positively was not lying. I could tell. You can tell when a person is lying, and he was too natural about the whole thing. There was no mistaking it. Anyhow, the way to lie about this would be to admit knowing her because that in itself was unimportant so why get tripped up over it, but just deny that you had ever been seeing her. That would be the clever way, and Nickie is nothing if not clever. No, I knew he was telling the truth. And I was sick about it, because there went your shabby little whitewash. I almost wish now you hadn't tried to justify yourself in that way, because it now seems the one really cheap thing in the whole business. The one I can't forgive." Tears welled in her eyes as she rose and flung the emery stick into the medicine chest and slammed it shut. "I'm glad we've got you home again and that you didn't die, Chick, but I don't see how I can forgive you." Her lip quivered. "Do you?" she added, and went out.

I sat in blank misery in the water. My mouth felt as though it had been stuffed with ashes and then gagged. My brain was a mass of maggots. After the first shock, it began to function again, enough at least to cope with the confusion that filled it.

I must thrash these facts out again, I thought to myself. There is something wrong here. If Nickie didn't know Beth Appleyard, then who did I see her get into a cab with that afternoon when I was having my shoes shined on a street corner? I could have sworn it was Nickie. I may have seen him only from the back, but you can recognize somebody you know from the back. It *must* have been he. The same erect shoulders and boyishly hollowed neck between the fresh haircut and the tweed coat collar. Perhaps the gait and manner had had a dash more of surface swagger than was usual with Nickie Sherman, but that . . .

I sat bolt upright. It hit me like a rock. I sprang to my feet and, clutching a towel from the rack, ran dripping into the bedroom where Crystal was sitting on the bed doing nothing.

"I've got it!" I said. "It was Johnny Velours she got mixed up with — or who got mixed up with her! Don't you *see*? That was why Nickie didn't remember — he couldn't. That's it, it must be. That's who I saw getting into a cab with her that time. It is, it *is*, I wouldn't lie to you about a thing like that! I knew at the time that's how it was, but completely forgot it."

The face she turned under the flowing tears was one that hungered to believe. And just as she knew Nickie hadn't lied then she knew I wasn't now.

"Dr. Bradshaw said she told him there was one man in particular she liked and who was single, but he never came back again," she said.

"He was *scared* away. Back into Nickie Sherman for keeps. Of course. It fits — it must. Two free spirits both running full tilt from the gaff they couldn't take. Here all the while I thought it was my psychology at work, and it was only a male scuttling for cover from a dizzy woman. That's what cured Johnny Velours out of existence. And makes the child truly anonymous, since it must be Johnny's because he was the first." I raced on in rapture, drying myself with the same furious speed at which I talked. "And so it ends as it began after all, resolved in that rich obfuscation from which it burgeoned, the father not only nobody we any of us really know but nobody we will ever see again. Because just as the whilom bones and blood and breath are gone of which the new was sprung — O inconceivable conception — so the new will on the instant of its materialization be the very seal and avatar of that Father obliteration. More. Will by its very deed of expungement perpetuate the Not-being, by the very apparition bland fortuitous and insolent of all Birth declare and embody that Anonymity of all flesh of which it is both apotheosis and usufruct, and thus by the infinitely subtractable tissues of human substance levels our little trouble till it is lost from sight in the eternal pattern woven out of all teeming random bonded sentient dust. — What are you getting that fresh linen out for? The bed is made."

"So I'll have the couch in your study ready when we get home." She shifted the sheets on her arm as she wiped away the truly last of her tears. She drew a long, quivering sigh of relief, but that was all. "You can take your things and move in there. Or you can sleep here and I'll go in the study. Whichever you prefer. You can have your choice. Because I don't want to upset you."

Four or five days later, I sat brooding in the study. How could I resolve my problem? On what note could I make the story play itself out? How, in other words, to get back from exile?

Would my writers be any help in tidying up the muddle? No! only in compounding it. Each had passed me on to the next in a worse state than he had got me from his predecessor. Our authors, the good ones anyway, are no guide to life — and the better they are the worse they are. And the poets, could one go to them for inspiration? Not the ones you can bear to read, today. Still, poetry . . .

One rainy evening when, alone still in my study, I was browsing among the bookshelves, I came across several old volumes that had been handed down in my family for generations. They included the *Home Book of Verse*, one of those unutterable anthologies of which the contents are classified under categories of human sentiment such as Love, Patriotism, Sorrow, the Home, and so on. In a section entitled "The Parted Lovers" I stumbled on the poem, *Jest a-wearyin' fer you*. It plucked my heartstrings. Sobs caught in my throat as, seated in my lonely chair, I read the lines so familiar as those of a song selection with which parlor and church audiences were favored by sopranos of yesteryear. I squeezed the volume back onto the shelf with eyes that saw not. Yet I knew a great peace. I knew the inscription I would put on a card to accompany a gift of a dozen roses tomorrow. The roses would be red, and the white card would say, simply, "Jest a-wearyin' fer you."

I was in my study the next afternoon, a Saturday, when the delivery truck drove up on the gravel drive outside. I heard the front door open, then a pause as the flowers were signed for. The door closed and there was another pause, broken by the rustle of tissue paper. Then another long pause, followed by a faint sniffling sound. I shot back to my chair as footsteps approached my closed door. I was sitting in the chair with my head bowed in my hand when the knob turned slowly and the door opened. I rose and we stumbled into one another's arms with tears in our eyes, one another's tears on our cheeks . . .

That brought the story to an end, that scrap of Frank L. Stanton (1857–1927) flapping like a torn flag above the shambles.

Other private resolutions in our joint complications I cannot vouch for in detail, but, from the short distance in which I am compelled to report, it looks as though Nickie (who of course has a B.A. degree) will soon get his teacher's certificate. I shall miss both him and Lila as well as their kids when they move to Nickie's first post, but I know that when the time comes I shall with a steady heart surrender him to Bennington or Antioch or whatever. Meanwhile on his holidays home from school I get along with him a good deal better than formerly. He's learned a lot. By and large he keeps his promise not to be needlessly adroit, in deference to my condition, but occasionally his tongue runs away with him in the childish need to create an effect.

Sweetie has had her child, a boy, and has moved to San Francisco, which has since, of course, superseded New Mexico as The Place To Go. Crystal helped see her through it all, which she was able to do in good part when it became fairly certain that I was not vitally involved. Too, she wanted to make sure I never saw the woman again, as, indeed, I never have to this day. I hear bits of news about her now and then, and learn she has enough money to get by, the will having been broken on the evidence that Appleyard probably pre-deceased Mme. Piquepuss in the plane accident, if only by a split second, and thus did not live to inherit the money to pass on to his wife. It all went in a direct line to Sweetie after all. Eve Bickerstaffe yielded, I am told, with good grace, but then she probably has enough harvested from previous husbands to live on in her house in Chelsea.

Recently in a dentist's reception office the name Beth Appleyard popped out at me from a page of a well-regarded magazine. It was signed to a poem entitled *Theme and Variation*, of which I instantly recognized the first stanza, as you will too. It was the stanza that had provoked the argument between us. Since then she had obviously had a great deal of time and reason to think about the subject of the poem, and seriously. In its final and published form it goes:

> *Coleridge caused his wife unrest,*
> *Liking other company best;*
> *Dickens, never quite enthralled,*
> *Sent his packing when she palled;*
> *Gauguin broke the marriage vow*
> *In quest of Paradise enow.*
> *These things attest in monochrome:*
> *Genius is the scourge of home.*

> *Lady Nelson made the best of*
> *What another got the rest of;*
> *Wagner had, in middle life,*
> *Three children by another's wife;*
> *Whitman liked to play the dastard,*
> *Leaving here and there a bastard.*
> *Lives of great men all remind us*
> *Not to let their labors blind us.*

> *Each helped to give an age its tone,*
> *Though never acting quite his own.*
> *Will of neither wax nor iron*
> *Could have made a go with Byron.*
> *Flaubert, to prove he was above*
> *Bourgeois criteria of love,*
> *Once took a courtesan to bed*
> *Keeping his hat upon his head.*

266

But mine is off to Johann Bach,
For whom my sentiment is "Ach!"
Not once, but twice, a model spouse,
With twenty children in the house.
Some fathers would have walked away
In what they call a fugue today.
But he left no one in the lurch,
And played the stuff he wrote in church.

At last she had written a poem that was not derivative — not technically, that is. This time it was the idea that carried a vague echo of something I had heard before. No, I hadn't heard it — I had said it. She had appropriated my side of the argument for a finish, or switch. At first I could think only of the snideness of creative talent, which steals from wherever and whomever it can. Then, behaving rather less childishly myself, I was able to see the growth represented in Sweetie's viewpoint. The task of rearing a child must have taught her a lot. Taught her that the conformity we often glibly equate with mediocrity isn't something free spirits "transcend" as much as something they're not quite up to. That convention calls for broader shoulders — and, for all I know, more imagination — than revolt. Yes, the job of bringing up a child must always be considerable, even without the added burden of a man around the house. Though I must in all fairness to Sweetie add that she hasn't married — so far, anyway. I understand she has a man hanging around her in San Francisco, a poet who reads from his works in night clubs, but she's still single. And, I am sure, to the best of her lights, singular. Still I was glad to see that rhymed salute from a free spirit to those of us who pitch our tents, as most of us, in the end, must, on more or less conventional terrain.

Which is where I close with the declaration of being content to remain. Crystal's emotions were shaken and her temper was really inflamed, for a good while there. But passions have cooled now, and we are again sleeping together in the great double bed which is also an heirloom of mine. I have had, for the record, one clear-cut instance of physical temptation since the events put down here. I don't imagine I need add that I resisted it. It concerned a woman I have known for years, freshly divorced when I came across her in a New York bar one night when I was staying in town. "Thanks just the same," I told her, "but I don't want any pleasures interfering with my happiness."

APPENDIX

NOTE: Since the preceding events, Beth Appleyard did marry. She married the West Coast sales manager of a retail shoe corporation, and has moved to the suburbs of Los Angeles. Her husband, whose name is Hubert T. Hanley, has two children by a previous marriage, so that Mrs. Hanley now has three lovely youngsters. Despite her household chores and the pressures of suburban social life, however, she still manages to find time for her writing, and recently had a new volume of poems published under the title *Omens and Amens*. A representative sampling from it appears in the following pages.

BACCHANAL

"Come live with me and be my love,"
　　He said, in substance. "There's no vine
We will not pluck the clusters of,
　　Or grape we will not turn to wine."

It's autumn of their second year.
　　Now he, in seasonal pursuit,
With rich and modulated cheer,
　　Brings home the festive purple fruit;

And she, by passion once demented
　　— That woman out of Botticelli —
She brews and bottles, unfermented,
　　The stupid and abiding jelly.

CHRISTMAS FAMILY REUNION

Since last the tutelary hearth
  Has seen this bursting pod of kin,
I've thought how good the family mold,
  How solid and how genuine.

Now once again the aunts are here,
  The uncles, sisters, brothers,
With candy in the children's hair,
  The grownups in each other's.

There's talk of saving room for pie;
  Grandma discusses her neuralgia.
I long for time to pass, so I
  Can think of all this with nostalgia.

SAVAGE

Back in the primitive past,
    He had a grape in his mouth,
I had a flower in mine.
    It was deep in the dulcet south.

Now he has seeds in his hand,
    I have a rake in mine,
Gathering twigs that are oak,
    Dreaming of leaves that are vine.

Our Paradise had a snake
    Who appeared in the grass and was gone,
Or rather turned into a hose
    For sprinkling the garden lawn.

When once its innocuous hiss
    Was plaguing the Protestant night,
I took an impromptu kiss
    From a swain who strayed into sight.

Then I knew that the primitive man
    Is something you cannot subdue —
From my sudden corroborative pang
    When the neighbors protested "Taboo!"

SACRED AND PROFANE LOVE,
OR, THERE'S NOTHING NEW UNDER THE MOON EITHER

When bored by the drone of the wedlocked pair,
When bromides of marriage have started to wear,
Contemplate those of the crimson affair:
    "I had to see you," and "Tonight belongs to us."

Skewered on bliss of a dubious sort
Are all adventurers moved to consort
With others inspiring this hackneyed retort:
    "I can't fight you any longer."

Some with such wheezes have gone to the dead,
Oblivious that Liebestod lurked up ahead,
That pistols would perforate them as they said:
    "This thing is bigger than both of us."

Experimentation in matters of sin
Pales on the instant it's destined to win;
Paramours end as conformers begin:
    "I don't want just this — I want you."

Explorers are highly unlikely to hear
Novelties murmured into their ear;
Checkered with such is the checkered career:
    "It's not you I'm afraid of, it's myself."

Such liturgies standardize lovers in league
That someone will cry in the midst of intrigue,

And someone will hear in the midst of fatigue:
"You don't want me — you just want sex!"

Strait is the gate and narrow the way
Closing at last on the ranging roué;
Who plucks a primrose plants a cliché:
"We're married in the eyes of Heaven."

The dangerous life is so swiftly prosaic
You might as well marry and live in Passaic;
It ends and begins in established mosaic:
"I'm all mixed up."

The lexicon's written for groom and for rake.
Liaisons are always a give-and-take.
Disillusionment's certain to follow a break.
"For God's sake be careful or someone will hear you!"

PSYCHIATRIST

His role is to invert the fairy tale;
  To give the wakeful Beauty sleep,
Change back the charming Prince into a frog,
  Or unmask him as the chimney sweep.
To him at last dear Cinderella,
  And not Rapunzel, must let down her hair,
Yield up the hopeless fetish of the shoe
  And much of what was dreamt below the stair.

Don't ask him tritely can he heal himself.
  Hope rather that his private dream
For living happily forever after
  Be not the fantasy that it may seem:
A village where the hunter's evening stride
  Betrays no more of strutter than of hobbler;
And Cinderella sleeps content beside
  The kind and well-adjusted cobbler.

STRATEGIC RETREAT

The blossoms that besot the bee
Once quite intoxicated me.
But that was in my squandered youth
(That still unopened bud of Truth).
Now, for the fairly simple reason
That foliage endures a season,
While days may bring a flower to grief,
I have begun to praise the leaf.

That thief and donor Time, who taught
Me thus to sing as sing I ought,
Shall bring me to the winter's kiss
As once he did from spring to this.
As one who from relinquished bloom
Has settled for each plainer plume,
I trust that then I shall not blanch,
But steadfastly extoll the branch.